GASLIGHT
AND
FOG

DEANNA MADDEN

ISBN-10: 0692665048
ISBN-13: 978-0692665046

Cover design by SelfPubBookCovers.com/diversepixel

Flying Dutchman Press

2016

For Doug and Gypsy

PROLOGUE

There were at least twenty of them as they came around the corner into Petticoat Lane following their tour guide, a man with shaggy grey hair wearing a black lined jacket against the chill night air. They were a hodgepodge of different nationalities, men and women of all ages, docilely trailing behind the guide but chatting with each other as they went. At least one, a reed-thin young woman in high boots and a long brown sweater, was talking on her cell phone and not paying much attention. Before rounding the corner, the guide had warned them that the area was unpredictable, dangerous even, known for low-lifes, pickpockets, and the occasional obstreperous drunk, so they should look sharp and stay close. Sure enough, as the group eddied sluggishly around the corner, a young man with a cigarette clamped between his lips leaned out of a second story window above them and dropped a bottle of cheap wine, which struck the head of a woman in the crowd, knocking her to the pavement unconscious and scattering the others like a flock of frightened birds.

CHAPTER 1

It was dark, and I didn't know where I was. I was lying on a narrow cobblestone street, or alleyway, hemmed in by tall bleak walls, the only light a faint yellow streetlight glowing in the distance through the fog. Nothing looked familiar. A chill ran through me, prickling my flesh. What was it? I felt more afraid than I had ever felt before in my life. The thought rushed through my mind that I was in the wrong place. I had to get out of there. I didn't know why. My head hurt. Not a headache, but a sharp pain, as if I had suffered a blow to my head. I had the sense that something terrible had happened, like a terrorist attack. A bomb had gone off, there had been an explosion, or something like that. If I lay still, soon someone would be coming to help me. Maybe there were others injured too.

Then a new fear swept over me. Where was Courtney? Had she been hurt too? The thought that my daughter might be lying nearby hurt made me forget my own pain as I lifted my head and looked about desperately. There was no one nearby. And yet I had the feeling I was not alone in the dark

1

alley. There was a sound—a sort of shuffling, a gurgle, gnawing, wheezing. I couldn't identify it, but it made my skin crawl. I wanted to cry out, but I was too afraid. There was something terrible in that alley with me, and I knew instinctively that I must not draw attention to myself. Was it an animal? A dog? A wolf? The sounds were like that of an animal feeding. If I lay still, would it go away without noticing me?

Cautiously I looked about again. Yes, this time I saw something. A shadow farther up the alleyway, not an animal but a man bending over something shapeless and inert. His back was to me and he was doing something to it. He squatted beside it, intent on his work. I felt I must not disturb him. He didn't know I was there. He thought he was alone. I would wait until he was gone and then I would try to move.

As if he had just sensed my presence, he froze, head lifted, alert, listening. I tried not to breathe. Was that a knife in his hand? He rose to his feet. Whatever the object was, he quickly wrapped something around it. A cloth maybe. Or a newspaper. He held it cradled against his chest as he walked toward me. He glided noiselessly across the distance that separated us. I closed my eyes tightly, held my breath, and hoped he wouldn't notice me. No such luck. He was standing over me. I didn't have to open my eyes to know that. If he squatted down beside me, what should I do? I didn't think I could jump up and run. I could tell him I didn't belong here. I could tell him it was all a mistake. I thought again of that knife. Had I just witnessed a murder? I would tell him I had seen nothing. I would swear to keep his secret. In the distance faintly I could hear a woman singing off-key. Did he hear it too? Please let her come this way, I prayed. He nudged my arm with his shoe. I kept my eyes tightly shut and wondered if he could hear my heart beating. It was beating so hard it hurt my chest. All I could think of was that at any moment he might plunge that knife into me. There was no one to stop him. Certainly I couldn't stop him. I wasn't even sure I could cry out.

Somewhere a bell began to toll. Once, twice, three times. Maybe it reminded him of the time. In any case, he strolled away then, whistling a tune I didn't recognize. As it faded away, I turned my head and saw him disappearing into the fog.

After that I must have lost consciousness. The next time I woke it was to the indistinct murmur of voices. Opening my eyes, I saw two men bending over the shapeless heap where the man had squatted before. I wondered if I should call to them and tell them I was hurt. Before I could make up my mind, one broke away and loped down the street toward the streetlight. He's gone for help, I told myself, and a wave of relief swept over me. Someone over there was hurt worse than I was, and they would help her first, and then they would help me. My head was throbbing and I didn't want to move it and make the throbbing worse. It was cold too, and I was shivering. It had begun to drizzle and my face felt wet now and my clothes unpleasantly damp. It didn't matter. I told myself everything would be all right now.

The man was soon back with a policeman, but such an odd-looking policeman with a quaint old-fashioned helmet on his head and a lantern in his hand. He didn't really look like a policeman at all but more like somebody wearing a costume. Maybe he had been called away from a party. It seemed strange, but then everything seemed strange—and in any case he had a light. That was what mattered. He held his lantern over the shapeless heap and let out an exclamation of horror. So that shapeless heap was a person. I had known that, hadn't I? Please God, don't let it be Courtney, I prayed, remembering my daughter might be badly injured, dead even. All three men talked together, but I couldn't make out what they were saying. Their British accents were too thick. Gradually more men arrived, stepping from doorways I hadn't noticed or materializing out of the fog. They all had to squat by that shapeless heap as if it were some kind of ghastly shrine. I knew the person must be dead; otherwise they would try to help him. Or her. One man came up the alley, leaned his hand against the wall, and vomited. I thought he would surely see me but he didn't. It was as if I were invisible.

"I came out to go to work and there she was, just lyin' there," one man said. "I thought it was a tarp at first that someone had rolled up and thrown away. I almost stepped on her before I realized. . . . Who'd do a thing like that?"

"Hey, bring a light over here," said a man's voice not more than a few feet from me.

There was a scramble of movement. I closed my eyes at the light that was held over me.

"Suppose that's him?" someone said.

"Some poor sod sleeping it off more likely. Can't you smell the wine?"

"Is that blood?"

"Back off, will you," ordered a gruff voice. "Let's get the surgeon over here. Dr. Ellman! There's another one over here."

I told myself I should open my eyes, but something held me back, like when I was a child and my mother had opened the bedroom door to check on me before going to bed and I had kept my eyes closed, pretending to sleep.

"Let's have a look then," said a new voice. "Has this one been cut up too?"

"Not so far as I can see," said another. Maybe this was the man holding the lantern. "But there's blood on his head."

I knew they were talking about me, but I didn't understand why they thought I was a man. Or was it just some peculiar British way of speaking, mixing up their pronouns?

I felt someone prod my forehead and let out an involuntary gasp at the pain which shot through my head. I opened my eyes and blinked at the glare of the lantern thrust in my face.

"Well, he's alive at any rate."

"Looks like someone hit him on the head. Nasty knock but he'll live. No knife wounds so far as I can see. Can you sit up, sir?"

I didn't think I could, but hands pulled me to a sitting position before I could protest.

"Blimey, it's a woman," someone said, and I fell back down as they let go of me. Of course I'm a woman, I wanted to say, but my head hurt too much to speak. I just wanted to curl up in a ball and sleep again.

"You think he hit her in the head?"

"If he did, she was lucky that's all he did."

"You don't need to stand around and gawk," one voice muttered, probably the surgeon.

They sat me up again like a rag doll. This time they propped me against the wall behind me. I whimpered in protest as the man touched my temple again.

"It's a nasty bump, but it's almost stopped bleeding. I'm going to bandage it up."

"Thank you," I said. My words were hardly more than a whisper. My throat felt dry and raspy.

"What's your name?" he asked as he wrapped my head.

I opened my eyes and looked at him. The lantern had been set nearby on the ground and I could see him now, an elderly man, kind-faced, with a short grey beard and glasses. He wore a round hat with a brim. No one wore hats like that anymore. Maybe he had been at the same costume party as the policeman.

"What happened?" I asked.

"Well, you got knocked on the head," he said.

"No, I mean over there." I looked toward the small knot of men.

He sighed. "Well, a poor unfortunate woman got herself murdered."

It wasn't Courtney, I told myself. Wherever Courtney was, she wasn't here.

"Where am I?"

"Buck's Row."

I had never heard of it. "Why am I here?"

"I don't know. Maybe you were on your way someplace. Or on your way home. Do you live around here?"

I tried to think and drew an absolute blank. I didn't know where I was and I couldn't remember where I lived. "I don't think so."

"What's your name?"

Now I began to feel frightened. Of course I knew my name. How could I not know my name? I just couldn't think of it right that minute.

"It's all right," he said. "You got a pretty hard knock on the head. A little rest and you'll remember."

"She see anything?" asked a short man with a bristly mustache who had just come up to us. He wasn't wearing a policeman's uniform but spoke with an air of authority.

The surgeon was standing now. He looked down at me doubtfully.

"Christ, she smells like she fell in a wine vat," said the other man in disgust. "And how come she's dressed like that?"

He was right about the smell. I could smell it myself now, a sickening sweetish stench. I had been half aware of it before but had thought it must be something else in the alley.

"Did you see anything?" asked the surgeon, looking down at me.

I thought about the man squatting by the shapeless heap. The awful feeling of fear and dread washed over me again, and I started to shiver uncontrollably.

"I'm afraid you'll have to question her later," the surgeon said.

"But maybe she could tell us something," the other man protested. "If she saw something—"

"Maybe she did, and maybe she didn't," said the surgeon. "Right now she can't even remember her name or where she lives. That doesn't make her a very reliable witness."

The man with the bristly mustache glared down at me, and I huddled closer to the wall, trying to stop my teeth from chattering.

"So what do we do with her? You want me to take her to the station?"

"No, I don't think that's necessary. Maybe I'll take her home with me."

The man scowled. "I don't think that's such a good idea."

"And why not? Do you think she'll steal the silver or murder us in our sleep?"

"She's probably a whore," the man said. "What else would she be doing out on the streets at this time of night? And clearly she's had a drop too much."

His words shocked me. I wanted to protest. I didn't know why I was there, but I knew I was not a prostitute and I certainly wasn't drunk.

The surgeon was called away then to examine the body

once more before they moved it. I lay my head on my knees and listened to their muffled voices. I felt unbearably lost and alone. I wanted to go home, but I had no idea where that was.

Perhaps I lost consciousness again. The next thing I knew the surgeon's hand was on my shoulder, gently shaking me. I looked around, confused. Where was I? A narrow alleyway, men with lanterns, a smell of decay and sewers, the chill night air. It came back to me in a rush. A woman had been murdered. Involuntarily my eyes sought the spot. Yes, the shapeless heap was still there. I glanced quickly away, not wanting to see it.

The surgeon was holding out his hand to help me to my feet. With effort I got up.

"Easy now," he said.

I was surprised how stiff I was. I had sat too long on the hard cobblestones. And I was dizzy. If it had not been for the surgeon's arm, I would have fallen.

He led me toward the streetlight. It was an old section of the city, a cobblestone street and gaslights, or electric ones made to look like them. Several horse-drawn carriages were lined up at the curb when we reached the corner. I looked down the dark foggy street. Not a car in sight. It was as if I had stepped into the past. I shivered.

The surgeon stopped when we reached the nearest of the waiting carriages.

"We're going to ride in this?" I said, surprised.

"Well, you're in no shape to walk," he said, holding the door for me.

I climbed in carefully, grateful there was a step by the door. Inside two seats faced each other. I took one and the doctor seated himself across from me. Our knees nearly touched. Perhaps cars weren't permitted in this section of

London, I told myself. Perhaps the city was trying to keep it authentic for the tourists.

The carriage lurched as it took off. I could hear the horse's hooves striking the cobblestones and the clatter of the carriage wheels. It bounced terribly, making my head hurt again. I raised my hand and tentatively touched the bandage wrapped around my temple. Through the window I saw dark dingy buildings roll by.

"What is this place?" I asked.

"Whitechapel."

The name seemed vaguely familiar. I was sure I had heard of it. It was famous, but I couldn't remember why.

"You aren't from here, are you?" the doctor said. "You have an accent. Are you from the States?"

The States? He meant the United States of course. "Yes," I said, relieved to have remembered something about myself. "Yes, I am."

"Well, that explains a lot," he said.

"Does it?" I had no idea what it explained, but if I remembered where I was from, maybe I could also remember who I was.

"Like the way you're dressed."

The way I was dressed? What did he mean? I glanced down at my jacket, my jeans, my walking shoes. They seemed familiar enough. I tried to remember when I had put them on. If I could remember that, I would know where to go back to. But it was all a blank.

"I wish I could remember!"

"Never mind," he said kindly. "Give it time. It'll come back to you. I've seen cases like this before. It may come back gradually in pieces or all at once."

"Amnesia," I whispered, the word floating up from the

dark well of my mind. I tried to think what I knew about amnesia. "Does it take long for the memories to come back?"

"That depends," he said. "Sometimes it takes weeks. Sometimes months. Sometimes even years."

"Years!" I felt a rush of alarm. I didn't have years to wait for my memory to come back.

"Don't fret about it. Chances are someone will come looking for you. Like your husband."

Did I have a husband? I couldn't remember. There was no wedding ring on my finger.

"Or another family member," he suggested.

"Courtney!" The image of my tall lovely daughter flashed into my mind. Of course. She would be wondering where I was.

"Courtney?" the doctor said, his glasses glinting as we passed a streetlight.

"My daughter."

"Well, there. You're starting to remember already."

My momentary joy at the thought of Courtney quickly gave way to anxiety. Where was Courtney? Was she also lying in some dark alleyway? Surely we had been together at the time of the attack, or whatever it was that had happened. No, there was no attack, I told myself. The surgeon would know about it. There would have been rubble if a bomb had gone off. No, there had only been that intense feeling of fear and the man bending over a shapeless heap.

"I saw him," I said.

"Saw who?"

"The man who killed that woman."

The doctor watched me through his spectacles. "You saw his face?"

"No, just his back."

10

He sighed. "I doubt that will help much."

We both lapsed into silence then. I looked out the carriage window at the dark buildings. Nothing looked familiar.

He pulled a big gold watch on a chain from his vest pocket and checked it. "It's nearly five. It'll be light soon."

"It's very kind of you to offer me a place to stay," I said.

"That's quite all right. I'm sure you'll be much more comfortable at my house than at the station."

The house at which we alighted was on a more spacious street, not hemmed in by buildings. It was lined with two and three story houses packed closely together. I saw no cars, which again struck me as strange. The doctor helped me climb out of the carriage, and it drove on, the clop-clop of the horse's hooves echoing away into the night.

He opened the door and I stepped into a narrow hall lit dimly by a lamp in the nearest room. Then he pulled a rope which summoned a young woman with pretty blonde hair curling around her face, blue eyes, and a robe that fell to the floor. She looked as if she had just woken up.

"This is Lucy," he said. "She'll show you where to freshen up. You should get out of those wet clothes too before we have a case of ague on our hands." He turned to the girl, who was looking at me with obvious disapproval. "Lucy, find her some clean clothes to put on. And get her something to eat if she's hungry."

"Sir, Mrs. Haslip won't like me poking about in the larder and it's only a few hours till breakfast," the girl protested.

"I'm sure Mrs. Haslip won't mind. Oh, and make up a bed for her, will you?"

"Will she be staying then?"

"I don't know. That all depends—" He broke off. "Yes, I suppose she will be."

Lucy looked me over again with distaste.

"I don't want to be any trouble," I said.

"Trouble? Nonsense," the doctor said. "And now I think I'll go upstairs and wash up and try to get a bit of sleep before I head for the mortuary."

He hung his hat on a hat rack near the door and then climbed the stairs.

"Well, don't just stand there, follow me," Lucy said. "I think the back room should do fine for the likes of you."

She led me into a kitchen and from there into a small washroom. The water that ran out of the spigot into a small old-fashioned looking sink was not warm, but I was able to wash my hands and splash water on my face. There was a small oval mirror over the sink and I could see myself in it. I looked tired, my hair was frizzy from the dampness, and the bandage wrapped around my head made me look like a war casualty.

Lucy stood in the doorway watching me with hostile eyes. "You ought to be ashamed."

"I beg your pardon?"

"You don't fool me. I can see what you are. You got a nerve coming into a respectable house like this."

"Like what?" I had no idea what she was inferring.

"You reek to high heaven of it," she said, wrinkling her nose.

I realized she meant the wine on my clothes. "I'm afraid I do," I agreed. "I have no idea what happened."

"You don't need to put on airs with me," she said archly. "I know what you are."

"What am I then?" I had no idea why she had taken such a dislike to me.

"You're a prostitute, you are."

This was the second person since I had woken up in the

alleyway to assume I was a prostitute. I glanced back at the mirror. I saw myself, tired, a bandage wrapped rakishly around my temple, blood smeared on my cheek, no makeup, a woman in her early forties. Why did they think I was a prostitute?

"I am not a prostitute," I assured her. "And I'm very tired and I would very much appreciate it if I could just lie down for a bit. My head hurts and . . . I saw a woman murdered tonight." Suddenly I felt as if I would start crying if she gave me any more trouble. I had reached my limit. In fact, I was well beyond it.

She blinked. "You saw a woman murdered?"

She must have seen that I was on the verge of tears because suddenly she looked contrite. "I'm sorry. I guess I better find some clothes for you to put on."

She led me to a little room near the kitchen with a narrow saggy bed, a small bureau, a hooked rug, and not much else, then went away, to return shortly with sheets and a blanket.

"I can make it," I said.

The young woman shrugged. "Suit yourself." She spread out a dress on the bed. It was floor-length with long sleeves and hooks up the back.

"What's that?" I asked.

"As you can see, it's a dress, and way too good for the likes of you, if you ask me."

I stared at it. Surely she didn't expect me to wear something so out-of-date? Was she serious?

"What's the matter?"

"I think I'd prefer to just wear my own clothes," I told her.

"But you can't. You've spilled wine on them. They need to be washed."

She was right. But still—that dress! The girl left the room so I could change. I removed my still damp clothes and folded them in a neat pile on the floor. Then I pulled the dress over my head and struggled into it. I had it on when she came back to get my clothes, but I had only managed to get half of the hooks fastened. She had to help me with the rest.

"Breakfast will be in about another hour and a half," she said when she had finished hooking me up. "If you'd like to nap, I can wake you when it's ready."

I looked in dismay from the dress to the black high-top shoes that sat on the floor beside my walking shoes. The two pairs of shoes looked incongruous sitting next to each other. A thought struck me.

"What's the date?" I asked uneasily.

"The day?" Lucy said. "Why it's Friday."

"No, the *date*."

"The thirty-first of August."

"I mean the year. What year is it?"

She looked at me dumbfounded. "That must be quite a knock you got if you don't even remember the year."

"*Please.*" I was trying not to panic.

"1888, of course," she said with perfect equanimity.

I caught my breath. It wasn't possible. This was some kind of joke—they did this for tourists, just like the horse-drawn carriages and the old-fashioned dress. They were all pretending to live in the past. That or they were all crazy.

Lucy was looking at me strangely. "Are you all right? Do you want me to fetch Dr. Ellman?"

I shook my head again, not trusting myself to speak. I wanted her to go away so I could think. There had to be some kind of explanation. It could not possibly be 1888. It was the twenty-first century. Lucy had picked up my clothes now and was headed toward the door.

"Wait!" I could hear the desperation in my voice.

She stopped in her tracks, wary.

"Where are you taking my clothes?" I tried to sound normal. I didn't want to frighten her.

"To wash them, of course."

"I don't want them washed," I said, feeling panic at the idea that I would have nothing to wear but the ridiculous old-fashioned dress. It was as if a piece of my identity were being taken away. Or my sanity. I had to have something of myself to hold onto, something to remind me who I was.

"But they're dirty," Lucy protested.

"I can wash them myself," I said, grasping at some excuse to keep her from taking them away.

"We aren't going to steal them, if that's what you're thinking," she said in an offended tone.

"I didn't mean that. I just meant, why should you have to go to the trouble of washing my clothes? I'm perfectly capable of washing them myself."

"It's no trouble." She eyed me narrowly.

I saw I was going to have to let her take my soiled clothes. If I kept arguing, she would think I was not right in my head and would probably tell the doctor. Until I could figure out what to do, I had to behave as normally as possible. I must not let myself go to pieces. If this was a game, I would have to play it, at least until I could figure out what to do.

Still watching me distrustfully, Lucy left the room with my clothes in her arms.

Once she was gone, I immediately leaped up and began to search the room, opening the drawers of the little bureau, looking under the bed, examining the small hooked rug on the floor. Discouraged at not finding anything that would prove it was not 1888, I sat down on the bed and stared at the two high-top shoes. One thing was for sure. They were made for someone with smaller feet than mine. They wouldn't fit me like my walking shoes. My walking shoes! I grabbed them up. There was my proof. Surely they didn't have shoes like that in 1888. I was tempted to put them back on. Certainly they would be more comfortable than the high-tops. But if these people saw them, they might take them away from me—my only proof that it was not 1888. No, it was probably better to hide them for now. I pushed my walking shoes under the bed until they didn't show. It wasn't an ideal hiding place, but they were certainly too big to hide under the lumpy feather pillow and were likely to be found if I shoved them into a drawer. Now I felt better. The pain in my head had subsided to a dull ache. I spread the sheets and the prickly wool blanket on the bed and lay down on it. On second thought I crawled under the blanket because I was cold. I didn't think I could sleep, but I had hardly closed my eyes before I drifted off.

CHAPTER 2

"Wake up then!"

Lucy's voice brought me awake. I was confused for a moment. I had dreamed that I was lost, wandering from room to room in a large house, pursued by an unseen stalker.

"I was beginning to think I'd have to call the doctor," she said. "You were dead to the world. I had to call three times."

"I'm sorry," I said, sitting up and touching my bandaged temple. Maybe I had a concussion.

"Well, come along then," she said with a sigh.

In the kitchen she introduced me to Mrs. Haslip, the cook, a large jolly red-faced woman with an ample bosom and a toothy smile. I sat down with them at a table and sipped the steaming cup of tea they set before me. There was also a plate of cold roast, a slab of cheese, a loaf of bread, and several oranges. I did not feel like eating meat this early in the morning and opted for just a slice of what looked like home-made bread and a small piece of cheese.

"Is that all you're going to eat?" Mrs. Haslip asked in

consternation after she had tried unsuccessfully to press half a dozen other items on me.

"I'm not used to eating a lot for breakfast," I explained.

Lucy and Mrs. Haslip exchanged significant looks. I realized at once that they had jumped to the wrong conclusion. I had not meant to imply that I lacked the wherewithal to provide breakfast or any other meal for myself. But how was I to explain that people didn't eat such large breakfasts where I came from—it wasn't healthy—without bringing up the matter of time difference—a very big time difference. I hadn't in fact convinced myself that this really was 1888. Maybe they had just put together a number of very authentic looking details. Maybe it was some kind of period piece movie set. But inside me was the nagging doubt that it was real and so I wasn't going to argue about it. Fortunately Lucy changed the topic.

"Tell us about the murder," she urged, leaning forward with barely contained excitement. Since the early hours of the morning she had thawed considerably. Evidently she had decided I was not so objectionable as she had first thought.

"You might wait till the poor thing's had a chance to drink her tea," scolded Mrs. Haslip.

Lucy just rolled her eyes.

"I'm afraid I didn't see his face," I said.

"Did you see him stab her?" She looked positively avid for details.

"Not exactly. He was sort of squatting by her."

"Well, did you scream for help?"

"No . . . I didn't want him to notice me."

"Of course not," said Mrs. Haslip. "What good would that have done? Then he'd have murdered you as well."

"I'd have screamed," Lucy said. "I'm sure I'd have screamed loud enough to be heard by everyone in Whitechapel."

"You do have a pair of lungs on you," conceded Mrs. Haslip.

Lucy ignored her. "Was he young or old?"

"Not old." I tried to remember. No, I didn't think he'd been young either. He'd been somewhere in between. A man of indeterminate age.

"I bet it's him again," she said over her shoulder to Mrs. Haslip. "Leather Apron."

I looked from one to the other. "You know who did it?" I asked, surprised.

Lucy leaned forward and whispered, "He's murdered at least two other women."

"Is that his name—Leather Apron?"

"Of course not. What sort of name would that be? They call him that because he wears a leather apron."

"He's a Jew," said Mrs. Haslip, as if that explained everything.

"I don't think the man I saw was wearing a leather apron," I said. "He had on a jacket . . . and a hat."

Just then the door opened and a well-dressed woman in her fifties or sixties with white hair stepped into the kitchen. Her dress too had a skirt that nearly brushed the floor, and she wore high-top shoes. Like Lucy and Mrs. Haslip, she had neatly pinned up her hair.

"Mrs. Ellman!" declared the cook.

"Don't get up, Mrs. Haslip. I just wanted to meet our guest." She smiled at me. She had a kind face. "How are you feeling, my dear?"

"Better, thank you."

"My husband said you can't remember your name."

"No."

"And that you are from the States."

"That's right."

"My husband's cousin is living there. Albert Simmons? I don't suppose you know him? No, of course not. And if you did, you probably wouldn't remember. Never mind. It's of no importance. I see Lucy has found something for you to wear."

"Yes."

"It looks quite nice on you."

"Thank you, but I'm not really used to . . . such long skirts."

"Yes, my husband told me you were wearing trousers when they found you. Is that some new fad in the States? I must say I don't approve of women dressing like men. I hope you're not a bluestocking."

"No." I had no idea what a bluestocking was, but I assumed I wasn't one. The tone in Mrs. Ellman's voice made it sound disreputable. I wondered if I should point out that I had been wearing jeans, not trousers, then decided it would only confuse the issue, and if this was in fact 1888, Mrs. Ellman might see little difference between the two.

"Good," said Mrs. Ellman. "The Doctor is very opposed to bluestockings and it would be awkward if the topic were to come up at dinner."

"I won't mention it," I assured her.

"Well, now that we've got that settled, if there is anything you need just let Lucy know." She turned briskly to the cook. "Mrs. Haslip, the Doctor has gone out to do the" —her eyes closed— "*post mortem* on that woman and will not be back for a few hours." She looked visibly relieved to have gotten the words out.

"Pardon me for asking," Lucy said, "but was this one stabbed, like the others?"

Mrs. Haslip shot her a disapproving look, which she pretended not to see.

Mrs. Ellman's hand flew to her throat and a look of distress crossed her face. "He said the poor thing's throat was cut."

Lucy's blue eyes opened wide. "I knew it."

"You oughtn't to tell her," said Mrs. Haslip. "She has a morbid curiosity about these attacks. It's all those novels she's been reading."

"There have been others?" I asked.

"Yes, indeed," Lucy said. "A woman was murdered in Whitechapel last April and another one just a fortnight ago."

"It's getting so it's not safe for a body to go out alone," said Mrs. Ellman.

"Leastways not after dark in the East End," said Mrs. Haslip.

"I'll bet anything it's Leather Apron again," said Lucy.

"If the police know who it is, why don't they arrest him?" I asked.

"They have to catch him first," Lucy said.

At that moment there were three raps at the front door. From the kitchen they were faint, but we could hear them.

"Who do you suppose that could be?" Mrs. Haslip asked. "Who would come visiting before tea time?"

"Dear me," Mrs. Ellman said, biting her lip. "Well, don't sit there, Lucy. Go answer the door."

"Yes, ma'am." Lucy jumped up and darted out of the kitchen.

We waited silently, listening for a telltale scream that would let us know Leather Apron was at the door. But there was no scream, and in a few minutes Lucy was back.

"It's a detective from Scotland Yard, ma'am. He wants to talk to *her*." She nodded at me.

"Very well. Show him to the drawing room," said Mrs. Ellman.

"I already did, ma'am."

"Do you feel well enough to see him?" Mrs. Ellman asked me.

"Yes, of course." I took a last sip of tea, which by now had lost its warmth, and stood up.

"All right then," Lucy said as if bracing for battle and swept out the door. With considerably less confidence, I followed her.

The drawing room held a curve-legged sofa, two wing chairs, and dour portraits of ancestors on the walls as well as one of Queen Victoria. A grandfather clock stood against one wall and a piano in the corner. Light filtered in through a window framed by lace curtains. The detective, who had seated himself in one of the wing chairs, leaped to his feet when I entered the room. He was a tall dark-haired man of middle age with a neat mustache and penetrating blue eyes that seemed to take me in at a glance. He was wearing a jacket, vest, and trousers, and held a sort of bowler hat in his hand.

"Inspector Abberline, Scotland Yard," he said. "I wonder if you'd be so good as to answer some questions for me?"

"I'll try," I said, seating myself in the other wing chair as he returned to his.

"Do you mind if I take notes?" He fished a pencil and a small notebook from his breast pocket.

"I'm not sure I can tell you much."

"That's all right, Mrs. . . . ?"

"I'm afraid I don't remember my name."

He didn't look surprised by this. Probably he had already been told about my memory loss. As if to confirm this, he glanced at the bandage still wrapped around my head. "How's your head?"

"It aches a bit and when I stand up too fast I'm a little dizzy."

"Do you remember how it happened?" The pencil hovered over the little notebook.

His eyes were disconcerting. Did he look at criminals he interrogated like that? I had the feeling he would know at once if I lied to him. At least I didn't have to lie about this. "No, I don't remember."

"And you don't remember why you were there or where you are from?"

"From the States," I said, using their term for it.

"Where in the States?"

I hesitated. I should have been able to answer such a simple question, but I couldn't. "I'm sorry."

"Quite all right. The doctor said your memory may come back quite suddenly."

"I hope so."

"Did you get a good look at our man?"

I shook my head. "No."

"Tell me what you did see."

"He was bending over—" I hesitated, not wanting to say *the body*. I saw it again in my mind, the man's back, the shapeless heap. Inspector Abberline watched me. I took a deep breath. "Then he was squatting. I didn't know what he was doing, just that it was something terrible."

"Did he see you?"

"Yes. Not then—when he was leaving. He stopped beside me."

The Inspector's eyes studied me intently. "Why didn't he attack you?"

"I don't know. Maybe he thought someone was coming."

"Was someone coming?"

"I heard a woman singing."

"Did you see her?"

"No, I just heard her voice. She sounded drunk."

He smiled. "She probably was. There are plenty of public houses around there."

I smiled back. What was a public house?

"Can you describe him at all? Was he tall or short? Young or old? Heavy or thin? A gentleman or a laborer?"

"I don't know. I only saw his back—and his shoes."

"His shoes?"

"When he stopped beside me, I could see his shoes."

"But not his face?"

"I was too afraid to look up."

He nodded. "It's just as well. If you had, you might have ended up like his other victim."

With a shiver I remembered waking in the dark alley, the gnawing sounds the man made, like an animal feeding, and my terror when he stood over me.

"Who was she—the woman he killed?" I asked the Inspector.

"We don't know yet, but a prostitute, like most of the women in the East End."

His eyes were impenetrable. What was he thinking? Was he wondering if I was a prostitute too? Surely he could see that I wasn't. But what was I then? I wanted to tell him the truth—that I didn't belong here. He looked like a kind man. Maybe he could help me. But if I told him that I came from another time, would he believe me or would he think I was crazy? Probably he would think I was crazy.

"If you remember anything else—" he said, rising and tucking the pencil and notebook back in his pocket.

"There is something else."

"And what would that be?" He watched me, as if trying to read my mind.

"I think my daughter's here too. I mean, in London."

"Your daughter?"

"Yes, Courtney."

"Courtney?" The little notebook and pencil were out again and he was scribbling. "Is that her family name or given name?"

"It's her first name."

He tapped his pencil on the notebook. "You remember your daughter's name but not your own?"

"That's right." I couldn't help what I remembered and what I didn't. "Look, I'm worried about her. She could be hurt—or lost."

"Why do you think she might be hurt? Was she there with you in Buck's Row?"

"I don't know." I felt as if I might start crying. If I only knew Courtney was safe, nothing else would matter. The thought of her alone and lost in a strange city made me want to rush out and run through the streets shouting her name.

"All right," he said quietly. "Can you describe her for me?"

I took a deep breath and blinked back my tears. "She's nineteen years old. She has brown eyes and brown hair—long brown hair—about my height, about 110 pounds."

"How was she dressed?"

I tried to think. Had Courtney been wearing her grey

windbreaker or her black jacket? I couldn't remember. Jeans at any rate, so I told him that.

He studied me thoughtfully. "Jeans?"

Hadn't he ever heard of jeans? No, maybe he hadn't, not if this really was 1888. "Pants," I said, wishing I had just told him I didn't remember.

The look on his face was blank.

"Trousers," I said reluctantly, "although they aren't really trousers. They're more fitted—" I stopped. "They're very popular where we come from." I waited for him to make some disapproving comment. It was ridiculous really. Why would any woman in her right mind want to wear long skirts? Except of course for formal wear, like high school dances. Or weddings. For a fraction of a second I saw myself in a wedding dress looking in a full-length mirror. Then it was gone.

"Go on," he said.

But I couldn't. I shook my head. "I don't remember. I'm sorry. It's all just a blur."

"You have a nineteen-year-old daughter?"

"Yes."

"Any other children?"

"No. Just Courtney."

Why was he looking at me like that—as if he didn't believe me?

"You look very young to be the mother of a nineteen-year-old daughter."

I lifted my chin. It was flattering to be told I looked young for my age, but I had to be sure he believed me. Otherwise he might not search for Courtney. "I'm forty-three," I said, looking him straight in the eye. This was no time for feminine vanity. Thank god I remembered my age.

He nodded and jotted that down in his little notebook.

"You do believe me, don't you?" I asked.

He closed his notebook. "You're a bit of a puzzle for us. We don't know who you are or where you're from. We don't know what you were doing in Buck's Row at three in the morning when our murderer was at work. We don't know if there's some connection between you and the murderer."

"Connection?" I repeated. What connection could there possibly be? It had been some awful random accident. Some freak trick of time. I was not supposed to be in that alleyway. And yet I had been. "I'm sure there's some perfectly logical explanation," I said. That of course was a lie. Would my voice give me away? Or my eyes? There was nothing logical at all about finding yourself thrust into the past. It was an impossibility. It only happened in books and movies. Or in the minds of crazy people. And I hoped I wasn't crazy.

"I guess we'll just have to wait for your memory to come back," he said, tucking his notebook into his breast pocket.

"I'm sorry I couldn't be more helpful," I told him.

He stood up, bowler hat in hand. "There'll be an inquest. Tomorrow, at the Working Lads' Institute."

I waited for him to explain. What was an inquest?

"We'd like you to come."

I wondered why he said *we'd*, not *I'd*. Did he want me to come or was he just speaking on behalf of Scotland Yard and the police? Of course that was a silly thought to flash through my mind, and anyway he was polite enough to make it sound like an invitation instead of a demand. If I said no, would he insist? But I couldn't say no because then I would look uncooperative, and if I looked uncooperative, he would wonder if I were hiding something, if there was some *connection* between the murderer and me.

"Of course," I said politely. "Although I don't know my

way around the city. Somebody will have to help me find the place."

"I'm sure you can ride with Doctor Ellman," he said as he walked toward the door.

I was tempted to rush after him and tell him the truth, that I was not from this time, but something warned me to be careful. I didn't know him. I didn't know any of these people. And who would believe a claim so outlandish when I couldn't even remember my own name?

I was halfway to the kitchen, where the other women would be waiting, when a thought struck me. Surely I had had my pocketbook with me in that alleyway. I never went anywhere without it. And in it would be my billfold with Courtney's senior photo, my driver's license, credit cards, and passport. If I found it, I would know who I was, and I would have proof—irrefutable proof—who I was and that I wasn't crazy. All I had to do was find it. I must have dropped it when I injured my head. I had been so confused when I woke that I hadn't thought to look for it. Wasn't it possible that it was still there in the alleyway? I had to go back and see if I could find it.

The cook, Lucy, and Mrs. Ellman looked expectantly at me when I entered the kitchen.

"He wanted to know what I saw, but I'm afraid I wasn't much help," I told them.

"I'm glad they've put Inspector Abberline on the case," Mrs. Haslip said. "He's one of their best. He'll get to the bottom of this."

"He's very handsome, for an older man," Lucy remarked.

"Don't you go getting any ideas," said Mrs. Haslip. "He's probably got a wife and half a dozen kids."

"Why, no, I don't believe he does," said Mrs. Ellman. "I think his wife died a few years ago—consumption if I remember right—and I don't think there were any children."

"There, you see," Lucy said.

"What happened to that lawyer you had your eye on?" Mrs. Haslip asked.

"Mr. Keating? Well, we're not engaged or anything like that."

"Oh dear, I hope you're not thinking about getting married!" Mrs. Ellman said. "Whatever would I do for a maid? I'd have to train a girl all over again! Oh, you can't think about marriage. You're far too young."

"I'm eighteen," Lucy said defensively. "There's lots of girls married younger than that."

"Well, I forbid it," said Mrs. Ellman. "What do you want with a husband? The next thing you'd have little ones to take care of. No, you don't want to get married. Get that thought right out of your head."

"I think it'd be exciting to be married to a Scotland Yard detective," Lucy said, undeterred. "I could help him solve his cases."

"He wants me to go to the inquest tomorrow," I told them.

They all looked at me as if they had forgotten I was standing there.

"Oh, can I go too?" Lucy said, turning to Mrs. Ellman. "I've never been to an inquest before."

"What exactly is an inquest?" I asked.

"Don't they have inquests in the States?" Mrs. Ellman asked, surprised.

"I don't think so," I said.

"Well, they look at the evidence and decide on a cause of death, if it's murder, or natural causes, or an accident," Lucy explained.

"But why do they want me there?" I asked.

"As a witness, I expect," said Mrs. Haslip.

"Oh, please say I can go!" Lucy pleaded.

"I suppose you'll give me no peace till I do," said Mrs. Ellman. "Oh, very well. No doubt she'll need someone to go with her and I'd rather not go myself. Inquests are always so unpleasant and when it's a murder there'll be all sorts of sensation mongers and reporters and whatnot there."

"Oh, thank you, Mrs. Ellman!" Lucy said, barely able to contain her excitement. "I can wear my new hat."

Meanwhile, I was impatient to get away. I wanted to go look for my pocketbook, which might be lying in that alleyway in Whitechapel. However, if I told them where I wanted to go, I was afraid they would try to stop me. Who knew—maybe blocks from here was the world I had come from. So I lied to them.

"If you don't mind," I said, "I think I'll lie down for a bit. My head is hurting again. You don't need to wake me for lunch. I'm not really hungry. I think if I could just lie down for a while and sleep I might feel better."

"Of course," said Mrs. Ellman, her voice full of sympathy. "Let us know if you need anything."

She was so nice about it that I felt quite ashamed of myself for deceiving her. Nevertheless, as soon as I was back in the little room behind the kitchen, I pulled off the high-top shoes, retrieved my own walking shoes from under the bed, and put them on instead. I was not going to walk in those cramped old-fashioned shoes, which were pinching my toes something fierce. I would also have liked to put on my own clothes, but if I asked for them, Lucy would be suspicious. So I had no choice but to go out in the ridiculous dress. If I was lucky, I would find Buck's Row and return before anyone came to wake me for dinner. Looking in the mirror above the sink in the little washroom, I took off the bandage and tried to hide the cut on my temple by letting my hair fall over it. Then I waited until I thought I could slip out of the house undetected and stole past Mrs. Haslip in the kitchen, whose back was turned as she peeled vegetables. I let myself out the front door, careful to make no noise when I lifted the latch.

As soon as I stepped outside, I felt suddenly free. I looked up at the overcast sky and hoped it wouldn't rain. Then I hurried toward the street, anxious to make my escape and fearful that someone looking out a window might see me and try to stop me. I knew which way the carriage had come from when I had ridden home with the doctor in the early morning hours and started resolutely in that direction. It had not been a long journey, so I thought I could walk it—just not in badly fitting old-fashioned shoes. I thought the dress would help me blend, but then the first carriage rolled past and the driver stared at me. Perhaps it was my hair, I told myself. I should have taken the time to pin it up like Mrs. Haslip and Mrs. Ellman and Lucy wore theirs. But I was on my way now and I did not want to turn back and risk getting caught. I would keep going. There were other people walking and they all stared at me. Maybe it was because I was a stranger. The men almost invariably wore hats and had mustaches or whiskers. The ladies also wore hats, and I began to wonder if this might be why they stared at me—not my hairstyle but my lack of a hat. I had made a fashion faux pas that was drawing their attention. Well, there was nothing I could do about it. I lifted my chin and looked straight ahead. I was not going to turn back for the lack of a hat.

The Ellmans' house was on a respectable street, but soon houses gave way to larger buildings of a decidedly seedier appearance and the men and women I passed looked seedier too. Just as I was trying to work up nerve to ask directions, I turned a corner and found myself in a bustling marketplace crowded with people. There was produce for sale, and pots and pans, and shoes. Venders were crying out their wares, vying for attention. Ragged, dirty-faced children darted about. I was wondering whether to try to cross to the other side or go around the area when I felt a tug at my skirts and looked down to see a dark-skinned boy of about seven holding out his hand.

"A ha'penny please," he said. He was Indian perhaps. His face was smudged, his nails dirty, and his feet bare, but the big dark eyes that looked up at me were bright and hopeful.

"I'm sorry," I said. "I don't have any money."

That didn't get rid of him. He fell in step beside me. It occurred to me that he might be able to help me.

"Do you know Buck's Row, where a lady was murdered last night?" I asked him.

He cocked his head to one side and dug a finger in his ear. Then he nodded.

"If you take me there and I can find my pocketbook, I'll give you two pennies."

I would have offered him more, but I doubted he would know what quarters were or dollars, and I didn't know the British equivalents.

The boy seemed quite content with my offer and took off at a jog toward a nearby street, looking over his shoulder to see if I was following. While I was in the marketplace, nobody paid me much attention because there were so many people, but once we were out of it, people began to stare again. We were definitely in a bad neighborhood now. We passed long run-down buildings where worn-out women and grimy children sat on the curbs. I saw a little girl who couldn't have been more than five or six holding a crying baby and a little boy peeing in the street. Everywhere I looked I saw dirt and poverty. It stank too—stank of decay and sewage and misery.

"Is it much farther?" I asked the boy, worried now about the danger that could lurk in a slum like this.

"Not much," he said and jogged on.

We had turned so many corners that I was not sure I could find my way back. And now a light rain began to fall. Glancing uneasily behind me, I noticed a man was following us. He was shabbily dressed and, like our surroundings, gritty looking. I couldn't see his face, which was shaded by his hat. Again it struck me that my surroundings might be more dangerous than I had realized. After all, a woman had been murdered here last night, and according to Lucy, there had been other murders recently.

I wondered uneasily where I could turn for help if need be. We had passed a pub a little way back. Maybe we could run back there, where at least there would be other people. What if the man following us was the killer, the man they called Leather Apron? No, that wasn't likely. But he might not be just strolling down the street either. He could be a thief, intent on robbing me. And if he was, would he be angry when he found out I had nothing worth stealing?

"There it is." The boy pointed toward a gateway cordoned off by rope—the crime scene. I recognized it with a shiver. At the same moment I saw out of the corner of my eye two more derelict-looking men. The alleyway looked as if it might be a dead end, and I didn't want to be trapped. It was raining harder now. I ran to the spot where I had lain. Please let my pocketbook be here, I prayed.

The men were closing in now. I looked around for the boy. He was standing by the entrance to the alleyway looking uncertainly at me.

"Help!" I screamed. "Someone help!"

CHAPTER 3

As the first man grabbed me, I kneed him as hard as I could and raked my fingernails at his eyes. It was what they said to do if you ever get attacked. He fell back, cursing. The other two men hesitated.

"I haven't got any money!" I shouted.

They took a step toward me, and I screamed again at the top of my lungs. "You touch me and I'll kill you!"

I don't know what would have happened if two policemen had not appeared at that moment at the entrance of the alleyway, where the boy had been standing seconds before. He was nowhere to be seen now.

"What's going on here?" shouted one of the policemen.

My would-be assailants hesitated and then backed away as the policemen approached.

"You shouldn't be here, ma'am," one policeman said when they reached me.

I began to shake all over. It would be all right now. I was safe.

"Maybe you better come along with us," the policeman said.

"First I have to find my pocketbook," I said, looking around on the ground.

"You lost your purse, did you?" They looked around too.

"Yes, last night. I mean this morning—when the murder took place."

"What about the murder?" said the second policeman. "You know anything about that?"

"I was here. That's when I lost my purse."

"Well, I don't see it now," the first policeman said.

"It's got to be here." I felt as if I would burst into tears in another moment. It was raining harder now and I was getting soaked.

"I think you'd better come along with us," said the first policeman.

My attackers had disappeared. Why hadn't the policemen arrested them? Now that the danger was gone, I didn't want to go with the police. I just wanted to get back to the doctor's house before anyone discovered I was missing.

One of the policemen put his hand on my arm. I debated whether to run. If I did, would they chase me or would they let me go my way, like the men and the boy? If they did give chase and caught me, it would probably make things worse. I would be guilty of resisting arrest and they might even hit me with their truncheons. Besides, could I outrun anyone when I was wearing a long skirt?

"I haven't done anything wrong," I said in a last ditch effort.

"Just come along with us." The first policeman tugged at my arm.

So I walked in the rain, flanked by a policeman on either side. I felt like a criminal being led off to jail. People watched us and steered clear. A horse-drawn wagon loaded with scrap rolled past. Fortunately we didn't have far to walk. The police station, a dreary brick building with grimy windows, turned out to be only a few blocks away.

Once inside, I had to face a desk sergeant with a thick black mustache, who looked at me with contempt.

"Name?"

I was not going to say I didn't have one. It would lead to too many questions. "Lucy," I told him, offering up the first name that popped into my head. He wrote it down in his ledger.

"Last name?"

This was trickier. What last name could I give them? My mind raced. "Smith." I figured there must be a great many Lucy Smiths. It was not likely a name they could trace.

"Charge?"

"Drunk and disorderly," said the policeman who had his hand on my arm.

"I am not drunk," I objected.

"Found her near the murder scene screaming her head off," said the other policeman.

"I can explain," I said. "There were some men who were trying to rob me."

The desk sergeant looked at the two policemen who had brought me in. The one with his hand on my arm shrugged.

"What were you doing there?" demanded the desk sergeant.

"I was looking for my pocketbook," I said.

"And why did you think it might be there?"

"I think I dropped it there."

"Did you now?"

I didn't like the way he looked at me—as if he thought I was lying.

"What happened to your head?"

I took a deep breath. "I bumped into a wall."

The policeman with his hand on my arm made a snort.

The desk sergeant wrote something down. "Don't think we've seen you here before. You new to the area?"

"Yes," I said.

"What's your address?"

"I don't have an address."

"Then what lodging house are you staying at?"

I didn't know the city well enough to lie about an address. I decided to be truthful. "I'm staying at Dr. Ellman's house."

The desk sergeant eyed me skeptically.

"On Whitechapel Road," I added, proud that I knew the location.

No one said anything. I decided to push my luck.

"In fact, I should be getting back. They'll wonder what happened to me."

I thought that might persuade him to let me go, but it didn't. The desk sergeant signaled with a slight movement of his head to the policemen beside me and then each of them had a hand on my arms. I had no choice but to go with them again.

"Where are you taking me?" I asked nervously when I saw that they were not headed toward the door.

Without answering, they took me down a narrow hall to a cell occupied by seven women. I stared at them through the bars and felt panic rise within me as the policemen unlocked the door. How had this happened? I didn't belong in here with these bedraggled and hardened women. I could see at a glance that they were prostitutes and thieves. Murderers too, for all I knew. What if they attacked me?

The policemen could see my reluctance. They just pushed

me roughly through the door and locked it behind me. I stood with my back to the bars, facing the women. For a moment no one said anything. We just stared at each other.

Then a woman sitting in the corner spoke. "Looks like yer got rained on, dearie." She had a worn face and straggly greying hair that looked as if it hadn't been combed recently.

They all laughed.

"That's a swell dress," said a thin young woman with pasty skin and unkempt hair.

"What'd you do to your hair?" asked a flat-chested girl who was barely more than a child. She had dark smudges under her eyes like bruises. "Did you cut it off?"

"Can't you talk, dearie?" said the woman in the corner. "Cat got your tongue? Or are you daft?"

They laughed at this one too, but half-heartedly.

"What's your name?" asked another, her voice kind.

"Lucy Smith." What other name could I give them? I had none.

"What you in for, Lucy Smith?"

I was going to say it was a mistake. I hadn't done anything wrong, but looking around at them, I couldn't say that. "Drunk and disorderly," I told them, repeating the words of the desk sergeant.

This brought howls of laughter.

"Ain't we all," said the woman with the kind voice.

"You talk funny," said another. "Where you from, Lucy?"

"The States." It was beginning to come out naturally now. Not America, but the States.

"My uncle went over there," said one of the women. "Haven't heard from him since."

"Is that where you got them shoes?" asked the youngest, who couldn't have been more than twelve or thirteen.

They were all staring at my walking shoes now.

"Yes, I did," I said, trying to hide them under my long skirt.

"I never seen shoes like that before," the girl said.

"They're the ugliest shoes I ever seen," said the woman in the corner, and they all laughed. This time I laughed too.

My fear of them soon evaporated. They were just women who had been treated badly by life. They were prostitutes because they had to survive. The youngest, Lizzie, was out on the streets because there were younger children in her family to feed. Not much older, Alice was obviously in poor health—that cough, the rail-thin arms, the sore on her lip. Nettie had been tossed into the cell for drunkenness. She had sobered up some but was still under the influence and her words were slurred. She kept breaking into song:

On a tree by a river a little tom-tit
Sang "Willow, titwillow, titwillow."
And I said to him, "Dicky-bird, why do you sit
Singing "Willow, titwillow, titwillow?"'

It seemed familiar, but I couldn't remember where I had heard it before. Jane was in for getting into a fight with another woman. She had a bruise on the side of her face. Nancy had a black eye which she said her man gave her. Kate had been caught stealing a man's watch. And the Duchess had been arrested for hitting a constable.

"I'd do it again in a minute," she said. "It was wonderfully satisfying."

"So what's your story, Lucy?" Kate asked. "We all told you ours. It's your turn now."

So I told them about going to Buck's Row to hunt for my

pocketbook, which I thought I might have dropped that morning when I'd witnessed a murder.

The cell became very quiet except for Nettie, who went on singing.

"Are you saying you saw Polly Nichols murdered?" Kate asked.

"Was that her name?"

"Aye," said Jane. "She was christened Mary, but everyone called her Polly."

"You knew her?"

"We all knew Polly," said Kate.

"One thing's for sure," said Nancy. "She was in her cups when it happened."

"Drunk, dearie," said the Duchess, who must have noticed my look of incomprehension.

"She liked a good time, Polly did," said Jane.

"She had her faults, but she didn't deserve to die like that," said Nancy.

"You saw him, did you?" Alice asked.

"Only his back."

"Were he a big man?"

"I don't think so."

"Did he do that to you?" Nancy pointed at my temple.

My hand flew up self-consciously to the cut near my hairline. "I don't know. I don't remember."

"I saw her at the morgue," said Jane. "Poor thing. Throat cut."

"They say he cut more than her throat," said the Duchess from the corner of the cell.

"I heard that too, but she was covered up with a sheet when I saw her. I only saw her face. They wanted to know if I knew her. I said as soon as I saw her, sure enough, that's Polly

Nichols. Just last night she was as alive as you and me, showing off her new hat and tossing down her gin at the Frying Pan Pub."

"It ain't safe out there," muttered Nancy. "A working woman can't walk the streets without fearing for her life. What are the coppers going to do about it? That's what I'd like to know."

"You think they care about what happens to the likes of us?" said Kate.

"How are we supposed to earn a living with lunatics like him walking the streets?" said Nancy.

A man's voice answered. "I can assure you ladies that we are doing everything in our power to find the man who did this crime and see that justice is done." Inspector Abberline was standing on the other side of the bars. I hadn't noticed him come in, nor had the other women apparently.

As soon as I saw him, I felt embarrassed. What must he think seeing me there among women who sold themselves for a living? For a fleeting second I hoped he might not recognize me. But, no, he was looking directly at me.

"Constable, can you unlock this door?" he called over his shoulder. "I know this woman."

The constable ambled over with his keys and unlocked the door. Now I felt embarrassed at being released when the rest of the women were still locked up. I glanced back at them, hoping they would not hate me for being freed. But there was no time to say good-bye, and I couldn't help feeling relieved to be free again.

"I can explain," I said as I followed Abberline down the narrow hall. Without a word he opened a door to a room with a table and two chairs, one on either side. A policeman stood discreetly by the door while Abberline sat down on one of the chairs and indicated for me to take the other.

"So you remember your name?" he said when we were both seated. He spoke with cool professionalism. "You told them that your name is Lucy Smith. Is that correct?"

"No. I mean, yes, I said it, but it isn't true."

He watched me evenly. It was impossible to know what he was thinking. Was he angry? Was he disappointed in me for lying? It hadn't occurred to me that he might find out. But what did it matter anyway? Why should I care what he thought?

"I had to tell them something."

"Why not the truth?"

"I didn't think they'd believe me."

"So who are you really?"

"I told you. I don't know. I don't remember."

He studied me with his relentless blue eyes. "Why did you go back to Buck's Row?"

I sighed. "I thought I might have dropped my pocketbook there."

"Your pocketbook?"

"I thought if I could find my I.D. I would know my name and where I'm from."

"I.D.?"

"Identification."

He looked at me blankly. Would he know what a driver's license was? I had seen no cars. Did they have passports? I was afraid to ask for fear they might not.

"Did you find your pocketbook?" he asked.

"No. But I didn't have much time to look. It was raining, and some men were following me. There was a boy—" I stopped. What was the point?

"I'll tell my men to take a look."

"Thank you."

"Was there money in it?"

"Yes, I'm sure there was."

"Was it much?"

"I don't remember." I had probably been carrying traveler's checks, but why bother to tell him that? He wouldn't know what they were.

"If there was money in it, it's probably gone."

I nodded, not trusting myself to speak. How could I explain to him that the money was not important? What I was concerned about was my driver's license and passport. Never mind that they were of no use to me here. I would need them when I went back.

"Are you ready to go back?"

I blinked at him. It was as if he had read my mind. Then I realized he meant back to the Ellmans' house.

When we left the station, it was drizzling. A horse-drawn cab waited at the curb. The driver, who had his jacket collar turned up and a cap on his head, looked as stoical about the weather as his horse. Inspector Abberline held the door for me and offered me his hand as I climbed in, then climbed in after me, taking the seat opposite as the doctor had the night before. I realized with a sinking feeling that meant I would be subjected to more scrutiny during the ride. I was right.

"Those are very unusual shoes," he commented as the cab started rolling.

I tried to tuck them under my skirts and made a mental note not to wear them again. They were attracting far too much attention.

"May I have a look?"

Reluctantly I lifted one foot. He leaned forward and examined my shoe thoughtfully.

"Interesting. I've never seen anything like it."

"It's a new fashion," I said, which was technically true. "Comfortable for walking."

"Rubber soles?"

"Yes, I suppose they are."

"You know, you were very lucky today that those men didn't attack you."

"Yes, thank goodness there were policemen nearby," I agreed, generously not pointing out that they had arrested *me* but not my attackers.

"Why didn't you tell me this morning that you had dropped your pocketbook there?"

"I thought of it later, after you'd left."

He watched me steadily until I looked away like some guilty criminal. I suspected he was very good at getting confessions. "If you think of anything else, will you please tell Dr. Ellman and he'll get word to me. It isn't safe for you to be wandering around the streets of Whitechapel. We've got a killer on the loose."

"I know that," I said, my eyes resolutely fastened on the passing buildings.

"It could have been you with your throat slit this morning instead of that other poor woman. You realize that, don't you? Next time you might not be so lucky."

"Did you know her?" I asked, looking him in the eye.

He shook his head. "I know some of them, but there are so many. Whitechapel is teeming with them."

"Such a pretty name for such a dangerous place," I observed.

He smiled. "I suppose it is. It takes its name from the church at the end of High Street."

"Do you live here?" I asked, curious. "In Whitechapel, I mean."

"No, I live in Clapham."

"Is that a nice place to live?"

His mouth twitched in a half-smile. "It's not Whitechapel, but it's not St. James's either."

The cab jolted and our knees bumped.

"You haven't asked about your daughter," he said.

My heart stopped. "Courtney? Have you found her?"

"No, there's no word. I just thought it was curious. Before you were so concerned for information, but now you haven't mentioned her once."

I realized with a pang this was true. How could Courtney have slipped my mind? I had been so busy. I had been thinking about my pocketbook. Was my pocketbook then more important than Courtney? Of course not. Somehow she seemed far away. I no longer felt that she was in danger. "I don't think she's here."

He was watching me. "Before, you seemed so certain she was."

"I know. I can't explain it."

"So you were alone after all?"

I closed my eyes and sighed. "I thought she was there with me, but perhaps I was mistaken. It's all very hazy now."

"You think she's back in the States?"

"No. I mean, yes. Maybe. I don't know."

"You really shouldn't be out walking the streets after taking such a knock on the head."

"I suppose not."

The cab stopped in front of the Ellmans' house.

"Thank you for all your help," I said. "It was very kind of you."

"You won't go out again, will you?" he asked.

I hesitated. "No, of course not." I didn't meet his eyes. It was a promise I couldn't make.

We reached for the door handle at the same time and our hands touched. I pulled mine back, but not before he had given me a quick, startled glance. Evidently he wasn't used to women opening their own doors. I waited for him to open the door and climb out first.

When he reached a hand up to help me, I took it, taking care not to trip over my long skirt. I wondered if he could tell that I had had no practice climbing out of horse-drawn cabs. He put his hand on my elbow, guiding me as we went up the walk. When we reached the door, he lifted the brass knocker and knocked.

"Shall we call you Mrs. Smith then?" he asked. "At the inquest we'll have to call you something."

"Mrs. Smith is fine," I agreed.

CHAPTER 4

When Lucy opened the door, her eyes went wide with surprise.

Inspector Abberline tipped his hat. "Mrs. Smith went out for a walk and got lost. Perhaps you can find some dry clothes for her before she catches a cold."

"Of course, sir," said Lucy, bobbing him a curtsy.

He tipped his hat to me. "I'll see you tomorrow then at the inquest."

We watched him stride back to the cab and climb in without a backward glance.

"Mrs. Smith, is it?" Lucy said as I stepped across the threshold. "So you've remembered your name, have you?"

"No, it's not really my name," I said. "It's just something people can call me until I remember my own name."

"Lucy!" She jumped at the sound of Mrs. Ellman's voice at the top of the stairs.

"Quick. In the drawing room."

I ducked into the drawing room as she suggested. All the

portraits on the wall seemed to look at me with disapproval, especially Queen Victoria.

"Who was at the door?" Mrs. Ellman called down.

"The Inspector from Scotland Yard," Lucy called back.

"What did he want?"

"He was looking for the doctor."

"Did you tell him to try the Infirmary?"

"Yes, of course, ma'am."

Lucy waited in the doorway for a minute and then motioned for me to follow her. We tiptoed through the house until we reached the little room in the back of the house where I was supposed to be sleeping.

"Why'd you sneak off like that?" she demanded in a low voice. "I came in here to check on you and you were gone. Mrs. Haslip and I looked everywhere. We didn't want to tell Mrs. Ellman. She would have been worried sick."

"I had to go back there."

"To Buck's Row? Whatever for?"

"I thought I lost something there."

"What?"

"My pocketbook."

She rolled her eyes. "And I suppose you thought the kind folk of Whitechapel would just leave it lying there for you to come back for." She shook her head in disbelief.

"I thought it might be there," I admitted.

"It isn't safe for a respectable woman to walk the streets of the East End," she said primly, forgetting that just that morning she had thought me not respectable. "You're lucky the Inspector found you."

"He didn't find me. A couple of policemen came to my rescue when I was about to be attacked by some men."

Lucy stared. "There—didn't I tell you it isn't safe?"

I decided to omit the part about being thrown in jail with half a dozen prostitutes. It might make her doubt my respectability again.

She put her hands on her hips and surveyed me. "Well, I suppose I should find you something dry to put on, like the Inspector said. You'd best get those damp clothes off." And with that she turned and bustled off on her mission.

Alone again, I went into the washroom and looked at myself in the small round mirror over the washstand. My hair hung limply and my eyes looked anxious. I looked like a battered woman with that ugly cut on my temple. I tentatively touched it with my fingertips. A bluish bruise was forming. It was all very tender. I washed my hands using the piece of soap lying on the sink and splashed water on my face. I longed to take a shower. Did they have a shower in the house I wondered? I would have to ask Lucy. I reached behind my back and began to unhook the back of my dress, which was not easy to do.

Soon Lucy was back with another dress almost identical to the first. The same long sleeves, the same long skirt, the same mousy brown color, and the same tedious hooks. I sighed. She expertly finished unhooking the rest of my dress in a matter of seconds, chattering nonstop about the murder. "It's in all the newspapers," she said.

She had brought a newspaper to show me, and after she had finished hooking me into the new dress, she spread it out on the bed for me to see. It was like no newspaper I had ever seen before, full of black and white illustrations with captions. The headline on the front page shouted 'MURDER IN WHITECHAPEL,' and below it was an illustration of a policeman standing over a woman's body with his lantern held high.

"That's her," Lucy said. "Mary Ann Nichols. The woman you saw murdered. Everybody's talking about it."

I studied the illustration. The woman in it could have been any woman. It made the murder seem unreal.

"It's an outrage that women aren't safe in the streets of London," Lucy declared. "Of course she wasn't a respectable woman and oughtn't to have been out at an hour like that—" She stopped and looked guiltily at me. "Sorry."

"It's all right," I said. "I wish I knew why I was there at an hour like that and in a place like that."

"You still don't remember anything?"

I shook my head. "No. Nothing. It's all a blank."

"You don't think you are—" Lucy looked away, embarrassed.

"A prostitute? No, I'm sure I'm not."

"How can you be sure?"

"I just am."

"It makes no sense." She frowned.

"I think I was there by mistake. I probably got lost."

"You must have been staying somewhere," Lucy said. "At a hotel, or with a family. I'm sure someone will report you missing, and then the mystery will be solved."

"Or I'll get my memory back."

"Yes." Lucy folded up the newspaper. "And now I hope you're not too tired from your walk because dinner is almost ready and Mrs. Ellman wants you to join her and the doctor for dinner."

Mrs. Ellman was standing by the fireplace looking elegant in a grey silk dress when I walked into the dining room. There was a small chandelier over the table and china and wineglasses and silverware precisely laid out on an immaculate white tablecloth.

"I hope you had a good sleep, my dear," Mrs. Ellman said.

"I did, thank you," I said, not meeting her eyes. I couldn't very well tell her I had had no sleep at all because I had been too busy getting arrested. I just hoped that she didn't find out.

"And you're feeling better now?"

"Yes, I am."

The doctor walked into the room, pulled out his pocket watch, and scowled at it. Mrs. Ellman moved to a chair at one end of the table. "Sit here, dear," she told me, gesturing toward a nearby chair. When we were seated, Lucy swept in bearing a roast on a platter. The smell of it made my mouth water, and I realized I was quite hungry.

"I heard they want you at the inquest tomorrow," the doctor said, staring so intently at the potatoes that it took me a few seconds to realize he was addressing me.

"Yes, Inspector Abberline—"

"I don't know what they expect to learn from you. You don't know how you got that bump on your head, and you can't even remember your name."

"I'd be glad to help if I can. That poor woman—"

A quick intake of breath from Mrs. Ellman stopped me.

"Yes, of course," the doctor said. "Quite. Sorry, my dear."

There was a brief silence.

"Mrs. Haslip has done a wonderful job on the mutton, as usual," said Mrs. Ellman, "although the pudding is a bit overcooked."

The doctor made a grunt of agreement, his mouth now full of food.

I took a bite of the meat, then stopped chewing. Mutton? Wasn't that sheep? With effort I forced myself to resume chewing and swallowed.

"I don't believe they raise many sheep in the States, do they?" Dr. Ellman asked when he could talk again.

"No, they don't," I agreed.

I wondered if Mrs. Ellman would be offended if I didn't eat more of the mutton. I lifted a fork and started on the stew. At least most of the ingredients were familiar.

"So is your President Cleveland going to win the election in November?" asked Dr. Ellman.

I stopped, fork halfway to my mouth. President Cleveland?

Mrs. Ellman came to my rescue. "Do you expect her to remember that when she's forgotten her own name?" she scolded.

"The mind is an extraordinary organ," the doctor said. "There was a case of a man in Scotland who had amnesia. He could remember his dog but not his wife."

"How convenient," said Mrs. Ellman. "Can you remember nothing at all, my dear?"

"Just my daughter—Courtney."

"Who was with you," the doctor declared as he reached for the pudding.

"Yes, although perhaps I was mistaken."

"Mistaken?" He frowned.

"I'm not so sure now that she was with me."

"You were quite sure this morning."

I could not explain. It was as if Courtney had been there, and then she wasn't. If I kept insisting Courtney had been there, they would keep looking for her, and now I felt fairly certain they wouldn't find her. She was in London, just not *this* London.

"You're right about the pudding," the doctor said. "I think it *is* overdone."

"You must miss her terribly!" Mrs. Ellman said, tears of sympathy welling up in her eyes.

"Yes, we're very close," I agreed, tears welling in mine too. I could hear her voice. I could see her in my mind. It was strange really how vividly I remembered Courtney but couldn't remember anything about myself. I was like the man in the doctor's story.

"Odd name that," the doctor remarked. "Is it French?"

"Courtney? It's not so unusual where I come from," I said.

"Of course not," Mrs. Ellman said. "No doubt it's a family name that's been handed down."

I didn't think so, but I didn't want to disagree.

"I'm sure your people are looking for you," Mrs. Ellman said. "It's just a matter of time until they find you."

"Yes, of course." I took another bite of stew to keep from saying more. Maybe my family was looking for me—just not in this time period. Maybe I would be stuck here forever. I pushed that thought away. I had to get back to my own time somehow. I didn't belong here. In fact, maybe none of this was real. Maybe I was dreaming it. But I didn't really believe that. The chair I sat in could not have been more solid, nor the table before me, nor the silver flatware, nor the wineglasses. I could feel the warmth from the fire and hear its crackle and taste the savory stew in my mouth. All this was as real as anything I had ever experienced. It was Courtney who seemed not quite real. It was my previous life, a grey blur in my mind, which seemed unreal. I suddenly realized tears were trickling down my face.

"Oh, I'm sorry," said Mrs. Ellman. "I didn't mean to upset you. I'm sure everything will be all right. And in the meantime you're quite welcome to stay with us. I hope the room is comfortable?"

"Yes. You've been very kind." It would have been churlish

to bring up the shortness of the bed or the outdated plumbing of the washroom. And after all, to them the bed was not too short or the plumbing out-of-date.

"Would you like to join us after dinner in the drawing room?" Mrs. Ellman asked. "Mr. Ellman reads and I do my needlework. Do you do needlework, dear?"

"No, I'm afraid I don't." At least that was one thing I was sure of.

"Oh," said Mrs. Ellman, looking disappointed. Then her face cleared as a new thought struck her. "Perhaps you would like to read? You're welcome to borrow a book from the study."

"Thank you," I said. "I'll do that." I wondered what sort of books would be in the Ellmans' study. Perhaps a good book was just what I needed to take my mind off my situation.

"I hope you're not one of these tiresome women who think they ought to have the right to vote," Dr. Ellman remarked.

I stopped in mid-bite and glanced at Mrs. Ellman. She did not appear to have heard and was scrutinizing the rug as if she had just noticed a spot on it.

"I expect we'll have the right to vote someday," I said cautiously.

"That may be true," he said. "I just hope I'm not around to see it."

When had women gotten the right to vote? In the 1920's, right? Or had it been earlier in England? I was still mulling this over in my mind when the doctor pushed back from the table. Apparently this was the signal that the meal was over. Mrs. Ellman stood up so I did too. I reached for my plate and wineglass, intending to take them to the kitchen.

"Lucy can do that," Mrs. Ellman said.

"I can help."

"There's really no need."

She was avoiding my eyes with such a pained expression that I realized I had made some kind of blunder, but I knew I would feel guilty if I let someone else pick up after me. I was not used to being waited on by servants. As if on cue, Lucy swept into the room and began to gather up the dishes with quiet efficiency. I felt silly standing there with my plate and glass in my hands, so I decided I would do what I set out to do. Lucy didn't say a word.

I followed her into the kitchen, where Mrs. Haslip had filled a large pan in the sink with hot water and was scrubbing a pot. I set my dishes down beside the ones Lucy had just piled next to the sink.

"I could help wash up," I offered.

"Whatever for?" said Mrs. Haslip.

"Is that how it's done in the States then?" Lucy asked.

"Yes, it is." I didn't add that at least *in my time* it was. In fact, what would she say if I told her that in my time most people didn't have servants? And for that matter, how could she be sure I wasn't a servant? After all, she had thought I might be a prostitute. I decided to ask her.

"Aside from the fact that you don't know your way around a kitchen, your hands," Lucy said promptly.

I looked down at my hands. No rings, no nail polish. They told me very little about myself.

"See," Lucy said. "Those aren't the hands of a working woman. They're smooth and tender as a baby's bottom."

She was right. "You'd make a good detective."

"Don't be telling her that," Mrs. Haslip said. "You're just encouraging her."

"Look," Lucy said and drew a small book from her apron pocket. The cover was tan with the title in red, *A Study in Scarlet*, followed by the author's name, Conan Doyle. "It's about a murder," she explained, eyes bright with excitement. "Well, actually two murders. And there's this detective, Sherlock Holmes."

"Yes, he's quite famous," I said.

"Have you read it then?" she asked in surprise.

"Well, no," I admitted. "I've only heard about it." I didn't add that I had seen Sherlock Holmes movies. Probably movies hadn't been invented yet. "Shall I dry?" I asked Mrs. Haslip, to change the subject.

"That's Lucy's job."

Lucy shrugged. "You can if you want. I don't mind." She handed me a dishtowel.

And so for the next fifteen minutes, while Mrs. Haslip washed, we dried and Lucy told us about *A Study in Scarlet*. A gentleman is found dead but there are no clues to the identity of the murderer or even how the gentleman was murdered. Baffled, the police call in Sherlock Holmes, who will use his prodigious skills of deduction and powers of observation to solve the murder.

"Do you suppose Inspector Abberline is like that?" she asked.

I picked up another plate to dry. "I have no idea, but he seems very intelligent. I wouldn't want him as an adversary."

"You're right there," said Mrs. Haslip. "He's not a man to be trifled with."

"What sort of husband do you think he'd be?" Lucy said. "Do you think he'd let his wife work with him?"

"I have no idea," I said. "I only met him today."

She sighed. "It's a pity he's so old. He must be at least in his forties. But I still think it would be interesting to have a detective for a husband."

Mrs. Haslip just shook her head.

After we were finished washing and drying the dishes, Lucy took me to the study and we looked over the books. There were medical books and treatises, but I had no interest in them. I spotted Darwin's *Origin of the Species*. The novels occupied the lower shelves and there I spotted a copy of *Ivanhoe* and next to it *Rob Roy*. *Pickwick Papers* sat next to *Pilgrim's Progress*, followed by several Trollope novels, a worn copy of *Silas Marner*, and several novels by a Mrs. Henry Wood, whom I had never heard of. Many of the books had beautiful covers with ornate titles and were illustrated. I lifted out one after another, handling each with care. I wished I could tell Lucy that in my time they didn't make books like this anymore, and any books as old as these were fragile and rare. One would have had to pay a small fortune to acquire them.

"Have you read this?" Lucy pulled out a plump red book and handed it to me—*Varney the Vampire or The Feast of Blood*. The cover was illustrated with bats and a skeletal demon with bat wings rising from an open tomb. I had to admit I had never heard of it.

"Then that settles it. You must read it. I promise once you start, you won't be able to stop."

I was not so sure this was true, but since she recommended it with such enthusiasm, I couldn't very well turn it down. So for the next hour while the doctor sat in a high-backed wing chair reading a book and his wife perched on the curve-legged sofa doing cross-stitch, I pored over *Varney the Vampire* in the yellow light thrown off by a gas lamp.

I can't say the novel lived up to Lucy's recommendation. It was written in a breathless melodramatic prose that moved at a snail's pace. It took the entire first chapter for Varney to enter a young woman's bedroom and bite her neck. By the end of the hour I was yawning. When the grandfather clock chimed nine, I said goodnight to Mr. and Mrs. Ellman, excused myself, and retreated to the little back bedroom. A long white nightdress with sleeves had been laid out on my bed—no doubt by Lucy. I didn't want to wear it, but I couldn't very well sleep in the dress I was wearing, which would have been even more uncomfortable. There seemed no choice but to don the wretched thing. "When in Rome—" I muttered to myself as I went into the little bathroom, which had no bath or shower but at least had a toilet and washstand with running water. Never mind that the water was lukewarm at best. I washed up as well as I could and vowed to ask Lucy tomorrow for a toothbrush. I just hoped she knew what a toothbrush was.

I tried to read *Varney* for a bit longer by the light from the lamp beside my bed before I gave up, put out the lamp, and snuggled under the blanket. It felt good to be in bed. In spite of being saggy, creaky, and rather short, it was comfortable and so was the feather pillow. I fell asleep almost at once and was dead to the world until I woke in the middle of the night from a bad dream, my heart racing. It took me a few seconds to remember where I was. I had dreamed I was being followed through dark narrow streets. At first I had walked faster, and then I had run. I had woken up terrified, in a sweat. As I lay there, a church clock chimed. I tried to count the number of times but lost track. It must have been eleven or midnight. I waited for my heartbeat to slow. I told myself I was safe. I was in a strange place and a strange time, but I was not in any imminent danger. Things would seem better in the morning. Somehow I was going to get back to my own time. I just had to be patient and not lose hope. In fact, maybe I would wake up in the morning and be back in my own time and all this would seem like a dream. Or maybe I would not even remember what had happened.

CHAPTER 5

The next thing I knew it was morning and Lucy was throwing open the curtains to let a grey dawn seep in.

"Come on," she said. "You've got to get dressed for the inquest."

She was wearing a pretty dark blue dress that made her waist look impossibly small. Watching her made me feel old. I just wanted to go back to sleep. Had I ever been that young?

"And we've got to do something about your hair," she added.

"My hair?"

She sighed. "Whatever possessed you to cut it so short?"

Short? I reached up and touched it. It was hardly short. It fell to my shoulders.

I flung myself out of bed, stumbled to the little washroom, and splashed cold water on my face. A bleary-eyed woman no longer young looked back at me. But now I was more awake.

"Is there some deodorant I could use?" I called to Lucy in the other room.

"What's deodorant?" Lucy called back.

I groaned, then stepped into the room and pantomimed, lifting one arm and then the other. Surely they did something about body odor?

"Oh, powder," Lucy said, suddenly enlightened. She pointed at a round container sitting on the bureau.

Powder? I had my doubts about whether that would work, but if that's all they had, it would have to do.

When I next emerged, she had made the bed and laid out a long grey skirt, matching jacket, and a white silk blouse with tiny pearl buttons. It was a definite improvement on the mousy brown dress of the day before.

"Whose is it?" I asked.

"It belonged to Mrs. Ellman's daughter."

"I didn't realize she had a daughter."

"Poor thing died giving birth to a little boy, who also died. It near broke Mrs. Ellman's heart."

Once I was dressed, Lucy pinned up my hair. When she finished, she stood back to inspect her handiwork.

"Well, that'll have to do," she said.

I looked in the mirror again and was amazed by the transformation. Gazing back at me was a proper Victorian woman. I hardly recognized myself.

"You should eat breakfast now," Lucy said. "You don't want to go to the inquest on an empty stomach."

Breakfast was laid out on the buffet in the dining room: cold roast, buttered bread, hot tea, and a bowl of fruit. Mrs. Ellman was sitting at the table having her tea when I walked in.

"I hope you slept well," she said.

"Thank you. I did." I had decided not to tell anyone about my dream. After all, it was only a dream, and it was no wonder I had had it after seeing a woman murdered.

"Oh!" Mrs. Ellman said with a quick intake of breath. She stared at me with a startled expression.

"What is it?" I froze as I reached for an orange in the fruit bowl.

"Nothing." Mrs. Ellman passed her hand across her eyes as if she had a headache. "It's only. . . . Forgive me, my dear. I did tell Lucy she could find something of Henrietta's."

I realized it was the dress that had startled her. The sight of her daughter's dress had dredged up the old hurt of losing her daughter.

"Should I take it off? Should I wear something else?"

"Oh, no. It's quite all right. It was just a shock for a minute. I shouldn't be so sensitive. It's been twenty years."

I poured myself a cup of tea and carried it to the table along with the orange and a slice of toast and sat down across from her. "Was she your only child?"

"We had a son who died of cholera in India."

"I'm sorry for both your losses."

"Thank you, my dear. It's a risk we take when we bring children into the world, isn't it? We think we'll have them forever, but it doesn't always work out like that."

The bite of toast I had just taken stuck in my throat as I thought of my own daughter. Would I ever see Courtney again? Or was she as lost to me as Mrs. Ellman's daughter and son were to her?

After that we ate in silence, both lost in our own thoughts.

The inquest was held at the Working Lads' Institute on Whitechapel Road. It was a large brick building that looked something like a library and was intended to serve young working men, Lucy explained. With Dr. Ellman and Lucy, I joined the throng of people streaming in through the open double doors. Once inside, we were herded toward the Reading Room, which was furnished with a number of long tables and lots of chairs. As the crowd grew, it was noisy and there was considerable jockeying for seats. Inspector Abberline came to our rescue. He tipped his hat. "Mrs. Smith, Dr. Ellman, Miss—?"

"Callaghan," said Lucy, flashing him a pretty smile.

"There are chairs up front for witnesses," he said, then guided us to them. Once we were seated, he went back to his own seat beside another detective from Scotland Yard.

"Isn't it exciting?" Lucy said, looking about.

I noticed a man perhaps in his fifties, stern-looking, with horn-rimmed glasses and a mustache, enter the room from a side door.

"That's the coroner," Lucy said.

He walked straight to the table at the front of the room and sat down. The chairs near him were all occupied by men.

"Why are there no women sitting over there?" I asked Lucy.

"That's the jury."

"Is it a trial?"

"Of course not. It's an inquest."

I would have asked more questions, but the proceedings had begun.

The first witness was the dead woman's father, an old man with a troublesome cough and a gravelly voice. After asking him to state his name, his address, and his relationship to the deceased, the coroner asked him what sort of woman his daughter was.

"Our Mary Ann was a good girl," the old man said, looking around the room, "but she drank and it caused her no end of trouble. I tried to tell her to give it up, but she wouldn't listen. Said a drop never hurt anyone. Course she never could stop at a drop."

"Can you tell us her age?" the coroner asked.

"Forty-three this past August."

"And did she have any children?"

"Five of 'em, the youngest just eight. They live with their father. He and their mother were separated not long after the youngest, Charley, was born."

"When did you last see your daughter alive?" asked the coroner.

"I don't exactly remember, but it's been at least two years."

"Can you tell us if she had any enemies?"

He shook his head. "No, no enemies. Everybody liked Mary. It's just that she drank too much. Couldn't hold on to a farthing. Whatever she got, she spent it on drink."

The second witness to be called up was the first police constable to arrive on the scene, a lean red-haired man with a flushed face.

"Can you describe what you saw when you found the body of Mary Ann Nichols?" asked the coroner.

"Well, she was still warm, so I knew she hadn't been dead long," the constable said. "Her eyes were wide open. Her bonnet was lying nearby. Her throat had been slit. I saw that right away." He drew a finger across his own throat to demonstrate. "We found no money on her, just a bit of mirror and a broken comb. It was later after she was taken to the mortuary that they discovered she'd been disemboweled."

At the word 'disemboweled,' the room broke into a pandemonium of voices. Beside me, I heard Lucy gasp. I remembered again waking in the alley, my disorientation, the man bending over the woman's body, the grisly sounds of an animal feeding. Now I understood. He had been disemboweling his victim. The realization made me feel nauseous. Lucy reached for my hand and held it tightly. Why hadn't someone told me? Surely Doctor Ellman had known. Inspector Abberline too. Why hadn't they said something?

The room was still buzzing when the red-haired police constable returned to his seat. Next Doctor Ellman was called forward to be deposed.

"I was fetched to the scene at four o'clock on Friday morning," he said after he was seated in the witness chair. "After examining the victim and ascertaining that there was no pulse or heartbeat, I pronounced her dead. Her throat had been cut so brutally that she was nearly beheaded. I didn't notice any other wounds at the time. Her skirts were down and concealed them. It was only later at the mortuary that we discovered the wounds to the abdomen."

"And would you describe those wounds?"

"There were several long incisions running left to right, and several running upward. The weapon for all the wounds appeared to be the same—a long-bladed knife."

There was a murmur from the audience.

"Is there anything you would care to add?" asked the coroner.

"Yes, there is. I think the killer might be a left-handed person since the abdominal wounds ran left to right, but of course I could be wrong."

After Doctor Ellman had finished answering the coroner's questions, I was called to the stand. I felt self-conscious as I took the chair facing the packed room. There were so many faces and it was growing uncomfortably warm in the room. I tried to focus on what the coroner was saying. He asked me to state my name.

"Mrs. Smith."

"Christian name?"

I hesitated. I could not borrow Lucy's name again, not with her sitting right there.

"I don't remember."

"Please speak up," said the Coroner.

"I don't remember," I said again, louder.

A murmur ran through the crowd again.

"And would you explain to the court why you don't remember?"

"I was hit on the head."

"So in fact your name is not Mrs. Smith?"

"No. I mean, that's correct."

"And you were in Buck's Row the night the victim was murdered?"

"Yes."

"Would you tell us what you saw?"

"I saw the killer—from the back—as he bent over the . . . body."

"You didn't see his face?"

"No."

"Why didn't you call for help?"

I hesitated. How could I explain that I had woken in that alley not knowing what had happened or where I was? I looked out at the sea of faces. I didn't belong here.

"Why didn't you call for help?" he repeated.

"I was afraid."

"You were afraid he might attack you?"

"Yes."

"Can you describe the man you saw that night?"

"No. It was too dark. I never saw his face."

"Is there anything else you would like to say?"

I shook my head. "No."

"Very well. You may take your seat. Next witness."

I walked quickly back to my chair, grateful to slip back into anonymity.

My mind was in such a turmoil that I could barely concentrate on what the next witness was saying. He was the second constable who had appeared on the scene, a plump man with a bristly mustache.

"I shone my bull's-eye down on her and saw her throat had been cut ear-to-ear."

"Did you see any sign of her attacker?"

"No, sir. But I knew she hadn't been dead long. She still felt warm when I touched her."

At the close of his testimony, the coroner announced that the inquest would adjourn until Monday. Instantly the room erupted into noise and motion and there was a rush for the door as reporters ran to turn in their stories.

"Thank goodness that's over," Dr. Ellman muttered, picking up his walking stick.

We joined the crush of people flowing out of the building. As we left, a church clock began to toll the hours. The sound was becoming familiar. Almost unconsciously I counted the chimes. Noon. Overhead the sky was grey and oppressive. As we paused on the sidewalk, waiting for the crowd to disperse, Inspector Abberline walked up. "Mrs. Smith." He tipped his hat to me. "Doctor." A slight nod of his head to Lucy. "Miss … Callaghan. A nasty business this."

"It is indeed," Doctor Ellman agreed. "The sooner they catch this madman, the better."

"We're working on it."

"Why'd he cut her up like that?" Lucy asked boldly.

Abberline shook his head. "I don't know." He looked at me with concern. "Are you all right, Mrs. Smith?"

The crowd around us was jostling and high-spirited, like children just let out of school. I looked at them, then back at him. "Why didn't you tell me?"

"I beg your pardon?"

"Why didn't you tell me she had been disemboweled?"

He glanced at the doctor.

"There was no reason to tell you," Dr. Ellman said. "We didn't want to upset you."

"We knew we couldn't keep it from the press for long," Abberline said. "Once people know, there's going to be mass hysteria. Well, they'll know now."

"It's a shame you didn't see his face," Lucy said.

I looked at the people still streaming out of the building. Some of them stared at me. What was I doing in this place? Was it my fault Mary Nichols was dead? Was it my fault she had been disemboweled? What could I have done to stop it? I lifted a gloved hand to my temple. "I should have screamed. I should have done something."

"There wasn't anything you could do," Abberline said. I felt his hand on my elbow. "Come. Let's find you a cab."

CHAPTER 6

I did not want to think about Mary Nichols, but for the rest of the day I found I could not get her off my mind. Before the inquest she had been just a dead woman. Now I found myself imagining her as she might have been alive. She had had parents who cared about her, a husband and children. She had had a hard life and turned to drink and prostitution. Inspector Abberline had said most of the women in Whitechapel were prostitutes. It was a way to earn money, to pay for a bed for the night and a bite of food and gin. She was forty-three—the same age as me—and if I had been born in this place and time and in poverty, who was to say I might not have ended up like her. She had met a man in a dark alley in the early hours of the morning from whom she expected four pence for a bed to sleep in in return for sex, and he had cut her throat and slit her stomach open, then pulled down her skirts to hide his handiwork and walked away whistling as if he hadn't a care in the world.

I didn't want to be here. I wanted to be home—wherever that was—a place so far away I couldn't remember it. To distract myself, I picked up *Varney the Vampire* and tried to read, but I couldn't concentrate. I kept thinking about Mary Nichols and the squalid alley where she had died and my own past hidden in the fog of my mind.

Laying aside the book, I wandered into the kitchen, where I found Mrs. Haslip wielding a meat cleaver on a bloody chunk of meat on the table. I wondered if it was on the menu for dinner. If it was, I didn't think I was going to have much of an appetite tonight.

"Is there anything I can do to help?" I asked, hoping to make myself useful.

"Can you pluck a fowl?" she asked.

"I don't know," I said. "Perhaps if you show me how."

"Never mind. Maybe Lucy can find something for you to do."

Lucy had just walked in.

"I thought you were supposed to lie down," she said. "The doctor told us not to disturb you."

"I couldn't sleep."

"Well, I don't have time to stop and talk. I have rooms to dust and I have to run to the chemist's before supper to pick up a bottle of medicine for Doctor Ellman."

"I could help you," I offered.

Lucy looked from me to Mrs. Haslip, who shrugged. "She's no use to me. She doesn't know how to pluck a fowl."

"I suppose you could dust the drawing room," Lucy said tentatively.

"Yes, I could do that." I felt a weight lift from my shoulders. I had no desire to pluck a fowl, but I could dust.

"Mind you don't break anything," she added.

"I'll be very careful," I promised.

Five minutes later I was standing in the doorway of the

drawing room, a dust cloth in my hand. I surveyed the room. A pair of figurines of a lady and her swain stood on a small oval table. No doubt they were among the items Lucy was thinking of when she had warned me not to break anything. She might also have been thinking of the grandfather clock and the ornately framed portraits on the wall. What else would need dusting? Maybe the curved legs of the sofa and chairs, and of course the piano. I would save the piano for last, I told myself. While I dusted everything else, it would be there waiting for me, like a reward. I started on the figurines of the lady and her swain, picking them up carefully. As I worked, the pendulum of the grandfather clock ticked monotonously. It was a soothing sound which seemed to complement the silence. I got down on hands and knees to dust the three intricately carved claw feet at the base of the small oval table. All this decorative detail! So useless but beautiful too. When had people ceased to like these extravagant flourishes? I thought of the simple functional design of furniture in my own time. So much more practical. And who hung portraits of ancestors on their walls anymore? Soon landscapes and abstract paintings would replace these dour-faced predecessors, and surely that was progress.

At last I had dusted everything but the piano. I stood for a minute looking around the room to see if I had missed anything. When I was satisfied that I had not, I approached the piano. It was not new but looked in good condition. It was a style of piano I wasn't familiar with, smaller than a grand but shorter than an upright. I dusted the surface gently, then opened the keyboard cover and gazed at the ivory keys. Was it in tune? Tentatively I tried middle C. The note hung suspended in the air, and I closed my eyes for a moment to listen to it. With a small sigh of pleasure I sat down on the stool and spread the fingers of my right hand across the keys. As if it were as natural as breathing, my fingers knew what notes to play, and then my left hand, unable to resist, joined in. The music spoke to me like an old friend. A feeling of quiet joy welled up in me.

Within minutes Lucy came flying through the doorway, eyes wide, and the spell was broken. I stopped playing.

"You!" she said, astonished.

With a stab of guilt I remembered I was supposed to be dusting, not playing the piano. "I'm sorry," I apologized. "I didn't mean to—"

"I should have warned you," she said.

Before I could ask her what she should have warned me about, Mrs. Haslip rushed up behind her, clutching a dishtowel to her bosom. "I can't tell you what a start it gave me," she said. "I was just putting a pan of water on to boil when I heard it. I thought—"

They both turned. Mrs. Ellman stood there with the strangest expression on her face and one hand pressed to her heart. She must have run down the stairs. She stared past them at me.

"Beethoven," she said, tears shining in her eyes.

"Yes," I said, feeling as if I had been caught in the act of doing something forbidden. "Für Elise."

"Henrietta used to play that. It was one of her favorites."

"I'm sorry, Ma'am," Lucy said. "It's my fault. I should have told her not to play the piano."

"Nonsense," Mrs. Ellman said. "Why shouldn't she play the piano?"

"But—"

"You play very nicely, my dear," Mrs. Ellman said. "I'm afraid I've gotten out of the habit. But every young woman ought to learn. . . ." The thought trailed away. "Please continue. Don't let us stop you."

"I'm afraid that's all I remember," I said, not wanting to cause her pain. My playing would only remind her of the daughter she had lost. Gently I lowered the cover over the keys.

That night I had the dream again. I was walking through the rooms of a dark house, trying to escape someone who was following me. It woke me in the dead of night, and afterward I was not able to go back to sleep. I lay there listening to the distant church clocks that chimed the hour and tried hard to remember my past. What if my memory never came back? What if all I ever remembered was that I had a daughter somewhere far away? And would my memory of her fade with time? Could I bear a fate like that? I felt overwhelmed with the hopelessness of my situation. I don't want to be here, I thought. It's a mistake. Maybe it's not even real. And I curled up and tried to drift away—to find my way back to my own time.

Then it was morning and Courtney was in the room trying to rouse me. No, not Courtney. Lucy. With a feeling of despair I remembered. It all came rushing back. I was in the wrong place. This wasn't my world. I tried to block out the light and Lucy's cheerfully intrusive voice. I didn't want to get up and pretend everything was normal. I didn't belong here. I wanted her to go away and leave me alone. I wanted to sleep and then wake up in my own bed knowing who I was and that I belonged there.

"Come on then," Lucy said. "You can't lie in bed all day. Breakfast is waiting."

Her voice buffeted me. I wouldn't listen to it. I pulled the blankets over my head.

"Are you feeling poorly?" she asked.

This isn't real, I told myself. I'm not really here. If I ignore her, maybe she'll go away.

And finally she did give up and I was alone again.

But not for long. She was soon back with reinforcements. She had brought Mrs. Haslip with her, and Mrs. Haslip was not so easily put off.

"What's this now?" she said in her firm no-nonsense voice. I pictured her standing there with her hands on her hips. "You can't just lie in bed all day. Now come out from under those blankets."

I didn't answer. If I ignored them long enough, maybe they would just go away again. I felt someone tug at the blankets and gripped them tighter. I was not going to get up. They couldn't make me.

"Now we'll have none of this nonsense," said Mrs. Haslip. "You should be ashamed of yourself."

Ashamed? Why? I thought defiantly. Couldn't they just go away and leave me alone? Didn't I have the right to stay in bed if I felt like it?

"Should we fetch the doctor?" Mrs. Haslip demanded. "Are you sick?"

Oh great, just what I needed, more people! I imagined the room overflowing with them. "No," I choked out from my refuge under the covers.

"We know you've been through a lot," Mrs. Haslip said. "Come out and let's talk about it."

I felt the blankets being gently but firmly pulled from my grasp until my head was free. I opened my eyes and saw Mrs. Haslip's concerned face looking down at me.

"I don't belong here," I said and promptly burst into tears.

Mrs. Haslip took me in her arms and held me like a child while I sobbed. She murmured like a mother and patted me on the back until my sobs subsided.

"Feel better now?" she said. I noticed she was wearing a shawl, as if she had been on her way out when Lucy had come to fetch her.

"It's so awful not remembering anything," I tried to explain. "I don't even know who I am. What if I never remember who I am?" I thought it best not to add that I wasn't even in the right century.

"Well, we'll just have to give you a new name then," Mrs. Haslip said briskly.

It was not the response I had expected. I had expected her to assure me that my past would all come back eventually. It hadn't occurred to me I could simply give myself a name. Could I do that?

"How about Virginia?" she suggested. "Would that suit you?"

"Or Mary," said Lucy in the background. "I always thought Mary was a nice name."

Mrs. Haslip shushed her.

Virginia. I turned that over in my mind. Virginia Smith. Why not?

"All right now," Mrs. Haslip said. "I think a change of scene might do you good. Get dressed. You're coming with me."

I noticed the shawl again. "Where are you going?"

"It's Sunday, and I'm off to see my family."

"You have a family?" I don't know why this surprised me. I guess I had not pictured her having a life apart from her job working for the Ellmans.

"Indeed I do. Now get dressed before the morning's half gone. We've a train to catch."

Mrs. Haslip lived in Banstead, some fifteen miles south of London. We didn't have far to walk from the train station. When we arrived at the little house on a quiet street, five children of various sizes came running out the door to greet us. They paid no attention at all to me but vied to hug their mother. Everyone had to be hugged, from the toddler to the oldest daughter, a sweet-faced girl of fifteen.

"Where's Father?" Mrs. Haslip asked. "He hasn't wandered off I hope?"

"He lost his spectacles," a little boy volunteered.

"Did he now? Then we best go in and help him search for them."

"Did you bring us something?" asked the younger girl, eyeing the basket on Mrs. Haslip's arm.

"Well, maybe I did. If you're very good, there'll be cakes tonight."

This announcement was met with universal enthusiasm.

"Liza fell down two days ago and cut her knee," the oldest girl announced.

"This is my Jenny," Mrs. Haslip said, beaming proudly at the girl. "I don't know what I'd do without her. When I'm not home, she's in charge and I couldn't ask for a more capable helper."

Besides Jenny there were four others: Harry, who was ten; Will, a few years younger; Liza of the cut knee, who was five; and the toddler, Susan.

The room they squeezed into seemed hardly large enough to hold them all. It was furnished sparsely, and everything looked mended or worn out, from the children's clothes to the chairs and the curtains at the small window, through which light crept in, and yet it managed to be cheerful and homey. An old man on his hands and knees peering under a sagging armchair when we trooped in looked up in surprise and blinked.

"I wondered where everyone had gone," he said. "I thought perhaps you were playing hide and seek."

"Mother's home," said Jenny.

"Where have you been?" He threw Mrs. Haslip a reproachful look. "I've lost my spectacles and you know I can't see anything without them."

"Father's a little forgetful," Mrs. Haslip explained in a low voice.

"I found them," said Harry. "They're on the table beside your chair."

The old man looked nearsightedly at the table in question. "Well, now how did they get there? I'm sure I never put them there."

"Father, this is Mrs. Smith," said Mrs. Haslip, raising her voice. "She's come to pay us a visit."

He was on his feet now, and after setting his spectacles back on his nose, he squinted at me. "You're very welcome to our humble abode. Do I know you?"

"No, I'm afraid we haven't met before," I said, offering my hand.

He shook it vigorously. "I didn't think so, but then one can never be sure. There are ever so many people in the world, so many faces, so many names—it's difficult to remember them all."

"Yes, you're quite right, I'm sure."

Mrs. Haslip had her shawl off now and was tying on an apron. She appeared to be about to start cooking.

"May I help?" I asked.

"No, you're our guest," Mrs. Haslip said. "You just sit there and relax. And besides, this is what I look forward to all week long. Instead of cooking meals for other folk, I get to cook for my own dear ones."

So while Mrs. Haslip busied herself in one corner of the room over an odd little cast-iron stove, I held Susan, and Liza showed me her doll, Will his latest missing tooth, and Harry a small slightly chipped blue bottle he had found in a gutter. Mrs. Haslip's father persisted in removing his glasses at frequent intervals and then required help to find them again, but no one lost patience with him. It was a warm family circle and they generously included me in it without any hesitation or self-consciousness.

"Do you have any children?" Jenny asked, pulling a chair close. She had gentle brown eyes and a sweet smile.

"I have a daughter a few years older than you," I said.

"And is she back in the States?"

"Yes, she is." There was no need to explain that Courtney was not there now but in some future time.

"I'd like to travel and see the States someday," Jenny said wistfully.

"Then who'd take care of us?" asked Will, looking up from a marble he was rolling across the floor.

"I didn't mean now," Jenny said. "I mean someday when we're all grown up."

"Could I go too?" Will asked.

"Of course you could."

"I want to see a cowboy."

"For that you will have to go out West," I said.

"Have you been there?" Will asked.

I hesitated. "I'm not sure."

"Why aren't you sure?" he asked, curious.

"I got hit on the head. It made me forget a lot of things."

"Grandpa forgets things too."

"At least he remembers who he is."

Will looked at me, considering this. At that moment Susan decided she no longer wanted to be held and squirmed to be free. I lowered her gently to the floor.

"You remember your daughter," Jenny observed while keeping an eye on Susan, who had just spotted the marble. "Will, don't let her have the marble. She'll put it in her mouth."

"Yes," I admitted. I remembered my daughter.

"And your name."

I shook my head. "My name isn't Virginia Smith. I don't know my real name."

"Poor thing." Jenny patted my hand. "I can't imagine what it would be like not to know one's name."

"Leather Apron hit her on the head," Mrs. Haslip volunteered as she worked on the stew she was preparing.

"I've lost my spectacles," the old man announced.

"The Whitechapel murderer?" Jenny asked, surprised.

Before I could answer, Susan lost her balance, sat down hard, and began to cry. Jenny expertly scooped her up in her arms and comforted her.

"Did you see him then?" Jenny asked when Susan had stopped crying.

"Yes, I did."

"Weren't you frightened?"

"Yes."

"Was he a big man?"

"Not really."

Jenny bounced Susan in her lap, and the little girl laughed in delight. I couldn't help wondering how much time Jenny had had to be a child herself before she had taken on the role of caretaker for her younger siblings.

"Do you go to school?" I asked suddenly.

She sighed. "When would I have time? Who'd look after grandfather and Liza and Susan? Will and Harry go to school. They'll have to be the scholars in the family."

"You don't mind?"

She kissed the top of Susan's head. "It's just the way it is. No use fretting about it."

Her cheerful resignation impressed me. It also made me feel ashamed of my own despondency that morning. Jenny, despite her tender age, was coping with adversity far better than I was. She was right. There was no use wallowing in self-pity. I vowed to be more positive in the future. I also vowed that I would help Jenny if I could. I didn't like being stuck in the past, but since I was, I might as well do something useful.

The rest of the day passed in happy domesticity. All too soon it was time to say good-bye and catch our train back to London. When we got back to the Ellmans' house in the early evening, I felt like a different person. I was glad Mrs. Haslip had taken me home with her. Everything seemed more in perspective. I felt hopeful again. I had been very weak to despair of my situation so soon. It had been only two days since I arrived. I had gone through a door to get here and maybe I could find that door again and go back. I must have faith that I could get back to my own time again. In the meantime I would have to be patient. Perhaps I was here for a reason. Perhaps I was meant to do something, or to learn something, and then when I had done it, I would miraculously return to my own time.

CHAPTER 7

The inquest resumed the next day. Although Dr. Ellman and I had given our depositions, Lucy pleaded for us to go again, and after only a little grumbling, Doctor Ellman consented. I suspected he secretly wanted to attend. The case was drawing a good deal of attention in the press, and he felt personally involved because he had been summoned to the scene of the crime and had done the post-mortem examination.

Inspector Abberline was also in attendance, polite and inquisitive as usual. After helping us find seats, he asked if I had remembered anything else, and I said I had not. He was about to turn away when Lucy blurted out, "She can play the piano."

"Can she?" He looked at me with a raised eyebrow, waiting.

I felt myself flush, much to my annoyance. What was it to him if I could play the piano or not? I could have throttled Lucy for letting that slip out, although what did it matter?

"You should hear her," Lucy gushed, oblivious to the warning looks I shot her.

He looked at me with curiosity, waiting for me to speak, but what was there to say? Playing the piano was probably a skill like riding a bicycle. Once you knew how to do it, your body remembered. But did that bring me any closer to knowing who I was? No. Fortunately, at that moment the coroner walked into the room, and as on the previous occasion, conversations died away. Abberline had no choice but to leave us and take his seat.

The first witnesses called to depose were two men who had been on their way to work who had seen the body lying in Buck's Row and stopped to examine it. Then the dead woman's husband, who had been separated from her for eight years, testified that she had been a good wife and mother until she took to drink. The fourth witness was a young prostitute who had been the last person to see her that night except for her killer. She explained she had met Mary Nichols shortly after midnight. Mary lacked the four pence to pay for a bed at a lodging house for the night but said she would soon have it. She was wearing a new bonnet and seemed in good spirits, although a little the worse for drink. A woman who lived just above where Mary Nichols was found was called up next and swore she had heard no scream. After her, a constable described how he had run for the doctor. Then two mortuary workers, one after the other, described how they had undressed the body and discovered the horrific wounds to the abdomen. They were followed by an Inspector who told how he had made inquiries at the houses in Buck's Row to see if anyone had heard or seen anything. No one had.

At the close of the session, the foreman of the jury, a man with greying hair and bushy side whiskers, requested permission to speak. After it was granted, he said, "It's the general opinion of the jury that if a reward had been offered after the earlier attacks on two unfortunate women, this latest murder wouldn't have happened."

There was a widespread murmur of agreement from the crowd. The coroner rapped his gavel on the table for order. When the room had quieted, he looked about with steely eyes. "The Metropolitan police are opposed to such a reward as it might encourage unscrupulous individuals to turn in innocent victims in hopes of collecting the reward." This time the room maintained a respectful silence, like children in a schoolroom who had been reprimanded by their teacher. He then adjourned the inquest until the following Saturday.

"There's more?" I asked incredulously as we filed out of the building. I didn't see how there could be anything left to say.

"As many as need be," said Dr. Ellman, "until all the facts are known."

"Sometimes they go on for months," said Lucy.

"But does it bring them any closer to catching the killer?" I asked.

"Oh, they'll catch him eventually," Dr. Ellman said. "I have every confidence in Scotland Yard and the Whitechapel police."

I looked around for Inspector Abberline but saw no sign of him. I told myself he probably had more important matters to attend to. He couldn't always be hanging about, asking if I remembered anything. It wasn't as if I held any special knowledge that would help him catch the killer even if I remembered who I was or why I had been in Buck's Row. So why did I feel disappointed?

On our ride home, Lucy chattered blithely, while Dr.

Ellman seemed preoccupied with his own thoughts. Meanwhile I asked myself how I would manage if I were stranded in 1888 permanently. I couldn't expect the Ellmans to support me indefinitely. I had no relatives or friends or a source of income. How would I survive?

The next day Mrs. Haslip insisted I go with her to market. I didn't mind. It was better than moping about the house feeling sorry for myself, which was probably why she asked me to go along. She seemed to have a sixth sense about when I was feeling low. In her no-nonsense manner, she thrust a basket at me and tucked another under her own arm.

We set off in the opposite direction from what I had walked before when I had gone back to Buck's Row yet ended up in the same crowded market street I had been in before where there were stalls of food and many vendors hawking their wares.

Mrs. Haslip seemed to know them all, and they all seemed to know her. She also knew exactly what she wanted to pay and haggled over every transaction. I was impressed by how good she was at this.

While she was engaged in these transactions, I couldn't help but look around with curiosity. I had never seen anything like the market. So many people, so much confusion, such a din of voices, as if they were all trying to outshout each other.

"Now don't let anyone grab those out of your basket!" Mrs. Haslip warned as she set a cabbage and several oranges she had just purchased into my basket.

"Pippens!" shouted a freckled-faced young girl walking by.

"Strawberries," shouted another.

I looked around, enthralled.

"Haven't you seen a market before?" Mrs. Haslip asked, amused.

"Ours are different," I told her. She had no idea how different. I wondered what she would say if I described a modern supermarket to her.

At that moment a boy careened into me, nearly making me drop my basket. I stared at him. He was the Indian boy who had led me to Buck's Row. I was sure of it. But before I could say anything, he darted off.

I looked around, wondering if I would recognize anyone else—like the ruffians who had followed me to Buck's Row. There were so many people thronging the street. Maybe even the Whitechapel murderer was there, I thought, looking around uneasily. I wondered if I would know him if I saw him. In the alley I had only seen his back. His back and his shoes. That wasn't much.

"Virginia!" Mrs. Haslip said.

I jumped.

"You're a million miles away. Whatever are you thinking?"

"Nothing," I said guiltily. "I saw a boy I thought I knew."

"There are certainly a lot of lads about. Quick-fingered little devils who'll steal you blind. Mind that basket."

I pulled the basket closer. Satisfied, she turned to a burly man selling turnips and began to haggle again. After that, I kept an eye out for the boy but didn't see him again.

Later I was sitting at the kitchen table watching Mrs. Haslip make a meat pie when I found myself thinking about Jenny. Ever since Mrs. Haslip had taken me home to meet her family, I had been thinking off and on about the girl. If Jenny had been born a century or more later, her life would have been completely different. She would have been in high school, looking forward to college, instead of taking care of her grandfather and younger siblings. What did she have to look forward to? Would she be doomed to a life of poverty and servitude? Perhaps it was because she was not much younger than Courtney that this disturbed me so much.

"Jenny ought to go to school," I said as Mrs. Haslip deftly chopped up beef into small pieces with a butcher knife.

"But then who'd look after Father and the little ones?"

I didn't have an answer for her. "What happened to Mr. Haslip?" I asked, curious.

"He left us. Just walked out the door one day and disappeared."

This surprised me. It was hard to believe that a woman as practical as Mrs. Haslip could have a mystery in her past. "What do you think happened to him?"

"Probably went off to Canada or Australia to make his fortune. He was always going on about how he would make his fortune one day."

"Do you think he'll ever come back?"

"Not likely. I think he made up his mind before he walked out the door, and he wasn't the sort to look back."

"Did you love him?" I asked.

She shrugged. "When we were young, yes. My folks tried to warn me, but I wouldn't listen. And to give Alfred his due, he stuck by me for fifteen years. He was a clerk, but he wanted more from life. He loved the children, but they tied him down. I was pregnant with Susan when he left. He never saw her. I figure he just couldn't face the fact that there would be one more mouth to feed."

"And that's when you had to go to work?"

"What else could I do but go into service? Someone had to

bring in the money. And Mrs. Ellman's much more understanding than some would be. She lets me take Sundays off once a fortnight to go home."

She looked up. "Did you hear that?"

We both listened. Someone was knocking on the front door.

"I wonder who that can be," she said, frowning.

"Shall I go see?" I asked.

"Lucy will answer it."

I watched her hands moving dexterously with the knife. "Do you like being a cook?"

She shrugged. "It puts a roof over my family's heads and food in their mouths."

"But if you had a choice?"

Before she could answer, Lucy burst into the kitchen.

"It's Inspector Abberline," she announced, all smiles. "He wants to talk to you." She looked at me.

"Do you suppose they've caught the murderer?" Mrs. Haslip asked.

"I don't know," Lucy said, "but he said it was urgent."

I could not imagine why Abberline had come looking for me. Surely I could not be of much help to his murder investigation. All the same, I was looking forward to seeing him again as I hurried to the front of the house.

Lucy had left him standing at the open front door, scowling out at the street, where carriage traffic rolled by.

"Inspector Abberline," I said, trying to sound formal yet friendly.

He turned but didn't smile. "Sorry to show up like this without warning, Mrs. Smith. Can you come with me? I'm afraid we've found . . . a body."

"A body?"

"Of course we're not sure. That's why I need you to come with me, but she matches the description you gave me."

I felt as if a fist had clutched my heart and I couldn't breathe. Was he saying he had found Courtney? It wasn't possible. She wasn't here.

"I don't understand," I said.

"I think we've found your daughter."

"Alive?" It came out as little more than a whisper.

"Same height, long brown hair, about nineteen years of age."

"What was she wearing?"

He looked away. "If you'd just come with me. We need you to identify—"

I shook my head. "It's not her."

"I'm sorry."

I closed my eyes and tried to breathe. It could not be Courtney he had found. It had to be some other nineteen-year-old girl. Courtney was back in the 21st century.

"Did she have ID on her?" I asked, trying to be calm and rational.

"I beg your pardon?"

"Identification. Papers. Anything?" I couldn't keep the desperation out of my voice.

"She had nothing on her. I'm sorry."

"Clothes?" I choked out the word.

"Nothing."

He stood there watching me with troubled eyes.

"Is everything all right?" Lucy asked anxiously. She had come up behind me without my noticing.

I brushed a hand across my forehead as if to clear the cobwebs. It was a mistake. It was a misunderstanding. It couldn't be her.

"Inspector Abberline thinks they may have found my daughter. He wants me to go with him to identify—" My voice trailed away, unable to say *the body*. "But I'm sure it's not her."

"Shall I come along?" Lucy asked.

I shook my head. It was not Courtney. It could not be Courtney. I refused to believe it.

"No, that won't be necessary," I said, turning back toward Abberline.

"Wait," Lucy said. "Your hat. Don't forget your hat."

She dashed off and was soon back, a little out of breath, with the burgundy hat trimmed with pink flowers that Mrs. Ellman had given me to wear to the inquest. Just the day before I had thought it a pretty hat, but now it seemed a silly, frivolous thing. Without a word I set it on my head.

Once I was in the horse-drawn cab with Inspector Abberline, I began to recover somewhat from my original shock. A young woman had been found. That didn't mean it was Courtney.

"Where was she found?" I asked, forcing myself to speak calmly.

"She was pulled from the Thames."

"I see. And where is she now?"

"At the London Hospital morgue."

The word *morgue* sent a shiver down my spine. I nodded and stared out the cab window without seeing anything. I had been so sure that Courtney was back in our own time, not here. Maybe that had been because I so desperately wanted to believe it. What if she had been here all along? What if she had been wandering about with amnesia, and no one had taken her in as the Ellmans had taken me in? What if she had thought she was lost and alone in the past? I could hardly bear it, but far worse was the thought that she might be dead. I prayed that it would not be her.

Inspector Abberline seemed to understand and did not press me to talk.

The mortuary was a small brick building adjacent to the much more imposing large brick building which was the hospital. I wondered if this was where Mary Ann Nichols had been brought. I felt dread at entering the building. How many other bodies would be there? Inspector Abberline offered me his arm and I took it gratefully. He did all the talking, telling the attendant that we were there to look at the young woman who had been pulled from the Thames yesterday. I covered my nose and mouth with my hand to block out the odor of death and disinfectant that hung in the air. Light slanted in through several windows but couldn't banish the dismal atmosphere of the place. It fell on six narrow tables, and I realized with a shiver that on every table lay a body covered by a sheet. The attendant led us to one of these.

"Are you ready?" Inspector Abberline asked me.

I nodded, although I knew I would never be ready for this. I closed my eyes, and when I opened them again I was looking at a young woman who lay before me with closed eyes like some waxwork figure. Her skin looked strangely puckered, no doubt from the water. The attendant had drawn the sheet back to reveal only her head, not her nude body, for which I was grateful.

"Well?" said Abberline. "Is it her?"

I shook my head. "No, it's not." My relief was enormous. I wondered who she was. She did look a bit like Courtney, but it wasn't Courtney, thank God. I had been spared.

"Are you sure?" Abberline said. "Take a good look."

"It's not her," I said, beginning to cry.

"If it's not her, why are you crying?"

I shook my head, too choked up to explain.

He motioned for the attendant to cover the young woman's face again.

CHAPTER 8

Do you always manage to identify them?" I asked when we were back in the cab and my emotions were under control again.

"Not always."

"What happens then?"

Abberline sighed. "We bury them in an unmarked grave."

I wondered if that would be the fate of the young woman I had just seen. "Do you know how she died?"

"She drowned." His words sounded cold, but then he was used to dealing with death and I was not.

"But was it murder or suicide?" I persisted.

"Does it really matter?"

"It would matter to me if that were my daughter."

"I'm sorry for having to put you through that."

We rode in silence for a few minutes. I listened to the clop-clop of the horse's hooves mingling with the sounds of the other carriages and wagons on the street.

"Do you like your job?" I asked suddenly.

"I suppose I do," he said. "I've been doing it for nearly

fifteen years now. I don't know what else I'd do. I started out working for the Metropolitan Police as a common constable twenty-five years ago and now I'm Inspector First Class for the Central Office at Scotland Yard."

"I bet you're good at your job," I said.

"I try to be."

"You're not married, are you?" It was forward of me to ask, but I was beginning to feel like I knew him. Maybe the relief I felt after our visit to the London morgue had made me bolder than I otherwise would have been.

"What leads you to ask that?"

I glanced out the window. "You strike me as the sort of man who is married to his job."

"I suppose I am," he said. "God knows I don't have much time free. It's not a job with regular hours. Sometimes when I'm on a case I barely have time to eat or sleep."

"So you live alone?"

He nodded. "I was married once. My wife died. Consumption."

Now I remembered Mrs. Ellman had said that. "I'm sorry," I said. "No children?"

"No. Although I have a number of nieces and nephews to keep me busy."

"I don't think I could do a job like yours—murder and dead bodies and"—I grimaced—"autopsies."

He smiled. He had a warm smile that crinkled his eyes and relieved any awkwardness I was feeling. "It's not all like that. Sometimes it's like a puzzle, and I have to use every bit of skill I possess to put the pieces together, and when I do, well, it feels like I've won a prize. You know?"

I nodded.

"Now take yourself," he said. "You're a bit of a puzzle. I

keep moving the pieces around, but I can't quite get them to fit. You appear out of nowhere. You don't know your name or where you're from."

I started to protest, but he held up a hand to stop me.

"You don't know why you're here, and no one comes forward to report you missing."

"Well, surely it's not something Scotland Yard needs to concern itself with," I said.

"That might be true, except for the fact that the spot where you appeared was the scene of a murder."

"Surely you don't suspect me of killing Mary Ann Nichols?" I said.

He looked at me pleasantly enough, but I had the uncomfortable feeling the thought had crossed his mind.

"Am I a suspect?" I asked, a little offended now. After all, I had trusted him. I thought he was helping me, but maybe all the time he had been watching to see if I was going to exhibit any homicidal tendencies.

"I would not be good at my job," he said, "if I did not suspect everybody. You may not be a piece of the puzzle, but then again maybe you are. What were you doing there in Buck's Row? That's what I don't know. Is there some connection between you and the killer?"

At that moment the cab halted in front of the Ellmans' house. Before he could reach for the door handle, I reached for it myself, and this time I didn't wait for him to climb out and help me but got out by myself. I would show him that I didn't need his help.

He sprang out behind me and in a few steps caught up since he had no long skirts to contend with.

He looked mildly amused as he rapped on the door with the brass knocker, but I was not amused.

"I'm glad it was not your daughter," he said.

At once all my anger melted away. How silly I was being. Just an hour earlier I had been in mortal dread of learning Courtney was dead and now I was taking offense over something so trifling. What did it matter if he thought I was a murderess? What was he to me or I to him? We belonged to different worlds. It had been some kind of temporal fluke that we had ever met at all.

"Thank you, Inspector Abberline," I said politely, offering my gloved hand for him to shake, which he did after a look of surprise flitted across his face. "I know you're just doing your job and I appreciate it."

Lucy opened the door while we were standing like that and her eyes widened. Annoyed, I swept inside and did not look back.

"What happened?" she asked after closing the door.

"It was not Courtney," I said, taking off my gloves and hat.

"Was it another murder?"

"It was a drowning."

"You saw the body?"

I nodded, the image of the drowned young woman's face surfacing again in my mind. I resolutely pushed it away.

"Poor thing!" Lucy said. I wasn't sure if she meant me or the drowned girl.

Suddenly I felt exhausted. I stepped inside the drawing room and sank down on the nearest chair. "He thinks I'm connected to the murders."

"No!" The indignation in her voice was just the sympathy I needed. "Come to the kitchen and we'll make some tea. You'll feel better then."

I stood, a little shaky, and Lucy hooked her arm in mine. A

wave of gratitude swept over me. At least she was willing to give me the benefit of a doubt, even if Abberline wasn't.

In the kitchen, Mrs. Haslip also fussed over me. The teakettle was put on to boil, and soon we were all three drinking tea at the kitchen table and, as Lucy had predicted, I was feeling considerably better.

"If we could just figure out who you are!" Lucy said. "Maybe you're a Russian princess or something like that."

"You're forgetting she's an American," said Mrs. Haslip. "A Russian princess would have a Russian accent, wouldn't she?"

"I suppose so," Lucy conceded reluctantly.

"At least I'm pretty certain I was just visiting," I said.

"With your daughter," Mrs. Haslip added.

"Yes." I thought again of the young woman in the morgue and shivered.

"Maybe someone hit you over the head, robbed you, and then dumped you in Buck's Row," Lucy suggested.

"And why would they dump her in Buck's Row?" Mrs. Haslip asked skeptically. "What would be the point of that?"

"To cover their tracks," Lucy said. "To confuse the police."

"And her daughter?"

"Maybe they took her for the white slave trade."

"The *what?*" I asked faintly, a new fear springing up. Suppose I had been wrong about Courtney being back in our own time? Suppose something terrible *had* happened to her. Something just as bad as drowning.

"Now stop that," Mrs. Haslip scolded Lucy. "There's been quite enough talk of murder and dead bodies and such. "You're just upsetting her."

For a few moments we were silent, sipping our tea, each lost in her own thoughts.

"I know!" Lucy said. "I could take her to Madame Tussaud's."

"And why would you take her there?" Mrs. Haslip asked, lifting an eyebrow.

"Well, it would take her mind off things," said Lucy. "She could see one of the sights of London. After all, she came here to visit. She said so herself. Why shouldn't she enjoy herself a bit while she waits for her memory to come back?"

"Why not take her to someplace more respectable, like the British Museum?" suggested Mrs. Haslip.

Lucy rolled her eyes. "Madame Tussaud's is respectable. Besides, we can go to the British Museum some other time."

"You'll have to get Mrs. Ellman's permission. You can't just go traipsing off."

"Of course."

"And you should ask Virginia if she wants to go."

They both looked at me. Lucy's face was expectant.

"What's Madame Tussaud's?" I asked.

Madame Tussaud's, Lucy informed me, was a phenomenon not to be missed. No other city had anything like it. It was a sort of museum of famous people whose likeness had been caught in waxwork by Madame Tussaud herself, who as a young woman had barely escaped being beheaded during the French Revolution and had fled to England. Her creations were uncannily lifelike. People from all over Europe came to see them.

By Friday Lucy had convinced Mrs. Ellman that it would be a sort of philanthropic gesture to give her the afternoon off to take me to Madame Tussaud's and to pay the entrance fee and the omnibus fare. I was not entirely comfortable about this arrangement, especially since I was already feeling guilty for imposing on the Ellmans for as long as I had, but once Lucy had got it into her head that I should see Madame Tussaud's, there was no stopping her. I could only hope the entrance fee was small by the standards of the day.

My excursion with Lucy indeed proved to be therapeutic. Even in the twenty-four hours leading up to our outing, I began to catch her excitement. It was infectious. Had I ever been that young and full of energy? While I could not remember my life before waking up in Buck's Row, I didn't think I had been that enthusiastic about anything for a long time.

She pointed out all that we passed—shops, carriages, houses, parks, statues, and people. She was as eager to get to our destination as a child on the way to an amusement park, although from what she said I gathered she had been there at least a dozen times before. Madame Tussaud's was located in Marylebone Road, crouched among cramped houses and little shops. We joined a short line of people waiting to enter, paid the entry fee, walked down a dim narrow passage, and found ourselves in a cavernous gaslit gallery lined with waxwork figures. The figures indeed looked lifelike except for the fact that many were dressed in costumes of the past—in powdered wigs, silk breeches, an abundance of ruffles, and voluminous skirts.

"Aren't they wonderful?" Lucy whispered in awe.

'Wonderful' was not the word I would have chosen. 'Eerie' might be closer. They were quite lifelike, but being surrounded by them was disconcerting.

The room exuded elegance in the form of urns, sconces, red draperies, white pillars, gilt flourishes, dangling chandeliers, and a great many mirrors. The guests milled about, speaking in hushed voices and studying the wax figures as they might have studied paintings in a museum.

Lucy reverently pointed out Robespierre, George III, Oliver Cromwell, and Madame du Barry. She was surprised that I could recognize none of these and attributed it to my amnesia. She was particularly shocked that I did not recognize a tableau of the royal family—Prince Albert, Queen Victoria, and their nine children. In fact, the only waxwork figures in the room I could identify were Benjamin Franklin, George Washington, and Napoleon. Lucy was disappointed, but her bubbly enthusiasm never wavered. When we reached an ottoman at the end of the gallery, we took advantage of it to sit down for a moment. Lucy had launched into a story about the prime minister, Lord Salisbury, which I wasn't following—in fact, I didn't know who he was, but presumably he was there in wax—when suddenly I had a flash of Courtney standing next to a waxwork figure, posing for a photograph I was taking. I had been here with Courtney! I looked around. No, it was all different. There had been movie stars and rock stars and famous people from history like Hitler and Winston Churchill. For a split second I saw it, a completely different Madame Tussaud's.

"What is it?" Lucy asked.

"I think I may have been here before."

"Perhaps your memory is starting to come back. Oh, I knew it would help to bring you here!"

I looked around the large hall of waxwork figures and curious visitors. What would Lucy think if I told her how it would look in the future?

"You remember it?" she asked.

"Not exactly."

"Do you remember visiting the Chamber of Horrors?"

"The what?"

"Oh, you must see it. It's my favorite part of the museum."

She could not wait another minute to show it to me, so I let her lead me down a narrow winding staircase to a dank underground dungeon of cells with bars. The bars I assumed were there to keep people from touching the waxwork figures, but they gave me the unpleasant feeling of touring a prison. The lighting was dimmer here, steeping the tableaus in menacing shadows, and there was an unpleasant whiff of decay. In the first cell we saw a guillotine and a basket of bloody severed heads.

"It's a real guillotine brought over from France," Lucy explained.

I had to admit it was authentic-looking, right down to the blood on the blade.

In another cell we saw Marie Antoinette, waiting for her execution. Then Marat sitting in his bath, throat cut, while Charlotte Corday hovered nearby, the bloody knife still clutched in her hand. After that there were other murderers I didn't know, but Lucy did and she chattered away, recounting their stories. I was only half listening. I was trying to remember something. I looked around for a clue as to what it might be, which was when I noticed a man by himself not far behind us. I glanced back a few more times and noticed he kept the same distance behind us, moving forward when we did, stopping when we did. There was nothing unusual about him really. He was respectably dressed and wore a hat, but then so did the other men around us. I couldn't see if he had a beard or not because he didn't turn his head and the dim lighting made it difficult to see.

"What is it?" Lucy asked. "What are you looking at?"

"That man behind us. I think he might be following us."

She turned and stared at him. He might have been a waxwork, standing there so still, walking stick in hand.

"I think you're imagining it," she said. "He's just a law clerk or an accountant, no one out of the ordinary. If he follows us when we leave, I'll tell an attendant."

I tried to remember if I had seen the man in the gallery upstairs, but I hadn't noticed him there. Then again, as Lucy said, there was nothing unusual about him—unless you counted the fact that he was alone. Everyone else seemed to be in pairs or groups.

Perhaps it was because of the man that I found myself anxious to leave. Lucy would have liked to stay longer but reluctantly agreed to go. I was relieved when we emerged from the musty Chamber of Horrors. The man did not follow us when we exited the wax museum a few minutes later. I felt rather silly then and told myself it was just the oppressive atmosphere of the underground dungeon that had played on my imagination, but later I was not so sure. Something about the man I had seen disturbed me, and I had had the uncomfortable feeling that he was watching us. I found myself comparing him to my memory of the man in Buck's Row as he walked away. They were about the same size, similarly dressed, the same style of hat. It could have been him, but of course I couldn't be sure.

After we got back to the house, I kept thinking about what Abberline had said about a connection between me and the murder. I had been so quick to take offense that I hadn't really thought it through. Was it any wonder he should suspect me when I had appeared so mysteriously in the alley where the murder took place? I knew I was not the murderer, but perhaps there was a connection. Maybe not one I understood, but a connection all the same.

That night I dreamed again of being pursued through the narrow crooked streets of Whitechapel until at last I found myself in a blind alley with my pursuer closing in. I could hear his footsteps crunching on the cobblestones, and with no place else to run, I crouched down with my eyes closed like a frightened child hoping he couldn't see me. I woke drenched in sweat, my heart racing. There was no possibility of falling asleep again after that. I lay listening for the church clocks to chime the hour and morning to come.

CHAPTER 9

As soon as I heard Mrs. Haslip moving about the kitchen, I got up and dressed. She was surprised to see me up so early. I asked if she would mind if I fixed myself a cup of tea.

"You do love a cup of tea in the morning, don't you?" she said as she placed a skillet on the cast-iron monster of a stove.

"I usually drink coffee," I said and then stopped, startled, because it had just come out of the blue. I stood there, trying to conjure up the cup I drank my coffee from or the room I sat in while I drank it, or a face across the table, but nothing more came. There was only that fleeting memory of morning coffee. Still, I clutched at it like a sign of hope. It wasn't much, but it was something. Now I knew one more thing about myself: I drank coffee in the morning.

Meanwhile Mrs. Haslip had not even noticed.

I had just put the teakettle on to heat when we heard a frantic knocking at the front door. Mrs. Haslip looked at me, a spatula in one hand and a large wooden spoon in the other. "That will be someone looking for the doctor and Lucy's still in bed."

"I can get it," I said.

She looked uncertain, then nodded. "All right. Go see who it is."

I hurried down the hall and opened the door to a young red-haired policeman who was out of breath. "They sent me to fetch the doctor," he gasped. "There's been another murder."

I looked at the dark street behind him. A hackney cab stood waiting. "Another murder?" It felt like déjà vu.

"Can you wake the doctor? There's no time to lose."

"Yes, of course," I said, collecting myself. "Won't you step inside?"

I didn't know if I should be the one to wake the doctor, so I left him standing in the hallway and hurried back to Mrs. Haslip to tell her what he'd said.

"I'll wake the doctor," she said, wiping her hands on a dishtowel.

I followed her back to the entry, where the young policeman was waiting, looking as if he were anxious to be off again. She climbed the stairs, and within five minutes the doctor was dressed and rushing down. He grabbed his hat from the hat rack and headed out the door with the young policeman on his heels.

The commotion woke Lucy, who soon joined Mrs. Haslip and me in the kitchen.

"Was it another murder?" she asked me.

"Yes, that's what the policeman said."

"Where was this one? Was it like the other?"

"I don't know."

"Didn't you ask him?"

"No."

She groaned. "Oh, if only I'd been up!"

105

"Perhaps it's not Leather Apron," I said, trying to make her feel better.

"I'll bet it is," she grumbled.

"Well, don't you be saying anything of the sort in front of Mrs. Ellman," warned Mrs. Haslip. "You know how she hates talk of murder."

When Mrs. Ellman came down for breakfast, I joined her in the dining room as usual.

"The doctor had to leave early," she said. "Some sort of emergency."

She didn't mention the murder, and I didn't either.

"I was thinking perhaps of going out today," she said. "I owe Mrs. Russell a visit. Would you like to come along?"

"If you don't mind, I think I'd prefer to stay here," I said. "I've got a bit of a headache."

"I'm so sorry," she said. "Is your injury still bothering you?"

My hand flew up to the laceration on my temple. It was healing now. "No, it's not that. I haven't been sleeping well."

"Insomnia," she said. "Sometimes I have that too. Yes, I fear it's giving you dark circles under your eyes. Well, perhaps you should stay here and rest."

Of course instead of resting I read. And when I got bored reading about Varney the Vampire attacking young women, I wandered into the library and seated myself at the piano. The ivory keys felt like old friends under my fingertips. At the first notes I felt a great calmness wash over me. At first I played Beethoven, as I had before, but then I started to play something else, a tune that was nagging at my mind. I couldn't remember the composer or the title, just the sound of the music.

"What's that?" Lucy asked, ducking her head into the room.

"I wish I knew," I said. "It keeps going through my mind."

"Well, I'm sure you'll remember sooner or later, just like with Beethoven. Anyway, I'm off to buy a newspaper and see if I can find out anything about the murder."

"Can I come with you?" I asked on impulse.

"Of course, why not?"

Mrs. Haslip grumbled when Lucy informed her we were going out. "Are you forgetting there's a murderer out there on the streets?" Lucy just rolled her eyes. When Mrs. Haslip saw we were not going to change our minds, she gave up. "Mind you're back before Mrs. Ellman comes home," she warned. "I won't go telling tales to keep you out of trouble."

I thought we would go to the corner and buy a newspaper from a newspaper boy, but instead we set off walking briskly and ten minutes later, after we had already passed several boys selling newspapers without buying one, I asked Lucy where we were going.

"You'll see," she said mysteriously.

We caught a horse-drawn cab then, which took us to Fleet Street in the West End. The street was teeming with people, horses, carriages, cabs, omnibuses, and wagons piled high with goods. After the cab dropped us off, Lucy led the way into one of the buildings, where we climbed a narrow flight of stairs to the second story and entered a door emblazoned with the word *Star*. Inside were a number of desks scattered about and people—mostly men—sitting at them or walking between them. Lucy made her way to a desk in the corner, where a young man sat with his chair tilted back precariously, frowning at the papers scattered in front of him. His eyes widened at the sight of Lucy, and he let his chair fall forward on all four legs.

"Miss Callaghan!" he said. "To what do I owe the honor?"

"I thought you might like to meet someone who's actually seen the man who's been murdering women in the East End," Lucy said. "An eyewitness."

The young man looked at me skeptically.

"This is Mrs. Smith," she said. "Mrs. Smith, Bill Tanner."

He leaned forward. "Is she telling the truth? Did you see him?"

"Just his back," I said.

"Of course I'm telling the truth!" Lucy said indignantly. "And if you don't appreciate it, I'll just go next door and introduce her to someone at the *Times*."

He looked from me to Lucy. "Of course I appreciate it. But I can't do much with his *back*. It's his *face* everyone wants to know about."

Bill Tanner could not have been more than twenty. He had a good-natured face, quick to smile, a smattering of freckles. I liked him right off.

"There was another murder this morning," he said, lowering his voice. "Hanbury Street."

"We know," Lucy said, also lowering hers. "They fetched the doctor early this morning."

"So you know as much as I do."

"Actually we don't. I was hoping you could tell us."

He glanced around to see if anyone was listening, but everyone seemed busily at work or absorbed in conversation.

"We don't know her name yet, but they say it was another prostitute. Throat cut, just like before. Stomach too, worse than before."

"Did you see her?" Lucy asked.

"No, but I know someone who did. Photographer chap. They called him in to photograph the murder scene and the body. He said it made him puke. Never saw anything like it. Really bloody. Intestines pulled out and draped over one shoulder." He made a face. "They're calling him the Whitechapel Fiend. Got a nice ring to it, doesn't it?"

"Anyone see anything this time?" Lucy asked.

"No, I don't think so. But everybody says he's got to be a foreigner. No Englishman would do a thing like that."

She frowned. "Why do you suppose he draped her intestines over her shoulder?"

"How would I know? He's probably a lunatic. Who else would cut a woman up like that?"

"You'd think someone would have seen him," she said thoughtfully. "How could he commit a crime like that and then just vanish?"

"You didn't expect him to just stay there and wait for the police to come, did you?"

"No, but—"

"How'd your friend get a glimpse of him?" he said, looking at me.

Lucy glanced at me too. If we told him, how would we explain what I was doing in the alley?

"She doesn't remember much because she got hit on the head," Lucy said. "Anyway, we'd better be getting back."

"You're going to take a cab, aren't you?" he said. "It's not safe out there for a woman alone."

"I'm not alone," she said. "Mrs. Smith is with me."

"You know what I mean," he said.

"Don't worry about me. I can take care of myself."

"I could see you got back safe."

"There's no need of that."

"I'm serious, Lucy. Don't you be taking any chances out there. You know how I feel about you."

109

"And I've told you a hundred times, Bill Tanner, that I'm practically *engaged* to someone else. We're just good friends, you and I, but if you can't get that through your thick head, I'll just have to stop dropping by."

He looked unhappy but didn't say anything. I felt sorry for him. Lucy was a pretty girl, and he was clearly smitten by her.

"Oh, let's not quarrel!" she said. "If I'd known we were going to quarrel, I wouldn't have come."

"Why did you come anyway?" he said. "Was it just to ruin my day?"

"I told you why we came," she said. "We wanted to know about the murder this morning."

"Well, now you know."

Lucy glanced at the door and hesitated. I could tell she didn't want to leave with ill feelings between them. She leaned forward and lowered her voice. "What do you suppose Sherlock Holmes would have noticed?"

He gave a quick glance around and lowered his voice too. "He could have noticed a boot print, I suppose, that told him how tall the killer was, and he would have known why the killer draped her intestines over her shoulder and half a dozen other clues the CID aren't picking up on. He'd have it all figured out by now and would know who the murderer is."

"Yes!" she said happily.

"You finished it yet?" he asked.

I think they had forgotten I was standing there.

"Almost."

He looked around again surreptitiously. "You read this one yet?" He pulled a slim book from his pocket and held it up just long enough for us to glimpse the title—*The Strange Case of Dr. Jekyll and Mr. Hyde*. "You'd like it," he said, slipping it back in his pocket as if it were pornography.

"I intend to read that just as soon as I finish *A Study in Scarlet*," Lucy declared.

"Is that so?" he asked, cocking an eyebrow.

"Tanner!" a man bellowed from the far side of the room, and we all jumped guiltily.

"Well, if you ladies will excuse me," Bill said, leaping to his feet and sticking a pencil behind his ear. "It seems I'm wanted."

"If you hear anything, let me know," Lucy called after him as he dashed away.

We watched him weave with practiced ease through the maze of desks and workers, then made our way back down the narrow stairs and out of the building.

"Are we going back now?" I asked as Lucy stood there looking up and down the bustling street with narrowed eyes. I hoped she was not planning for us to walk very far because my high-top shoes were pinching my feet.

"First I have to do something," she said vaguely.

The something turned out to be a stop at a bookshop in the next block, where she doled out one shilling for a paperback copy of *The Strange Case of Dr. Jekyll and Mr. Hyde*.

"Have you read it?" she asked when we were back on the street again and the book was tucked away in her reticule.

"No, I don't believe I have," I said, not adding that, like Sherlock Holmes, this too was famous in my time.

"You should," she said. "Everyone's talking about it."

"Maybe I will, after I finish *Varney the Vampire*," I said, although at the rate I was going, I doubted that would be anytime soon.

"What did you think of Bill?" she asked as we dodged a steady stream of horse-drawn vehicles to cross a busy street.

"He seems like a nice young man."

"Oh, he is. I've known him nearly a year now."

"He appears to care about you a great deal," I observed once we were safely on a sidewalk again. I wondered how many people trying to cross busy streets in London got run down by horses.

"Well, I don't want him to. As I said, Mr. Keating and I are practically engaged."

"I don't believe I've met Mr. Keating," I said.

"That's because he's very busy. He's a lawyer, you know."

It seemed to me that a lawyer was very much above her station, but I didn't point this out.

"And you're in love with this Mr. Keating?" I asked.

"Of course. I'm fond of Bill, but Mr. Keating would make a much more suitable husband. I have to think about my future, you know."

"Will you continue to work for Mrs. Ellman after you get married?"

She looked at me in surprise. "Certainly not."

"Well, surely it's a long way off," I said. "You've got lots of time before you have to make up your mind."

"I'm eighteen," she said, lifting her chin. "Lots of girls my age are married with little ones to take care of."

"You shouldn't be in such a rush. You should enjoy being young, single, and free."

"Free? I'd hardly describe myself as free. No thank you. I'd rather be married and mistress of my own home. It's clear you've never been in service."

I sighed. She was right of course.

We took a hansom cab back to Whitechapel, for which I was grateful. I thought about how anyone seeing us would just see two women out on an errand. No one would know from looking at me that I didn't belong. Even Lucy didn't realize how out of place I was. If I just understood why I had been transported to this time, perhaps I could figure out how to transport back. I looked down at my gloved hands resting on the brown skirt. I had been wearing my own clothes when I was so mysteriously transported to this time and place, and so maybe I needed them on to transport back. It had been a week since Lucy had carried them away to be laundered and she still hadn't returned them to me.

"May I have my clothes back?" I asked suddenly as our cab turned onto Whitechapel Road.

Lucy looked at me blankly. "Clothes?"

"The ones I had on when I came here."

"What do you want them for? Haven't we given you nice things to wear?"

"Everyone's been very kind, but I'd like my own clothes back. I'll need them when I go home."

"But you don't know when that will be!"

"It could be soon. And besides I have a right to my own clothes."

"A right? What a funny way to put it. You make it sound as if we're deliberately keeping them from you. How can you be so ungrateful?"

She grumbled for a while in this vein, but after we were back at the house she brought me my clothes, laying them in a small neat pile on the foot of my bed.

"You can't wear them here even if they are the fashion in the States," she warned. "Everyone will stare."

"I don't care."

"Women don't wear trousers here. People will think you're a bluestocking, like George Sand."

"You don't understand," I said. "I can't stay here. I have to go home. I don't belong here."

"But that bump on your head—"

"Lucy, if I stay, more women may die."

"What do you mean?" she asked, frowning.

I had said more than I meant to say, but it was too late to take it back. "I shouldn't be here."

"But none of this is your fault," she protested. "You can't possibly believe you have anything to do with the death of those women."

"Inspector Abberline said maybe there's a connection between me and the murders."

She stared at me. "Why would he say a thing like that? You must have misunderstood."

"But suppose there is? Suppose it wasn't coincidence that I appeared in that alley."

"You're making no sense," Lucy said. "And I don't see what your clothes have to do with it in any case." She looked at them lying there. "Why don't you let me just put them away somewhere until you need them?"

She started to reach for them, but I scooped them up first. I was not going to let her take them away again.

She sighed. "I'm afraid the laundress couldn't get all the wine stain off your jacket."

"It's all right."

"They're strange clothes," she said. "I've never seen material like that before, or buttons, or the metal fastener."

She meant the zipper on my jeans. I could explain to her that these were clothes from the future, that I was from the future, but she would think I was crazy. She probably thought I was crazy anyway.

"I oughtn't to have taken you out today," she said uneasily. "If Mrs. Ellman finds out, I'll be in trouble."

"I won't tell her."

"Perhaps if you just rest a bit."

"Yes," I agreed. "I think that's what I'll do. I haven't been sleeping well, you know. I have bad dreams."

"What do you dream about?" she asked curiously.

"I don't remember." I didn't want to tell her I dreamed about the Whitechapel killer.

"Well, you'll rest now, won't you?"

I assured her I would.

After a last regretful look at the clothes I was clutching, she left. Once I was alone, I began to undress. The hooks gave me no end of trouble, but finally I struggled out of the dress that was so confining with its long sleeves and tight waist and cumbersome skirt. Then I put on my own blouse, jeans, and jacket and, retrieving my walking shoes from under the bed, put them on too. Now that I had my own clothes on again, maybe I would find my way home.

I must have fallen asleep because the next thing I knew Lucy was shaking my shoulder. I was disappointed to find myself still in the past, but I wasn't ready to abandon my plan. Somehow I must get back to my own time.

"What time is it?" I said, sitting up.

"Almost six," she said. "You've got to dress. You can't go to dinner in those clothes. What will Mr. and Mrs. Ellman say?"

"I'm not hungry," I said.

"How can you not be hungry? You've hardly eaten all day."

"I have a headache."

She stood there uncertainly. "Well, it might make you feel better to eat something."

"I don't want anything."

"Virginia, *please.*"

I would have liked to make her happy, but if I gave in now, how would I ever get back? I stared at the ceiling and waited for her to go away.

Finally she did, but only to return a few minutes later with Mrs. Haslip.

"Lucy says you're not feeling well."

"I have a headache," I said. "I'm sure it's nothing serious. Please explain to Mr. and Mrs. Ellman."

"Perhaps you should undress and get under the covers," she suggested.

"No," I said quickly. Without my clothes on, I might not be transported back to my own time. I had come here in my own clothes, and so it seemed logical I had to go back in them. But I couldn't tell her this. She wouldn't understand.

"How long has she been like this?" Mrs. Haslip asked Lucy.

"Right after we came back she wanted her clothes. She said she had to have them to go home."

"Did anything happen to upset her today?"

Lucy hesitated. "Well, the murder this morning of course."

"But she wasn't like this until you got back?"

I didn't want Lucy to be blamed. This was not her fault. Anyway, I was fairly certain I was not going to be transported anywhere as long as they stood there talking.

"Look, it's just a headache," I said, trying to sound reasonable. "I'm sure I'll feel better in the morning."

"And your clothes?" Mrs. Haslip said suspiciously.

"I feel more comfortable in them."

There was a whispered exchange between them, after which they retreated. The room gradually grew darker. Then

Mrs. Ellman came in. There was just enough light in the room for me to see her standing beside the bed.

"I heard you have a headache, my dear."

"I'm sure I'll be better in the morning."

"Perhaps if you had something to eat? When I have a headache, I often find that if I have something to eat—"

"I'm not hungry."

"Then perhaps a cup of tea?"

"I'd just like to rest I think."

She stepped closer to the bed. "Are you upset about . . . what happened this morning?" She meant the murder.

I wasn't, but it occurred to me that maybe I should let her think I was. It would make more sense to her.

"I don't know how much you know," she said.

"Another woman was murdered." Maybe if I shocked her she would go away.

"Yes, poor soul."

"And mutilated," I added for good measure. I didn't mean to be cruel, but I wanted her to leave.

"Yes," she said faintly.

Neither of us said anything for a few moments. In the semi-darkened room her face looked sad. I felt ashamed of myself for having tried to shock her. She had been very good to me and deserved to be treated better.

"I know sometimes one feels like lying down and giving up, but you can't. You mustn't. You have to go on."

I was surprised. I thought she turned her back on the ugliness and pain of life and refused to see it. Perhaps, married to the doctor, she heard more than we knew. Perhaps forbidding talk of murder and death at the table was her way of maintaining a semblance of rationality in an irrational world. Maybe this was the hard lesson she had learned when her beloved daughter died in childbirth and her son of cholera in India.

"I'm sure I'll feel better in the morning," I said. With any luck I would be gone by morning.

She sighed and turned toward the door. I couldn't let her go like that. What if I really did transport back to my own time? What if this were the last time I ever saw her?

"Mrs. Ellman—"

"Yes?" She paused by the door, her hand on the knob.

"Thank you for all your kindness."

"You're welcome, my dear."

CHAPTER 10

The next morning I awoke with my heart hammering to find myself in the same small bedroom. I had not transported home. And I had had the same nightmare again. Well, not quite the same as the previous night. I had not been running through the streets of Whitechapel but through the house of many rooms, and I had fled from room to room, trying to escape from something dreadful that was following me. After I woke up, I could not shake the feeling that if I stayed here, that horror would stalk me in my dreams until he found me, and then someone would die. I couldn't stay. Somehow I had to get back to where I came from.

I'm not sure how much time passed before Lucy breezed into the room. She threw open the curtain, letting the grey light of morning fill the room. I flung one arm over my eyes to block it out and groaned.

"Mrs. Haslip has made muffins," she announced cheerfully, "and it would be ungrateful of you not to get up and have some."

"Thank Mrs. Haslip," I said, "but tell her I'm not hungry."

"Not hungry!"

Mrs. Haslip stuck her head in the door. "Is she still feeling poorly?"

"It appears she plans to starve herself to death," Lucy said.

"Lucy!" Mrs. Haslip sounded shocked.

Now Dr. Ellman ventured into the room. Why couldn't they all just leave me alone?

"Has she got a fever?" he asked.

Mrs. Haslip placed a warm hand on my forehead. "I don't think so. Could that bump she got on her head be causing this?"

They were talking about me as if I couldn't hear them. I closed my eyes and pretended to sleep. Soon they went away and left me alone. I got up and yanked the curtains closed again, then lay back down. It was strange to listen to the sounds of the house, muffled voices, footsteps, doors opening and closing.

What if I didn't transport back to my own time? Wouldn't I have to eventually get up and go on with my life? Maybe so, but not yet. I would give it a little more time. Maybe I could fall asleep again.

The minutes ticked by and no one came to persuade me to get up, but neither did I fall back to sleep. After about an hour I thought I heard rapping at the front door. I didn't have to lay there long wondering who it might be. Soon the door to my little room was flung open and someone entered. The curtain was thrown open again and light filled the room.

"They say you won't get up and you won't eat, Mrs. Smith. Are you sick?"

My eyes flew open. Why was Inspector Abberline in my room? Had they sent for him?

"Is this how she was dressed?" he demanded.

"Yes, sir," Lucy said, hovering near the door. "Those are the clothes she had on when she arrived."

"Why didn't anyone tell me?"

"I suppose because you didn't ask."

"Didn't it strike anyone as strange?"

"It struck me," Lucy said. "And now that she's got her clothes back on, she won't take them off."

"Go fetch a cup of tea," he snapped.

"Yes, sir." She turned and disappeared through the open doorway.

Dr. Ellman was also in the room now. "What do you think?"

"Well, we can't leave her like this. You're sure there's nothing the matter with her?"

"She doesn't seem to be sick. No fever or anything like that."

"They tell me it's somehow my fault that you're refusing to eat," Inspector Abberline said, sitting down on the bed beside me, which I thought was rather forward of him. "Lucy said you were going on about a connection between you and the murders. She said that you've got it into your head that there's a connection and that I was the one who put that idea into your head."

I realized that I was not going to be able to ignore them. Clearly they were not going to leave me alone. "You did," I said.

"Did what?"

I sighed. "You said there was a connection. And I think you're right."

"Well, even if I said it, I don't see why that should make you want to starve yourself."

I couldn't explain it to him, especially not with Dr. Ellman standing there.

Lucy sailed back in with the cup of tea.

"Oh, good," Abberline said. "Now sit up like a good girl and drink it."

I really didn't have a choice, so I sat up and reluctantly sipped the hot tea he held to my lips. Transporting back to my own time would just have to wait.

"Perhaps some toast too?" he suggested, and Lucy flew away again.

"Those really are unusual clothes," he said, scowling slightly as he looked from my jacket to my jeans to the walking shoes on my feet. "Trousers—but not like any I've seen before. What do you make of them, Doctor?"

"I don't approve of women running around dressed like men," the doctor grumbled. "Next thing you know they'll be wanting to vote."

"I have to go over to Colney Hatch today. Would you mind if I took her along?"

"Do you think that's necessary?"

"I think it might be a good idea for her to see it."

"Ah, I see what you mean."

Lucy stood behind Abberline now, holding out a small plate with a slice of buttered toast on it.

"Eat that and we'll go," he said, rising. He stopped by the door. "Oh, and you might want to change your clothes."

"What's Colney Hatch?" I asked Lucy when Abberline and Dr. Ellman had left the room.

"An insane asylum."

I was alarmed now and regretted I had not been more cooperative. "Why is he taking me there?" I asked. Surely they didn't think I was crazy? Last night I hadn't cared what anyone thought, but I saw now that may have been a mistake.

"I have no idea," Lucy said. "But I think you should wear something more sensible and watch what you say in front of Inspector Abberline."

I wondered if I could refuse to go but decided I shouldn't risk it. It might give them one more reason to question my mental stability.

"Please don't take my clothes away," I begged Lucy as I took them off again.

"I'll put them right here in a drawer for you," Lucy assured me. "Safe and sound."

I struggled into the dress she brought for me to put on and waited nervously while she hooked it up. My fingers were shaking too much to manage hooks.

"What about my hair?" I asked nervously.

"We don't have much time, but I'll see what I can do."

Within minutes she had pinned it up. I checked the results in the washroom mirror. A proper Victorian woman looked back at me, a worried expression on her face.

"My hat!" I remembered as I was about to leave the room.

Lucy grabbed the burgundy hat from the hatbox on the bureau and placed it on my head. "There, you're all set."

"If I don't see you again—" The words caught in my throat. I wanted to thank her for all she had done for me.

"Of course you'll see me again," Lucy said. "What sort of silly talk is that?"

I gave her a quick hug and then, taking a deep breath, walked out to meet my fate.

Abberline barely glanced at me before we reached the waiting carriage. I was surprised to discover that we would not be traveling alone. Waiting in the carriage was a young man with a high forehead and a pale complexion. Abberline did not introduce him until we both had climbed inside.

"This is Inspector Purkiss," he said. "Inspector Purkiss, Mrs. Smith. She'll be traveling with us to Colney Hatch."

If young Inspector Purkiss was surprised, he didn't show it. He merely nodded politely.

Abberline had sat down next to him, leaving me in the uncomfortable position of having to face them both. I wondered how long the ride would take. Was I expected to make conversation? I remembered Lucy's warning to watch what I said. I must give the impression of being in my right mind. If Abberline had any intention of leaving me at Colney Hatch, I must convince him that I didn't belong there.

"You're not wearing those interesting shoes I notice," Abberline remarked.

"No," I said. I wondered if he had forgotten he told me to change.

"She has an interesting pair of rubber-soled shoes," he told young Purkiss.

"Ah!" Purkiss said.

"A pity she didn't wear them. You would have found them interesting."

"They may look strange to you," I said, "but I assure you they are far more comfortable than these shoes I have on."

"She has some other clothes that are interesting too."

Inspector Purkiss did not look particularly interested. He was gazing out the window next to him with studied indifference.

"Mrs. Smith here is a bit of a mystery," Inspector Abberline said. "We found her in Buck's Row on the night Mary Nichols was killed. She has no idea how she got there."

"American?" Inspector Purkiss asked without looking at me.

"Yes," I said before Abberline could answer for me.

"But where in America?" Abberline asked. "And where was she staying here in London?"

"Traveling alone?" asked Purkiss, although he looked as if he didn't care one way or the other. I wondered if they always talked like this.

"With her daughter," Abberline informed him.

"Ah." Clearly conversation was not Inspector Purkiss's forte.

"No sign of the daughter. No one's come forward to claim her."

"No husband?"

"She can't remember. And it's not easy to trace a woman who can't remember her own name."

"She's not really Mrs. Smith then?"

I wondered if they were going to sit there discussing me as if I weren't there for the whole ride. "I'm Mrs. Smith for now," I said briskly. "I'm sorry I don't remember my real name. Just as soon as I do, I'll let you know."

"You remember nothing?" young Inspector Purkiss asked in a bored voice, his eyes flicking to my face and away again.

"I remember a few things," I said. "Every so often something comes back."

"Such as?" prompted Abberline.

I took a deep breath. "Coffee."

"Coffee?" He raised an eyebrow.

"I remembered the other day that I like to drink coffee with breakfast."

"Oh, that's going to help us," he said sarcastically.

I lost my patience. "Look, it doesn't mean I'm crazy just because I can't remember my name."

Neither man said anything for a moment. Inspector Purkiss looked as if he had suddenly noticed something of great interest about the buildings rolling past.

"Have you ever seen the inside of an asylum?" Abberline asked.

"No," I said. "I'm pretty sure I haven't."

"Then it might be instructive to see one. Not every American visitor gets the opportunity to see inside one of our asylums."

"It's hardly the sort of landmark a visitor would seek out," I suggested.

"But it's where any one of us could end up if we lose our grip on reality," he said meaningfully.

At that point I followed Inspector Purkiss's example and turned my attention to the buildings we were passing. They were dingy and uniformly ugly. As far as I was concerned, they could all be torn down without any great loss. They would no doubt be gone in another hundred years—sooner even—and replaced with apartment buildings or modern office buildings or tract housing.

As if to prove me right, the buildings began to give way to an area of houses with lawns and patches of open countryside spread out under a grey and sodden sky. I mistook the Colney Hatch Asylum for a country estate as we approached. It was a sprawling brown brick building with a domed tower and many small narrow windows and numerous chimneys located in a residential area of prosperous looking houses and surrounded by a broad swath of lawn enclosed by a tall wrought iron fence. After the gate was opened for us by a guard, our carriage rolled up to the front entrance and we climbed out, Abberline assisting me and I politely accepting his help, a model of sanity.

We were admitted by a thin balding man in a white lab coat. Abberline told him we would like to have a brief tour before we met with Mr. Pizer. The man just nodded, pulled out a large ring of keys, and we set off down a lengthy corridor, our footsteps echoing hollowly.

Despite its impressive exterior, Colney Hatch was quite as grim as I had imagined—bare whitewashed walls, bars on the windows, and locked doors. The men and women were confined in separate sections of the building. Some inmates were locked in their own small cells like prisoners and we could hear them screaming or crying out. Some were chained. Those who were less aggressive milled about in a large room. Some, lost in their own world, did not seem to notice us, while others glared or looked at us with dull lifeless eyes. One woman with disheveled hair and wildly staring eyes cried out to us: "Please, you've got to help me. You've got to get me out of here. I don't belong here. It's a mistake." She wore a dress that had once been elegant but was now ripped and stained. I wondered what she had done to end up confined in the asylum. Was that how I would look if I were locked away in that grim place? I shuddered at the thought.

If Abberline had intended to frighten me, he had succeeded. I vowed that in the future I would be careful what I said and did. I saw now that my situation could be worse. Much worse.

We said little as we made our way through the bleak hallways and maze-like warren of rooms. No one commented when we were shown a room where inmates were hosed down with cold water—what our guide casually called water therapy—or saw a room containing lethal-looking apparatus for administering electro-shock treatments.

"I think we've seen enough," Abberline said finally, to my relief. "Now let's talk to Mr. Pizer."

Mr. Pizer was evidently the primary reason for our visit. We were led into a room furnished only with a small wood table and several chairs. Like the other rooms in the asylum, this one had bars at the windows and bare walls. After we had been waiting for a few minutes, a rough-looking man with a thick growth of beard and shaggy hair was brought in by an attendant. The attendant sat down near the door while the man sat at the table with the three of us. His eyes darted about in a wild manner, and I wondered how fast the attendant could get to him if he chose to attack us.

"Mr. Pizer," Abberline said, pulling out his small notebook and pencil, "do you know who we are?"

"Course I do," the man said in a gruff voice. "Scotland Yard."

"That's right," Abberline said. "I suppose you know why we're here?"

"On account of people say I killed those women, but it's a lie! I never did it!" His blood-shot eyes flicked nervously from one face to another.

"Are you the man they call Leather Apron?" Abberline asked calmly.

"So what if I am? That don't mean I did it."

"The newspapers say you did."

"The newspapers lie!"

"They say you carry a knife. Is that true?"

"So what? Is it a crime to carry a knife? I got to protect myself, don't I?"

"They say you threatened some of the women who walk the streets. You said you'd cut them if they didn't pay you."

"I didn't cut nobody! It wasn't me."

"But you threatened them?"

He looked sullen now. "A man's got to make a living. There's others do the same."

"What else do you do for a living?"

"I make boots," he said.

"Did you know Mary Ann Nichols or Annie Chapman?"

"I tell you I didn't kill anyone," he said.

"Can you tell us where you were on the night of August 30th?"

"I was at my lodging house, same as usual. Just ask anyone."

"And Friday night last?"

"Yes, then too. Just ask. They'll tell you."

"We already did."

"Well, then, you know I didn't do it. If anyone told you different, they lied."

"So why didn't you come forward when we were looking for you?"

"I figured I wouldn't get no fair trial, and if that mob got hold of me in the East End, they'd just as soon hang me. No thank you. I'd rather be right where I am. No one in their right mind wants to be in Colney Hatch, but sometimes being locked up is the safest place to be."

"I understand," Abberline said, "but suppose we could make it possible for you to be cleared of all charges?"

"It's no more than what I deserve."

"Of course you'd have to promise no more threatening women."

Pizer looked as if he might object but then thought better of it. He nodded.

"And you'd have to appear at the inquest tomorrow."

"Why do I need to be at the inquest?" he demanded. "I just told you. I don't know anything."

"It's up to you," Abberline said. "You could go on hiding out here at Colney Hatch or you could come to the inquest and get your name cleared."

"Well, I suppose I could go," he said grudgingly, scratching his jaw. "But you've got to give me protection. You can't expect me to go back there without protection."

Abberline wrote something in his small notebook, tore the page out, and handed it to Pizer.

"What's it say?" Pizer growled, looking at it distrustfully. Evidently he couldn't read.

"You give it to the sergeant at the Whitechapel Road Police Station. It says he's supposed to keep you safe."

Pizer nodded. He stood up and shook hands with Abberline. "Thank you, Governor." Then he shuffled out of the room, followed by the attendant.

"What do you think?" Abberline asked Purkiss.

"Was he telling the truth?" Purkiss asked.

"Yes, as far as I can tell. He couldn't have killed either woman. We know what time he checked into his lodging house and when he checked out. It's there in the register and the landlord will swear he didn't go out."

Abberline turned to me. "What do you think?"

"I have no idea," I said, surprised that he should ask me.

"Could he be the man you saw in Buck's Row?"

I thought about the man I had seen that night crouching by the body of Mary Nichols. I saw him again in my mind. I heard again the gnawing noises. I remembered my fear that he would turn and notice me. I shook my head. "No. He's too big—and too nervous. The man I saw was calm. He was whistling as he walked away."

"Whistling?"

"Bloody hell," muttered Purkiss.

CHAPTER 11

Monday was the first day of the inquest for Annie Chapman, the woman who had been killed in Hanbury Street. The Reading Room at the Working Lads' Institute was packed and not all the crowd that had gathered outside could get in. Police stood guard at the doors. There was tension in the air and heated exchanges broke out over seats. I was there with Doctor Ellman and Lucy. I had been uncertain that I wanted to attend, but Lucy had begged me. If I didn't go, she couldn't go, and she desperately wanted to attend, so despite my qualms, I had asked Dr. Ellman if we could accompany him, and he had consented.

It was Mary Nichols all over again. A prostitute, aged forty-seven, an alcoholic, poor, separated from her husband, trying to earn the fee for a bed to sleep in. She had taken her killer through a narrow passageway from the front of a house to the small enclosed yard in back, where it was dark and they would be alone. That was where her body was found early in the morning by an elderly man who lived with his family in a room on the second floor and who had stepped out for a breath of air.

He was the first witness. He described how he found the deceased lying between the step and the fence, her throat cut so badly that it was nearly severed from her body, her skirt pulled up, her abdomen a gaping wound, her small intestines flung above her right shoulder, blood everywhere. He had not touched her but ran to the nearest police station to notify the authorities that there had been another murder.

Next a friend of Annie Chapman's explained how Annie had received bruises on her breast and head from a fight with another woman at her lodging house over a bar of soap and how she had felt poorly ever since. It was testimony that showed the deprivation and casual violence of her life but added nothing to solving the identity of the murderer, yet the audience listened raptly. No detail seemed too small for them to consider.

The third witness was the deputy of the lodging house where Annie Chapman usually rented a bed and the fourth was the lodging house night watchman. Both had identified the body. Both testified she had been drinking and had gone back out to earn the four pence for her bed. She had lost her life for that four pence, poor woman.

At midday the inquest adjourned. When it resumed two days later, Pizer, the man Abberline had interviewed at Colney Hatch and who was known among the prostitutes of Whitechapel as Leather Apron, took the stand and testified as to his whereabouts on the nights of both murders, after which the coroner declared that he was no longer a suspect in either crime. Pizer looked around the room with obvious satisfaction and then made a bee-line for the door, as if anxious to escape.

The following day Doctor Ellman took the stand. The first several questions were general questions about when and how he had been notified of the murder. Then the coroner asked if he could describe the murder weapon based upon his examination of Annie Chapman's wounds.

"It was a long knife," Dr. Ellman said. "Six inches or more. And very sharp." He hesitated. "I'd like to add for the record that the killer appears to have a knowledge of anatomy."

A murmur began, but the coroner chose to ignore it. He raised his voice.

"Why do you say that?"

"Because he knew how to find what he was going after. And he had to do this without much light to see by."

"Would you explain what you mean by that? What exactly was he going after?"

"I would prefer not to say," Dr. Ellman said. "Certain details might better be kept from the press and the public for the sake of the investigation and to prevent panic."

"To prevent panic?" Lucy said in a low voice. "There's already panic. What are they not telling us?"

"That is not our affair," said the coroner sternly. "This inquest is to seek out the details that will help determine what happened and how justice may be served."

"But there are ladies present," Dr. Ellman objected, glancing about the room.

"Shall I have them removed from the room?" the coroner demanded.

Dr. Ellman looked uncomfortable. He must have decided not to ask to have the ladies removed. With effort, he said, "Certain parts were missing."

The murmurs increased. The coroner threw a warning look at the audience.

"Could you tell us what parts?"

Dr. Ellman looked around again. Clearly he would have

preferred not to answer the question. "Certain viscera. Part of a kidney . . . her womb."

The room erupted into pandemonium then and the coroner had to rap repeatedly with his gavel to restore order. When the room quieted again, he asked:

"By what he was going after, do you mean her womb?"

"I do," said Dr. Ellman. "She was missing some rings, but as near as anyone can determine, they were of no value. Her womb, on the other hand—"

"So do you think our killer could be a doctor?" interrupted the coroner.

There was a groundswell of whispers.

"Possibly, or someone acquainted with the post-mortem procedure. Maybe an assistant or a medical student."

"Not a butcher?"

"Of course it could be a butcher," Dr. Ellman said. "A butcher would also know the location of the organs, and he might also have such a knife, for cutting certain parts of carcasses."

"And there are many butchers in the East End, are there not?"

"Indeed there are."

"And no one would question blood on his clothes or his hands."

"I suppose not. Certainly that is one of the puzzling features of this affair. Both of these murders involve a great deal of blood. What is the killer doing to clean himself, or is he walking away with blood on his clothes and hands? And if he is, why hasn't anyone noticed him?"

* * *

When the inquest adjourned, Abberline and Purkiss were waiting for us outside.

"Wynne Baxter is making a circus of this," Abberline declared. "The longer he drags it out, the more excited people get. He and the press had them wanting to lynch every Jew in the East End with that business about Leather Apron, and now they'll be wanting to lynch every butcher and maybe even a doctor or two."

"You forgot lunatics," Purkiss reminded him.

"Yes, we've got orders to round up lunatics too."

"Are there so many?" I asked.

"Far too many," Purkiss said.

"No one pays them much attention unless they kill someone," Abberline said.

"But it may not have been a lunatic," Dr. Ellman said.

"Surely only someone insane would commit a murder like this," I said. "It wasn't like a robbery or a revenge killing."

"Oh, but perhaps it was," Dr. Ellman said.

I didn't understand why he would say this. "You mean because they took her rings? But you said yourself that they had no value."

"No, the rings had no value, but her *womb*—"

"I don't understand," I said.

"Like Burke and Hare," said Purkiss cryptically.

"What?"

"They killed people," Abberline explained, "for their body parts."

This also made no sense to me. I was sure that in 1888 no one had figured out how to transplant a heart or a liver or a kidney, let alone a uterus.

"I'm sorry," I said. "I don't understand. What can they do with these body parts?"

"Sell them," Lucy said. She had just rejoined us after talking for a few minutes to Bill Tanner, who was there to cover the inquest for the *Star*.

"But why would anyone want to buy a dead woman's . . . womb?" I asked, bewildered.

"For medical studies," Dr. Ellman answered.

"You've never heard of Burke and Hare?" Abberline asked.

I shook my head. "It's horrible. How can you call yourselves civilized?"

There was an uncomfortable silence.

"The parts should come from a cadaver of course," Doctor Ellman said. "Only the very lowest type of human being would think of resorting to murder in order to profit in such a way."

"You're absolutely right," Abberline said, turning to me. "It is an uncivilized custom and encourages murderers."

"I don't condone murder of course," Dr. Ellman said, "but science must have access to specimens and cadavers if we are to have medical progress and trained surgeons."

"The Nichols woman didn't have any missing organs as I recall," said Purkiss, "so maybe the killer isn't out to collect specimens."

We all looked at him. Purkiss never said much, but he was clearly an intelligent and observant young man.

"If he didn't take Annie Chapman's womb to sell it, why did he take it?" Dr. Ellman asked. "It makes no sense."

"A lunatic perhaps," said Purkiss. "They've never been known for making a lot of sense."

"So we're back to our lunatic theory," said Abberline. "What do you think, Mrs. Smith?"

"I think you've got a serial killer on your hands," I said.

"A what?"

"A serial killer."

"And what is a serial killer?"

They were all looking at me blankly. Had they never heard of a serial killer?

"You know, someone who kills more than one victim. A series of victims. A serial killer."

"I'm not acquainted with the term," Abberline said, turning his laser-like gaze on me. "Is that an American term?"

"I suppose it is." I regretted having spoken without thinking. Now I would have to bluff my way through it.

"Don't tell me you've got so many maniacs like this fellow running about that you have a name for them?" Abberline said dryly.

"I guess we do."

"Well, then I'd say the States are not much more civilized than we are."

As the inquest continued, the coroner seemed determined to interview everyone who had known Annie Chapman in life or encountered her in death. We heard from neighbors who ran to view the body as word of the murder spread, police who responded, people who rented the rooms of the house where the crime had been committed, the dead woman's boyfriend, a man next door who may have heard the voices of the killer and his victim on the other side of the fence and may have heard her body fall against the fence, and a woman who may even have seen the killer.

This last witness was middle-aged with a red face and a limp. In response to the coroner's question she described the encounter.

"I passed a woman in the street at half past three in the morning walking with a man wearing a deerstalker hat," **she** testified. "He wasn't a young man, maybe forty, and he was foreign-looking, maybe Jewish. He was not dressed like a gentleman but neither was he shabby. As I walked by them, I heard him say, 'Will you?' and she says, 'Yes.' I didn't think anything about it until I heard the Whitechapel killer killed a woman on Hanbury Street that night. That's when I remembered."

"And how did you know this woman was Annie Chapman?" asked the coroner.

"They showed me the dead woman at the morgue and that was her. I'm sure of it. She was the woman I saw that night."

"Did you get a look at the man's face?"

She shook her head. "No, I didn't because just as they passed he looked down and his hat hid his face."

Each day of the inquest after listening to all the sad details of Annie Chapman's life and the grisly details of her death, I would go back to the Ellmans' house and take solace in playing the piano. I was surprised how easily the music came back to me and how much I remembered about the men who had composed it. It was ironic: I could tell you Mozart had married a singer whom his father disapproved of when he was twenty-six and that Beethoven had written some of his greatest works after he became deaf but nothing about the people in my own life apart from Courtney. That one piece of music puzzled me though. It was completely different from the others, and I couldn't remember who the composer was or how it ended. Each time I got stuck at the same place. I couldn't remember what came next, and I had the feeling that if I could, I would remember other things as well.

At least the inquest gave me a reason to leave the house. On days when it wasn't held, I was bored. Lucy had housekeeping duties to attend to and Mrs. Haslip was usually busy preparing meals, except when she went to market. Whenever possible I went with her just to have something to do. I had more or less given up on *Varney the Vampire*. The plot had become so convoluted that I had lost interest. The author wanted me to feel sorry for poor Varney, but I didn't. I couldn't help feeling that if he just had a little more will power, he could refrain from sinking his teeth into the necks of helpless young women.

Then one day Mrs. Ellman suggested I accompany her to a soiree. Eager for any diversion from my routine, I consented. I wasn't sure what a soiree was, but if it would get me out of the house for a few hours, I was up for it.

"My husband doesn't care for soirees," she explained. "The last time I took him he was barely civil to the other guests and complained all the next week."

I could scarcely imagine Dr. Ellman being uncivil, although he was a taciturn sort of man who liked nothing better than to lose himself in a newspaper or a book when he was at home.

"It will be a small select group of people," she said. "Madame Agoti will be there, and there will be a séance. Have you been to a séance before, my dear?"

Of course I had not. Who held séances in the twenty-first century? They had long since gone out of fashion like long skirts and horse-drawn carriages.

"No, I don't believe I have," I said.

"Then you must go," she declared. "Sometimes nothing

happens, but other times they can be quite extraordinary. I know many people, like my husband, think they are all tricks and fakery, but I've seen things I can't explain, and if there's a chance I can communicate with my Henrietta or poor Charles, why then I don't want to miss it." Tears glistened in her eyes.

"I understand," I said, squeezing her hand, for what extremes would I not go to if I thought I could talk to Courtney again?

CHAPTER 12

The soiree took place on a Saturday evening in mid-September the day after Annie Chapman was buried. I had been in Victorian London for two weeks, but I had not given up on the idea of going home. However, I didn't see what I could do about it, and since the visit to Colney Hatch, I was determined not to get myself locked away in an asylum. So the only sensible solution seemed to be to blend in. I must hide the fact that I was from the future and pretend to be one of them. Surely I could manage that.

Mrs. Ellman and I were picked up by her friends, Mr. and Mrs. Stevens, in their carriage after dinner. I was wearing another of Henrietta's dresses, a lovely evening dress of dark blue silk, and Mrs. Ellman had loaned me a sapphire pendant to wear. I had a black shawl against the chill air of an autumn evening. It was drizzling and the streets were wet and gleaming under the gaslights. The horses' hooves rang out on the cobblestones and the carriage wheels rattled—sounds that had now grown familiar.

On our way to the soiree I learned that Mr. Stevens, an

elderly gentleman who was hard of hearing, was not a believer in séances, but his wife, who had acquired the habit of talking loudly, probably so that he could hear her, had high hopes of contacting someone named Malarky. It took me a while to realize Malarky was their spaniel, which had died several months before.

The soiree was held in the drawing room of a house in Belgravia with an enormous chandelier dangling from the ceiling and large oil paintings on the walls of scenes from Greek and Roman mythology. Mrs. Ellman introduced me to people as Mrs. Smith, who was visiting from the States, and if anyone asked me questions about my background, she quickly changed the topic.

We had not been there long when she steered me toward a foreign-looking little woman with a round face dressed in black who seemed to be the center of attention. This was the medium, Madame Agoti. She was perhaps in her thirties but could have been younger or older. She had a kind face and grey eyes that seemed to miss nothing.

When Mrs. Ellman introduced us, Madame Agoti took my hand in hers and held it, looking deeply into my eyes. "I can see you are very far from home," she said, speaking with an accent which might have been Hungarian or Polish.

I told myself she was only referring to the fact that I was from America, but all the same, it gave me a shiver. I mustered a smile and agreed that I was indeed far from home.

Gradually more guests arrived, including, to my surprise, Inspector Abberline, who was dressed more formally than I had ever seen him before. He looked almost aristocratic in his white collar and dark suit. When our eyes met, he nodded, then turned his attention to Mr. Stevens, who had just asked him a question. Several other men joined them. Curious what they were talking about, I moved closer until I could hear. They were discussing the recent murders.

"I still say the police should offer a reward," said Mr. Stevens. "It's a shame they haven't done more."

"Don't they have any suspects yet?" asked a short man with bristly whiskers.

"We had plenty of suspects," said Abberline, "but in the end none of them did it."

"It had to have been a lunatic," said Mr. Stevens. "Can't you just round up all the lunatics?"

"It could be a sailor off one of the ships down at the docks," suggested the short man with whiskers. "I know a fellow who had it all worked out. Times of the murders coincided perfectly with when one of the ships was in."

"It was a Jew, I'll bet," said a rotund man with the gold chain from a pocket watch dangling from his waistcoat. "Whitechapel is crawling with them. It's a disgrace how they live. Like vermin."

"They need to improve conditions in Whitechapel," said a woman with a jewel sparkling in her dark hair and more at her throat and on her wrists. "This is what happens as a result of so much poverty. It was bound to happen sooner or later."

"They say he's like Dr. Jekyll in Stevenson's novel," said the rotund man. "A respected doctor by day and a monster by night."

"Oh, have you seen the play?" asked the bejeweled woman. "Go see it. That's the murderer. Richard Mansfield. No one could playact a killer like that unless they had done it."

Abberline turned to me as if he had just noticed me lurking at the edge of the group. "Mrs. Smith."

I greeted him as smoothly as if I had been attending soirees all my life. "Inspector Abberline. You seem to be everywhere."

"Ah, I wish that were so. If it were, we might have caught our killer by now."

"I'm surprised to see you here," I said. "I wouldn't have thought a séance was your kind of thing."

He raised an eyebrow. "My kind of thing?"

"I wouldn't have thought you believed in talking to dead people."

"Actually I'm here because my superior at Scotland Yard told me to come. I'm surprised you didn't know that. It was Mrs. Ellman who so kindly arranged for me to be invited."

"Did she?" I glanced toward Mrs. Ellman, who was engaged in conversation with our hostess. Had she forgotten to tell me that Abberline would be there? Or did she think I might have refused to come if I had known?

"So you're working?" I said.

"I guess I am."

"Do you think the Whitechapel Fiend might be here?"

"You never know. The killer may be hiding in plain sight. I've run into a few of the men in this room in the East End at night."

That surprised me. I looked about at the impeccably dressed men in the room and wondered which of them ventured into Whitechapel by night. Whitechapel was home to the dregs of London, but with its legions of public houses and prostitutes, it offered such men the lure of a walk on the wild side.

"And the women?" I asked.

"Certainly not by night," he said. "Although a few of them venture there by day, to do missionary work or shop at the markets."

"Couldn't the killer be a woman?" I suggested.

"I very much doubt it."

"And why is that? Do you think we're less violent than men?"

"The victims were all women," he said. "Generally women murder men—especially husbands or boyfriends who beat them. No, odds are our killer's a man. Besides, you saw him."

"I saw someone in the dark who *looked* like a man."

"I see your point. Appearances can be deceiving. You're absolutely right."

As he watched me, I wondered if he was thinking that my appearance might also be deceiving and hastened to deflect that thought.

"So why did your superior want you to come to a séance?"

"Actually I'm here because we're at a total loss how to solve this case. We've got two women dead, maybe more—there were a couple of cases earlier this year, but they weren't as vicious as the two recent murders—and not a clue to speak of. Scotland Yard is hoping one of the dead women will try to make contact and tell us who killed her."

I stared at him. Was he serious? Apparently. Although there was a hint of a smile at the corner of his mouth.

"You don't believe in this, do you?" I asked.

"I keep an open mind," he said. "I've learned from experience that if I don't keep my mind open, I may miss the clue that solves the crime."

"So you think Madame Agoti really can talk to the dead?"

He glanced at the diminutive lady, surrounded by women eager to talk to her. "I think most if not all of these mediums are frauds. But at least Madame Agoti isn't a table rapper and doesn't claim to be in contact with an American Indian spirit guide or Rasputin or anyone like that. It's all fairly straight forward."

I had no idea what he meant by straight forward, but now the hostess was encouraging all of us to move to the dining room and take a seat at the long polished mahogany table. Since I had been engaged in conversation with Inspector Abberline, he ended up sitting next to me. On my other side was Mrs. Ellman, who gave me an encouraging smile and patted my hand.

The gaslights in the room were extinguished, throwing us into near darkness, illumined only by two tall candles placed at either end of the table. Madame Agoti sat at one end and our hostess at the other. The rest of us were evenly divided, five on each side of the table. We were twelve in all. No doubt this had been planned in advance.

"I make no promises," Madame Agoti said in her accented English. "Sometimes the spirits come and sometimes they don't. Ladies must remove their gloves. Please refrain from talking unless you are asked a question. Now take the hand of the person sitting next to you and close your eyes."

The ladies all peeled off their gloves.

I started when Inspector Abberline took my hand and then hoped he hadn't noticed. The room grew still. We sat like that and the minutes ticked slowly by. After the first five minutes it felt as if our hands were welded together.

I wondered when something was going to happen. Finally I opened my eyes and looked around at the other guests. Everyone was still sitting there, hands clasped, eyes closed, except for the short man with bristly whiskers on the other side of the table, who winked at me. I quickly closed my eyes again. How long were we going to sit there like that? I uncrossed and recrossed my legs, accidentally bumping Inspector Abberline's leg under the table.

"Sorry," I whispered.

And then very close to my ear Courtney's voice said, "Mom?"

My eyes flew open again. I half expected to see her standing next to me, but only Mrs. Ellman was there, with tears coursing down her cheeks. I couldn't imagine why she was crying.

"Are you all right?" Abberline asked in a low voice.

The other guests were unclasping hands now. The séance was over.

"Did we make contact?" Madame Agoti asked, looking around the table doubtfully. She looked very small and doll-like sitting at the end of such a long table.

"Yes," Mrs. Ellman said. "My daughter spoke to me."

"I think my Alfred was here," said the dark-haired woman with the jewels. "I could sense his presence."

I stayed silent. After all, I hadn't really heard Courtney's voice, had I? It was my imagination playing tricks on me. Courtney wasn't there. And Courtney wasn't dead either, so how could she speak to me from the grave? I thought of the drowned girl in the morgue. No, hearing Courtney's voice didn't mean she was dead. I refused to believe that.

"Are you all right?" Abberline repeated.

"Yes, of course," I said. "Why wouldn't I be?"

"You practically broke my hand."

"I'm sorry."

"You didn't make contact with a ghost, did you?"

"No, of course not." I avoided his eyes. "How about you?"

"No, afraid not. I really didn't expect to anyway."

"I don't believe in ghosts," I said. "They're just figments of people's imaginations."

"I had a feeling you didn't. Hey, why did you kick me under the table?"

I apologized again.

For the rest of the evening I was in a daze. I hardly knew what I was saying when I was required to speak. Fortunately no one paid much attention to me. Madame Agoti was again the center of a circle of admiring women with an endless stream of questions for her. Mrs. Ellman thanked her profusely. From time to time I caught Inspector Abberline watching me across the room. I vowed not to tell anybody what I thought I had heard, but I was wondering now if maybe Courtney *had* spoken to me. Maybe I hadn't just imagined it. I didn't want to talk about it to anyone in that room, including Abberline. Especially Abberline. And not just because I feared ending up in Colney Hatch. To talk about it would be to lose it, and I didn't want to lose it. Somehow Courtney had spoken to me. Maybe she would do it again. Maybe next time she would say more. Maybe she would tell me how to get back.

People were beginning to leave now. Abberline appeared beside me as I was pulling on my shawl.

"I was wondering," he said. "Would you be interested in seeing the production of *Jekyll and Hyde* at the Lyceum? Half of London is talking about what Richard Mansfield does with it. He's a compatriot of yours, you know."

"You're asking me out?" I said in surprise.

He lowered his voice. "I'm asking if you would like to see it. I'd prefer your company over Purkiss's."

I hardly thought Purkiss could be the only alternative. Surely there were many other women around whom he could have invited.

"Oh, do go," urged Mrs. Ellman, who had been standing close enough to overhear the invitation. "It would do you good to get out and mix a bit with people. I know the doctor and I are awfully dull company. We don't get about as much as we used to."

It did sound far more appealing than another evening spent trying to read *Varney*. I supposed Inspector Abberline would use the occasion to try to pry more information out of me, but I doubted there was much for him to discover when I knew so little myself.

CHAPTER 13

During the next half week I repeatedly told myself Abberline had only asked me to go with him to the theatre because he had some ulterior motive related to his investigation. Probably he had no personal life. He was one of those men married to their work. He had said so himself. That was why I had been so surprised when he suggested I accompany him to the theatre. Of course I knew I shouldn't get emotionally involved with him. Any day now I might remember I had a husband or be transported back to my other life. Besides, he and I were too different. He was a product of Victorian England, and I was an American from the 21st century. He had no idea what I was. Even if you overlooked the differences between us, he was clearly a confirmed bachelor. If he was drawn to me, it was as a puzzle to be worked out or a riddle to solve, like one of his crimes. Then I would remember the feel of his hand firmly holding mine during Madame Agoti's séance. Was it really so hard for me to believe that he might be attracted to me? Besides, it was only an evening at the theatre. I was making far too much of it.

I think Mrs. Ellman and Lucy were almost as excited about my theatre outing as I was. Another dress of Henrietta's was produced—a lovely purple silk that made me revise my image of Henrietta. Evidently she had not been as staid as I had at first imagined. In fact, she must have harbored a love of lush elegant things.

Abberline arrived at seven wearing tails and a top hat. He really was quite dashing when he dressed up. I sensed that he was a little nervous about our evening out too.

Our cab bore us through the city to the Lyceum Theatre in Westminster. After having seen the people who lived in the backstreets of Whitechapel, it was always a bit of a shock to realize there were so many affluent Londoners. The women glittered with jewels and the men wore top hats and carried fashionable walking sticks. I felt as if I had stepped into another world, which of course I had.

"Surely you've been to the theatre before?" Abberline remarked with amusement when we had taken our seats.

I suppose I was looking about me with the excitement of a young girl at her first real theatre performance.

"It's different from our theatres," I said. That was becoming my standard response. No one questioned it, and it had some truth to it. But Abberline was not so easily duped as everyone else.

"Different how?"

"It's so—" I couldn't say *old* or *quaint* because to him of course it wasn't. I couldn't tell him it was the gaslight because then he would want to know what we had in the States if it wasn't gaslight.

"So magical," I finished.

He looked about. "Really? Magical? You do have a fanciful imagination."

"Do you come here often?" I asked, hoping to change the subject.

"No, I can't say I do. Until last year when I joined Scotland Yard, I worked for the C.I.D., and that often meant walking the streets of Whitechapel at night. I know those streets like the back of my hand. It's here in Westminster that I'm out of my element."

"I think you fit in perfectly well," I said. Better than me, I could have added.

"Well, then you are judging only by appearance," Abberline said. "And appearances can be deceiving."

I certainly knew that was true. Wasn't I relying on appearances to deceive everyone around me into thinking I was from their time? But I didn't understand what he meant in reference to himself.

"How are you different from any of these other men?" I asked, genuinely curious.

"You really want to know? Well then, I didn't go to Harrow or Oxford or Eton. I didn't inherit a country house. I don't live in Belgravia or Kensington. Every penny I have, I earned."

I thought I detected both resentment and pride in his voice.

"So you would rather be like them?" I asked.

He glanced at me sideways to see if I was serious, then cast his eyes upward despairingly, tried to stifle a smile, and shook his head.

Shortly after that the lights dimmed and all talking died away. The curtains parted to reveal young Dr. Jekyll in a laboratory distilling a vaporous potion. A murmur of anticipation ran through the audience. Young Jekyll was interrupted by the arrival of his older friend, Dr. Lanyon, and

Lanyon's attractive daughter, Agnes, who reminded him of the dinner party planned for that evening to celebrate their engagement. After he had promised to attend the party, they left. Alone again, he gulped down the vaporous potion he had been distilling and then clutched his throat as if poisoned. There were gasps from the audience. A man behind me murmured, "Oh, no!" Wracked with pain, Jekyll staggered off-stage, only to reappear seconds later transformed into Hyde, a stooped ogre who grunted like an ape and bared his teeth at us. The audience broke into nervous whispers. Hyde then donned Dr. Jekyll's top hat and set off for the dark corners of London where Jekyll would never go.

Each time Hyde appeared the audience hissed and booed. This was not because the acting of Richard Mansfield was bad, but because the audience had no inhibitions about expressing their feelings. They feared and hated Hyde. Hyde was pure evil. At first he relied on his potion to transform from the respectable Jekyll into the evil Hyde, from the evil Hyde into the respectable Jekyll. But then his evil side grew stronger and Hyde began to emerge without the aid of the potion. Unable to return home, he sought help from his friend Dr. Lanyon. As Dr. Lanyon watched in horror, Hyde drank the potion and was wracked by painful contortions. Until this point all transformations had occurred off-stage, but this time it occurred on stage in full view of the audience. Women screamed, men swore. The audience was horrified and they loved it.

Jekyll now wanted to be himself and regretted that he had brought Hyde into existence, but Hyde was too strong for him and the antidote no longer worked. Trapped in his laboratory, Jekyll pleaded for Dr. Lanyon to bring him more of the chemicals he needed to make the antidote, but the chemicals no longer worked. Lanyon's beautiful daughter tearfully begged him to open the door. Finally the police arrived, battered down the door, and found Hyde dying. As his sobbing fiancée held him in her arms, he transformed one last time into Jekyll before he died. The audience applauded wildly as the curtain fell, and Richard Mansfield was called back to the stage repeatedly to take another bow.

"So what do you think?" Abberline asked when it was over. "Could he be our killer?"

"I very much doubt it," I said as we made our way toward the aisle.

"You have to admit he's very convincing."

"Special effects," I said.

"Special effects? Another American term I suppose?"

I told myself I was going to have to be more careful of the words I chose, especially around Abberline.

When we got to the aisle, instead of following the crowd out the door, Abberline steered me against the tide, toward the stage.

"Where are we going?" I asked.

"You'll see," he said.

When we reached the stage, I saw a door to the right of it that I hadn't noticed before. Abberline opened it and waited for me to go through. It led backstage. In contrast to the sumptuous theatre inhabited by the audience, here it was bare, cramped, dingy, and ill-lighted with cables, ropes, and crates strewn about. The stagehands barely glanced at us.

"Watch your step," Abberline said, touching my elbow.

I did as he suggested. I did not want to trip over a stray cable in the long purple silk and end up turning an ankle or sprawling unceremoniously on the dusty floor.

Abberline led the way to a door where a gangly teenaged

boy sat tilted back on a broken chair reading a book. The boy looked up with bored indifference as we approached.

"Sorry. Mr. Mansfield doesn't want to be disturbed."

Abberline flashed his badge. "Scotland Yard."

The boy rolled his eyes but moved aside. Abberline knocked and in a minute the door was opened by Mansfield, still wearing his makeup but without his wig. I was surprised at how young he looked up close. He was perhaps in his early thirties.

"What is it?"

Abberline flashed his badge again. "Scotland Yard. I'd like to ask you a few questions."

"Is this about those murders in Whitechapel?"

"It is."

"I've already answered scores of questions. You people can't seriously think I'm involved."

"The newspapers seem to think you might be."

"You can't believe everything you read in the newspapers." Mansfield looked from Abberline to me. "Oh, let's get this over with." He threw open the door. "Do you mind if I take off my makeup as we talk?"

"Not at all. By the way, that's quite a show you put on."

"Thank you—I didn't catch the name."

"Inspector Abberline."

"That's right. I've seen your name in the newspapers."

"And this is Mrs. Smith. She's from the States."

Mansfield glanced at me in his mirror. "Is that right? Where are you from?"

Before I could stammer that I didn't know, Abberline intervened. "How do you do it?" he asked, fastening his intense blue eyes on the actor's in the mirror.

"What? Turn into Hyde?" Mansfield grinned. "You don't

really expect me to give that away, do you? Trade secret."

"Well, I can understand how you change your hair when you go offstage—the wig—and make yourself hunched over and the animal grunts of Hyde—that's all obvious enough—but how do you change your face like that on the stage right in front of our eyes? That's what I can't figure out."

Mansfield looked pleased. "You really want to know?" He reached for a small jar in front of him. "That's my secret. Phosphorus. I put it on my cheekbones and brow, and along my jaw. When the lights are up, you can't see it, and then I'm Jekyll, but when the lights go down, well, then I'm Hyde."

"That's very clever."

"Thank you," said Mansfield.

"I hear you're going to close the show."

"That's right. End of the month. There's too much hysteria with this Whitechapel Fiend on the loose."

"Some people think your show may have triggered the killings."

"I can't help it if some lunatic wanders into my theatre and then starts murdering prostitutes in Whitechapel."

"So you think he's a lunatic?"

"Of course. What else would he be?"

"Someone like your Dr. Jekyll. Would you say he's a lunatic?"

Mansfield started wiping off his makeup. "If your fiend is Dr. Jekyll, he could be anybody. He could be you. He could be me. You'll have to figure out how to look beneath the makeup, Inspector, won't you?"

"May I ask you something?" Abberline said as our cab rolled back through the wet streets to East London.

"Of course," I said.

"The other night at the séance—something happened, didn't it? You saw or heard something. What was it?"

I hesitated, debating whether to tell him. I could deny I had seen or heard anything, but he would know I was lying. He was not easy to deceive. His mind was sharp and he noticed everything. I decided to take a chance and tell him the truth.

"I thought I heard my daughter speak to me. Of course it was just an illusion."

He didn't bat an eye. "What did she say?"

"Mom." I teared up remembering.

"That's all?"

"Yes."

"Why didn't you tell me before?"

"You would have thought I was crazy."

"I don't think you're crazy," he said. "I knew something had happened. I could tell by the way you nearly broke my hand."

"I don't think it means she's dead," I said hurriedly.

He watched me. "What does it mean?"

"Maybe it means she's looking for me. Maybe it means she's waiting for me to . . . find her." I was going to say, *waiting for me to come back*, but I stopped myself in time. There was a limit to how honest I thought I could be.

"London has a great many young women fitting your daughter's description," he said. "Are you so sure she's . . . alive?" He hesitated just as I had. Had he been about to say something else? *Real*, maybe?

"Yes, I'm sure of it."

"So you think you made contact with your daughter during the séance. But you also think your daughter is alive. How do you explain that? If she's alive, how could her spirit contact you?"

I shook my head. "I don't know. Maybe her voice came from my subconscious."

"Your . . . ?" He frowned slightly.

"My mind." It was impossible to explain to him. We scarcely spoke the same language.

"You mean you imagined it?"

I wanted to say no, but how else to explain it to him? "Yes, I suppose I imagined it."

"Why do I get the feeling you're not being entirely honest with me? What is it you aren't telling me?"

We were getting into dangerous territory now. I was not about to tell him I was from the future. He might be open-minded, but not *that* open-minded. I had to distract him.

"I have tried to be honest with you, but I don't even remember my name. Do you know what that's like? I don't know why I'm here. I don't know who I am."

It was all true. Just not the whole truth.

"I'm sorry," he said. "You seem so normal in some ways. I keep forgetting. . . ."

"I don't belong here," I said, which was as close as I could come to telling him the truth.

"We've contacted New York and Chicago, but so far nothing. No one's reported you or your daughter missing. But it's a big country. I'm sure something will turn up. It's just a matter of time."

He was right about that.

"I'm grateful for all you're doing," I said. "I'm sorry to be such a nuisance."

"You're not a nuisance," he said. "A mystery, but not a nuisance."

CHAPTER 14

While the inquest for Annie Chapman was still underway, the fourth and final session of the inquest for the first victim, Mary Ann Nichols, took place on the 22nd of September, three weeks after it had begun. It was a Saturday with a grey sky threatening rain. Afterward Dr. Ellman, Lucy, and I lingered once again on the pavement outside the Working Lads' Institute with Abberline and Purkiss before heading home.

"Thank goodness that's over," said Abberline.

"The press is having a field day with all these inquests," lamented Dr. Ellman. "I really think it would be better to wrap them up."

"I agree," said Abberline. "I feel like I ought to be out hunting for the murderer instead of sitting about listening to drivel from every person who ever spoke to the victim. It's a waste of valuable time."

"Wynne Baxter likes being the center of attention," Dr. Ellman said.

"I fancy our killer does too," said Purkiss. "I wouldn't be surprised if he were hanging about here, lapping it up."

We glanced around uneasily, as if the killer might be lurking among the crowd that had just poured out of the Institute.

"Did you hear we've received a letter from him?" Abberline asked. "At least we think it's from him. It could be a hoax of course."

"What's he say?" asked Dr. Ellman.

"Catch me if you can—that sort of thing. Calls us imbeciles for not having caught him."

"You think he'll strike again?"

"He says he will. He says he won't stop until we catch him."

"Isn't there something more the police can do?"

"I don't see what. We can't post a man on every street in Whitechapel."

"You've heard about the Vigilance Committee?"

"I don't know what they think they can accomplish. We've got amateur detectives running around the streets now who think they can catch the Whitechapel Fiend. They're a bloody nuisance. My men trail someone they think is suspicious and he turns out to be some young toff from Pimlico who fancies he's a detective."

"Well, I can tell you, I don't look forward to seeing any more of his victims," Dr. Ellman said.

"Oh, and he's got a new name now, did you hear?"

"No, what's that?"

"He signed his letter Jack the Ripper."

"*What?*" I gasped. For a moment I felt as if the world had tilted on its axis. So that was why the name Whitechapel had seemed vaguely familiar. Who hadn't heard of Jack the Ripper?

He would still be infamous more than a century later. The most famous serial killer of all time.

"Mrs. Smith? Are you all right?" Abberline asked.

"I'm fine," I said tightly. But I knew I wasn't. My heart was pounding and I felt dizzy.

"I ought not to have let her come," Dr. Ellman said. "Women shouldn't be exposed to this sort of thing. It goes against their nature."

"She hasn't fainted before," Lucy said. "And today was only the summing up. It's not as if we heard anything shocking."

"Well, you'd better take her home," Abberline said. "She doesn't look well."

Soon Lucy and the doctor had me bundled into a cab and we were on our way home, clattering across the cobblestones. I didn't listen to what they talked about as the cab rolled through the streets. All I could think about was what I had just learned—the killer was Jack the Ripper.

As soon as Dr. Ellman had deposited Lucy and me safely at the house, he turned around and rushed off again to make his rounds at the London Hospital. I wanted to be alone to think so I told Lucy I was going to lie down for a bit. She looked at me anxiously and bit her lip.

"Not like before?"

"No, not like before," I assured her. I did not intend to put on my 21st century clothes in the vain hope of traveling back to my own time.

Retreating to my room, I took off my hat and Henrietta's tight-fitting high-top shoes, and lay down still wearing the grey dress I had worn to the inquest. Nothing had changed, I told myself. There was no reason to feel so frightened. It wasn't as if I were in any danger. The killer only attacked women in the streets and under cover of dark. So long as I didn't go out walking at night, I should be safe. And so long as I was in the Ellmans' house, I was safe. He didn't know where I was. But was that true? What about the man I had seen at Madame Tussaud's? Could he have been the Ripper? I thought so at the time. A shiver ran through me. And if he was, could he have followed us home that day? For that matter could he have followed us *to* the wax museum? He followed me in my dreams at night, didn't he? Was my subconscious trying to tell me that he was stalking me? The thought made my blood run cold. I didn't want to believe it.

I had not been lying there long, trying to control my mounting anxiety, when a faraway rap at the front door nearly made me cry out. What if it were him? Stop being ridiculous, I told myself. Jack the Ripper wouldn't come for me in broad daylight, nor through the front door of a respectable doctor's home. He would be like Hyde. He would come by night, stealing in through a back door or a window.

All the same I was relieved when Lucy appeared in the doorway to say Inspector Abberline was at the door and wanted to talk to me.

"I told him you were lying down but he said it's important."

I sat up, my hand flying to my hair as I wondered how badly I had disarranged it while lying on the bed.

Lucy smiled. "You look fine. If there's a hair or two out of place, I doubt he'll notice."

He was waiting in the drawing room, hat in hand, looking very serious.

"I hope you're feeling better now," he said stiffly as I

entered the room. There was no warmth in his eyes or hint of a smile, which surprised me. I wondered what was wrong.

"I don't know what came over me," I said.

"I think I do."

"What?" I said, confused.

"There's something you're not telling me."

"What do you mean?"

"Tell me," he said, his voice harsh. "What do you know about him?"

"Who?" I tried to sound innocent.

"You know who I mean."

I glanced quickly at the doorway, wondering if Lucy was close enough to hear.

"I'm afraid I don't know who you mean," I said.

"Come," he said abruptly. "We'll take a walk."

He had a grim determined look. I wondered if he would cart me off to jail to interrogate me if I refused.

"My hat," I said, remembering just as he threw open the door.

"Forget the blasted hat," he snapped.

It was overcast as we stepped outside. In spite of his foul mood, he offered his arm and I took it. Anyone seeing us might have thought we were a respectable married couple taking a stroll. I looked about nervously at the pedestrians and the cabs and carriages rolling by and could not help wondering if Jack the Ripper was lurking nearby. And if he were, would I know him if I saw him?

"So who is he?" Abberline demanded when we had walked in silence for a few minutes. "Don't tell me you don't know who I mean. I saw the look on your face when I said Jack the Ripper. You know something."

I shook my head. "I don't."

"Is he someone you know?"

"No."

"What aren't you telling me? Women are dying. Don't you care?"

"Of course I care," I said, stung that he would think I didn't. "You wouldn't believe me if I told you."

"Try me."

"I can't."

He swore under his breath. "Is he someone you're trying to protect?"

"No, of course not."

"Who is Jack the Ripper?"

"I don't know," I said quietly. "If I knew I'd tell you."

We came to the end of the street. A horse-drawn wagon rolled past, driven by a hunched man with his cap pulled low. Abberline made no move to cross the street or turn the corner. We just stood there.

"Ever since I first saw you, you've been a mystery to me," he said. "Each time I think I have you figured out, I find I don't really know you at all."

"If I could tell you, I would," I said.

"You can if you want to. Clearly you don't want to. You're hiding something."

For a few minutes neither of us said anything. I wanted to tell him the truth. I wanted that more than anything. But would he believe me?

"All right," I said, taking a deep breath. "I have heard of Jack the Ripper before. He's famous."

Abberline frowned. "What do you mean?"

"I mean he'll be famous in the future."

"Maybe, maybe not."

"No, I *know*. I know because I'm from the future." There, I had said it. It was out at last. Would he believe me?

He closed his eyes tightly for a few seconds. When he opened them again, he took my arm without a word and rather roughly steered me back in the direction from which we had come. I could tell he was angry. As we neared the Ellmans' house, he stopped and faced me.

"What you said back there, never say that again. Don't you remember Colney Hatch? No one but a crazy person would claim to be from the future. Do you understand?"

I felt as if the ground had been ripped away from under me.

"I understand."

A chasm had opened between us. I had told him and he didn't believe me. Why had I thought he would? I had just destroyed anything he might have felt for me. I doubted he would come around again to see me. I would be that crazy woman who thought she was from the future. Oh, why had I been so stupid as to tell him?

I glanced down the street again, blinking back my tears. Hansom cab drivers, carters, laborers—there were a dozen or more men about. Any of them could have been Jack the Ripper. Would that be my destiny? To die nameless and alone in the wrong century, the victim of a psychotic killer?

"I'll have someone watch the house if that will make you feel better," he said, not meeting my eyes.

I didn't want his help, not if he thought I was a lunatic.

"Don't bother," I said and left him standing there as I turned and walked back into the house with as much dignity as I could muster.

CHAPTER 15

I doubted that any number of men watching the house would keep Jack the Ripper at bay if he wanted to find me. The newspapers were right. The Whitechapel police were incapable of catching him. They were no nearer now almost a month after the first killing than they had been then. No, if he wanted to find me, he would. The only way I would escape him was if I could return to my own time. But I had no idea how to do that.

Realizing that I was upset, Lucy had a suggestion.

"Look," she said, "I'm going to visit my sister and her little boy on Saturday. They live in Epping. Why don't you come too? It would do you good to get out of the city."

I don't think I would have agreed if I had realized we would have to travel by train. I didn't like the idea of Lucy spending her hard-earned money on train fare for me, and of course I had none of my own. But by the time I realized it, we were in the train station, a bustling hub of activity with trains arriving and departing, people coming and going, and hawkers selling their wares. In spite of my concern about the expense, I began to feel excited about the outing. Maybe it would be good to get out of London. Lucy was bubbling with anticipation at seeing her little nephew, and her high spirits were infectious.

"My sister's little boy—his name is Jamie—is smart as a whip," she said as we sat together on the train and the grimy buildings and houses of London dropped away. "He's two years old now. You've never seen such blue eyes. And clever! You wouldn't believe how clever he is. Always trying to take things apart. Mark my words, he'll be a scholar when he grows up. And he's very attached to me. Cried something awful last time when I had to leave. It near broke my heart."

"Do you go there often?" I asked.

"Once a month, if I can. Mrs. Ellman's very good about it."

"Are your parents there?"

"Oh, they're both dead now. Got carried off by ague." She pronounced it *egg-yu*.

"I'm sorry," I said, wondering what ague was but not wanting to ask. It wasn't Chinese food at any rate.

She shrugged. "We all have to die sometime. It doesn't do any good to dwell on it. They raised me the best they could and now I'm on my own. I've got a good job with the Ellmans, and once I marry Mr. Keating, I'll have everything I could want."

"The elusive Mr. Keating," I said, glancing out the window at the grey countryside.

"He's not elusive," she said defensively. "He's just busy. He's always got some case he's working on. Like your Inspector Abberline."

I didn't say anything.

"You like him, don't you?" she asked.

"I don't know," I said.

"He likes you. A body would have to be blind not to see it. Otherwise he wouldn't come around so much. He can pretend it's on official business, but anyone can see that's just an excuse."

"I don't think he'll be coming around anymore," I said.

"Why not? Did you quarrel?"

"You might say that."

She flicked her hand dismissively. "He'll get over it."

I doubted that, but I didn't want to explain. "You're forgetting I may be married," I reminded her. "It could be one of those details I can't remember about myself."

"You might be, but I don't think you are."

I looked at her, curious. "Why not?"

She puckered her face, concentrating. "You don't *seem* married."

That was not very reassuring. "I have a daughter," I pointed out. "Usually where there's a child, there's also a husband."

"One can have a child and not be married," she said airily.

I couldn't help smiling. Had she expected to shock me?

"I wish I could remember," I said. "It's so frustrating not to be able to remember who I am."

"Perhaps you're a widow," she suggested.

I hadn't thought of this.

"That would explain the sad look you sometimes have."

I had not been aware I looked sad. But if I was sad, wouldn't that be a result of having been thrust into the past and losing everyone and everything I'd ever known and cared about?

Through the train windows the countryside was rushing by flat and rather bleak under a leaden sky, but when we disembarked at Epping, the sun was trying to come out, the air smelled fresh and sweet, and a bird was singing. We walked along the cobblestone streets into a quaint village with old brick houses and Tudor manors, Lucy chattering as we went. She pointed out an old church and a public house from the 18th century. The village was small and we soon left the shops behind and were walking along a row of small snug houses.

The door of the house where we stopped was opened by a sullen woman of middle age with a crying baby on her hip and a dirty-faced toddler clutching her skirt.

She acknowledged Lucy with a nod, then turned back inside, leaving the door ajar for us. There were more children inside, five little ones, along with a girl of ten or eleven who was helping take care of them. The girl had a sore on her lip and her hair hung in her eyes as she eyed us distrustfully.

Lucy introduced me to the woman, Mrs. Lynch, and the girl, whose name was Annie. I gathered Mrs. Lynch was not Lucy's sister but was employed to take care of her sister's children, although it was hard to believe that all these children could belong to one mother. Lucy did not stop to explain but ran to a little boy with fine blonde hair and swept him up in a hug.

"And this is Jamie," she said proudly. "Have you missed me, Jamie?" The little boy, who looked about three years old, stuck a finger in his mouth and stared at me. "He's ever so good. He hardly ever cries, do you, Jamie?"

He reached up one hand to touch a locket she had tied around her neck with a ribbon.

"Have you been a good boy?" she asked.

He looked from her to me and nodded.

"Well, then, I've got something for you." She pulled a small packet out of her reticule, and the little boy reached for it. She helped him unwrap the packet to reveal several sticks of hard candy.

"You'll spoil his appetite," Mrs. Lynch objected.

"Just one piece shouldn't hurt," Lucy said.

"The others will want some too."

"There's enough for everybody." She broke the pieces in two and began to pass them out to the other children.

I wondered when Lucy's sister would appear, but neither Lucy nor Mrs. Lynch mentioned her. Mrs. Lynch busied herself breastfeeding the baby while Lucy played with the other children. I didn't want to be judgmental, but it seemed to me a rather dirty environment in which to be raising children. I could not imagine why Lucy's sister did not try to find a more suitable situation.

By midafternoon it was time for us to leave and Lucy's sister had still not arrived. I saw Lucy count several pound notes into Mrs. Lynch's hand as we were about to leave. Then she knelt down by Jamie and kissed him on the forehead.

"You be a good boy until I come again," she said.

As we walked back to the railway station, she turned her head aside to try to hide her tears.

"He's yours, isn't he?" I said.

She nodded, her lip trembling. "But you mustn't tell anyone. Promise me you won't tell a soul."

"Of course I won't," I assured her. "Does Mrs. Ellman know?"

"No, and you mustn't tell her. She'd turn me out."

"Surely not."

"I mustn't lose my job. I might not be able to get another, and then what would happen to Jamie?"

"And if you marry Mr. Keating—?"

"I don't know," she admitted, biting her lip.

"You haven't told him about Jamie?"

"Of course not."

"But you're going to?"

She looked uncomfortable. "I thought I'd tell him Jamie is my sister's little boy, and after we're married, if my sister were to die in an unfortunate accident, it would be understandable as how I'd want the little fellow to come live with us."

"Do you have a sister?" I asked.

"I don't know. I had one, but she immigrated to Canada and I haven't heard from her since."

I felt sorry for Lucy. She was very young to be a mother. I wondered what would happen if things did not work out with Mr. Keating. For her sake I hoped he was a broad-minded man.

We talked about other things as we rode the train back to London. At one point she asked me about my quarrel with Abberline. "Is that why you're so down in the mouth?"

"It's not just that," I told her. "It's these killings. It's not being able to remember who I am."

"But it'll come back. Just give it time."

I sighed. "I keep asking myself what I was doing there. Why was I in that alley?"

"You were lost," she said simply. "You were in the wrong place at the wrong time."

I had been far more lost than she realized. Where had I been before I woke up in that alley? I still couldn't remember. *The wrong place at the wrong time.* The words echoed in my head, as if they were important. Then it hit me. Perhaps it was not the wrong place. Perhaps it was the right place and I just needed to be there at the right time. That was where I had come through and that just might be where I had to be to go back to my own time. Why had I thought I could lie in my bed at the Ellmans' in my own clothes and find myself transported back? That was the wrong place. I needed to be in the alley where I had come through. There was a window there—or a door—some kind of portal you couldn't see—but it was there all the same. I just needed to be there at the right time. And what was the right time? Well, it would be after midnight at any rate. Sometime between midnight and dawn. I didn't like the idea of walking to Buck's Row in the dead of night, but if that was my only way to go back to my own time, I would do it.

CHAPTER 16

To avoid arousing suspicions about what I was planning to do, I spent the evening in my usual fashion, plodding through more of *Varney the Vampire* while Mrs. Ellman bent nearsightedly over her needlepoint, and the doctor read a book. About nine I began to yawn and asked to be excused to turn in early. Then I lay in bed listening, and when I was fairly certain from the silence that everyone had retired, I got up and put on my own clothes. I wasn't sure that they were important to the time jump, but I was taking no chances. They would also help me to pass as a man in the dark. I regretted that I didn't have a man's hat as well and briefly considered taking the doctor's from the hall hat rack but decided against it. It would have been too much like stealing, and I didn't want to abuse the Ellmans' hospitality after they had been so kind to me. So I pinned up my hair as well as I could and hoped in the dark no one would notice I was a woman.

When I stepped outside, the night was damp and chilly, but at least it wasn't raining. I waited for a lone carriage to roll by and then set out on foot. I thought I could find Buck's Row easily enough. However, I was afraid that if I walked along Whitechapel Road, the gaslights might give me away and there would be police on patrol who might stop me. I would have to use the backstreets, which were less well lit, and hope that no one paid any attention to me. I walked quickly but before long was out of breath and had to slow my pace. From time to time I glanced behind me, nervous that someone might be following me. When I was still at least ten minutes away from my destination by my calculations, I saw a man not far ahead step into the shadow of a building. My heart leaped into my throat. There was a public house nearby with yellow light spilling out of its windows. I was tempted to duck in for temporary sanctuary, but just then three men stumbled out talking loudly, and I kept walking, anxious not to be noticed by them. A tipsy woman arm in arm with a man in a slouch hat gave me a curious look as they passed. I lowered my eyes and walked faster. A block farther, I glanced back again, and again I thought I saw someone following me. I tried to fight down my panic. Was this how it was going to end? Would I be found dead in a Whitechapel backstreet in the morning, my throat slashed, disemboweled? Perhaps it's not Jack the Ripper, I told myself. Perhaps it's just some lowlife hoping to rob me. I ducked down an alleyway, hoping it would not be a dead end. Still a shadowy figure followed. He wasn't close, but there was no doubt now that he was following me.

Then I heard a scream in the distance, faint but definite. My heart raced. I stepped into the inky shadow of a building. I could not believe how still the city was, as if holding its breath, waiting for something to happen. Surely others had heard that scream. I had not imagined it. My ears strained. I could hear a dog barking somewhere. Two men passed by talking without noticing me. When they were gone, I forced myself to continue on my way, but now I was uncertain in which direction to go. I cursed myself for having panicked and ducked into that alley. I was no longer sure where I was or even if I could find my way back to the Ellmans' house. I struck out again, trying to beat down my panic. When I saw two policemen up ahead under a gaslight, I took another turn to avoid them. Then I thought I heard a police whistle in the distance. Was the city always so full of menace at night?

I glanced behind me again. I didn't see my stalker, but I knew he was there. I couldn't help myself. I began to run with no idea of where I was going, just hoping that sooner or later I would hit a street I knew or stumble on something familiar.

Stumble in fact is what I did. The cobblestones were not good for running, especially in the dark. I tripped and fell to my knees. I knew from the pain in my ankle that I had sprained it. I could hear footsteps running toward me. I turned with pounding heart to face my assailant. In Buck's Row I had been too afraid to see his face, but this time I would know him even if I didn't live to reveal his identity.

To my surprise, I recognized the man who was bending over me.

"Are you all right?" asked young Inspector Purkiss, his pale forehead gleaming like alabaster in the moonlight.

"You!" I said, breathless. "What are you doing here?"

"I could ask you the same, Mrs. Smith. Are you hurt?"

"I think I've sprained my ankle."

"No wonder, running like that in the dark. You're lucky you didn't break your neck."

"Have you been following me?" I demanded.

"I suppose I have."

"Did Inspector Abberline tell you to watch me?"

He squinted, considering this. "You might say that. I've

been watching Dr. Ellman's house. Inspector Abberline thought you might be in some danger."

Again a police whistle. We both turned to look in the direction from which it had come.

"Something's happened," I said.

"Yes, it would seem so," Purkiss agreed.

I wondered if he ever got excited about anything.

"Well, shouldn't you go see what it's all about?" I suggested. "Maybe your killer has struck again."

"My killer?"

I bit my lip. I was not going to call him Jack the Ripper. It seemed like bad luck to utter his name.

Purkiss cast a wistful look down the street in the direction from which the whistle had come. "No, I think I'd better see you safely home. Inspector Abberline would have my head if anything happened to you."

"I find that hard to believe," I said. "He thinks I'm crazy, you know."

Purkiss smiled. "Does he?"

I got to my feet and tentatively took a step. I had definitely sprained my ankle.

"Can you walk?" Purkiss asked.

"Of course I can walk."

"Perhaps you could take my arm," he suggested as I took two more limping steps.

I had no choice but to swallow my pride and hobble along leaning on Purkiss's arm.

"So are those the strange clothes Inspector Abberline was telling me about?" Purkiss said, casting a sideways glance at me. "They don't look so strange to me. I've seen women in trousers before. The shoes are unusual though." Without warning he squatted down for a closer look. "May I?"

Reluctantly I lifted my sprained right foot so he could examine my shoe.

"I wouldn't half mind having a pair like those myself," he said. "Rubber soles, right?"

I sighed. "Yes."

"You know our killer wears rubber soles."

I doubted he wore athletic shoes but kept that to myself. "So you think I'm the killer?"

He squinted into the night. "Not likely. Our killer knows the backstreets of Whitechapel like his backyard. You haven't a clue where you're going."

"Well, you're wrong," I said. "I do know where I'm going."

"All right, which way is Whitechapel Road?"

I hesitated, then pointed to my left.

"Wrong," he said. "It's that way." He pointed behind us. "Just out of curiosity, where were you off to?"

"Does it matter?"

"You have to admit it's an odd hour to go for a walk."

"Am I under arrest?"

"Of course not."

"Then I'm free to go where I please?"

"No one's stopping you."

I started limping toward Whitechapel Road. There didn't seem much point in avoiding it now that I had Scotland Yard for an escort. Purkiss fell in step beside me. As we drew near to the thoroughfare, a helmeted policeman under a gaslight watched us approach warily. A horse-drawn carriage rolled past in the street and disappeared into the fog.

"Constable Collins," Purkiss said as we drew near to the policeman.

"You see anything back there?" the constable asked.

"No. Why?"

"There's been another woman killed. Over on Berner Street."

Just then we heard more police whistles.

"Maybe they caught him," the constable said without much conviction.

"I'll keep my eyes open," Purkiss said.

The constable looked at me suspiciously, but before he could ask any awkward questions, Purkiss steered me on.

"I've got a bad feeling about this," he said when we were out of earshot of the constable.

"Me too," I said.

"Mind if I take you back to Dr. Ellmans' house?"

"All right," I agreed. It had been a reckless plan to walk to Buck's Row in the dark. The idea that I would miraculously transport back to my own time from there now seemed a little silly. I was far more likely to get mugged, or end up in the gutter with my throat slashed.

"Will you promise to stay there?" Purkiss asked.

"Yes—for tonight anyway."

He glanced sideways at me. "You aren't afraid of running into our killer?"

"I can't just stay shut up in the Ellmans' house."

"Not even at night?"

I sighed. I could not promise him that.

"You know Inspector Abberline's concerned about your safety," Purkiss said.

"I can take care of myself," I assured him.

"Can you?" He glanced down at my shoes, or maybe at my injured foot. "You know, Inspector Abberline is actually a decent chap when you get to know him. One of Scotland

Yard's finest. That's why they gave him this case. If anyone can catch a killer, he can."

"I'm sure he's very good at his job," I said.

"Yeah, he is."

CHAPTER 17

Mrs. Haslip was wiping off the wood table when I limped into the kitchen the next morning.

"What happened to you?"

"I sprained my ankle."

"However did that happen?"

"I think I tripped over something in the dark last night. Maybe a shoe."

"Well," she said, "I suppose you haven't heard the news. Two more women were killed last night."

"Two?" I said, surprised.

"A lad came to fetch the doctor early this morning. Poor man had to rush off without breakfast."

"Does Lucy know?"

Mrs. Haslip nodded. "She ran out to buy a newspaper. Should be back any minute now."

"Is Mrs. Ellman up?"

"She's in the dining room having her breakfast. Mind, don't say anything about the murders. You'll just upset her."

I assured her I would not bring up the murders, then

limped into the dining room. Mrs. Ellman sat at the table with just a slice of toast on her plate and a cup of tea. She had a worried expression on her face but made an effort to smile when I entered.

"Good morning, my dear," she said. "I hope you slept well."

"I did, thank you," I said.

"The doctor's gone out. He was needed at the hospital."

She picked up her toast, took a small bite, then set it down again, as if she could not eat. "I thought I would go to church this morning. My friend Mrs. Stevens is stopping by for me. You're welcome to come along."

"Perhaps another time," I said.

She took a sip of tea. The worried look had not left her face. "You aren't planning to go out today, are you?"

"No, I'm not." I had had quite enough adventure the night before. My ankle was better, but I wanted to rest it.

She looked relieved. "That's good. There was a bit of trouble last night."

"I know. Mrs. Haslip told me."

She nodded and took another sip of tea. "I think I'll ask Mrs. Haslip to bake a pie for supper. A pie would be nice, wouldn't it?"

"Yes, a pie would be nice," I agreed.

When I returned to my room, Lucy was waiting with the newspaper spread out on my bed. We pored over it together. The first woman had been murdered in a little court off Berner Street. Her throat had been slashed, but she had not been mutilated.

"The police think that the killer was interrupted," Lucy

explained. "There was a man on his way home who discovered the body. They think he interrupted the killer before he was done."

The second woman had been killed less than an hour later in Mitre Square some fifteen minutes walking distance from the scene of the first crime. This time the killer had not only slashed his victim's throat but mutilated her face and disemboweled her.

"They're saying it's worse than Annie Chapman," Lucy said, her eyes wide. "People are scared. They don't understand why the police haven't caught the killer."

"Do they know who the women were?" I asked, hoping it was none of the women I had met in the Whitechapel Road Police Station.

"No, they haven't identified them yet, but it says they were prostitutes, both in their forties."

"Just like Mary Nichols and Annie Chapman."

"Yes."

Women in their forties, I thought. Just like me.

After Mrs. Ellman went out, I headed for the drawing room and soon I was immersed in a Beethoven sonata. Playing the piano always soothed me. It took me away to another, more serene, place. After I finished the sonata, I started the mysterious piece that kept haunting me. Soon Lucy popped her head in the doorway.

"You're playing that song again," she said. "The strange one."

"Yes, I guess I am. I just can't remember all of it. I keep thinking the rest of it will come to me."

"I expect it will," she said. "Anyway I'll be upstairs if you need me."

"Can I help?" I asked, feeling guilty to be indulging myself at the piano while she worked.

"I can go faster by myself," she said. "You go on playing. I can hear it from upstairs. It's lovely."

So I played for a while, stopping when I hit the blank wall of my amnesia. On that piece it was always at the same place. I didn't know what came next. It was like going down a road that suddenly disappeared. As my hands idled over the keys, I started thinking about my walk through the dark wet streets of Whitechapel the night before. I knew Purkiss would tell Abberline I had been out wandering about when the two women had been murdered. It would only be a matter of time before he showed up and demanded to know why I was there, so when there was a sharp rap at the door, I didn't wait for Lucy to come down to answer it but went to answer it myself, expecting it to be Abberline. But when I opened the door, to my surprise, it was Lucy's friend, the young man from the *Star*. He looked equally surprised to see me. For a few seconds we both stood there at a loss for words.

"You must want to talk to Lucy," I said, recovering myself. "I'll go get her."

"No!" he said quickly. "As a matter of fact, I've come to talk to you, Mrs. Smith."

"Me?" I couldn't imagine why he would want to talk to me. I also couldn't help noticing the quick desperate glance he cast beyond me, as if looking for Lucy.

"Lucy—Miss Callaghan, I mean—said you saw the Ripper."

"Yes, but I didn't get a good look at him, as I explained earlier. I'm afraid I can't be of any help to you."

"Could I ask you some questions anyway?" His eyes were full of pleading.

I hesitated, not wanting to be rude. "I'm afraid I don't know anything. I was hit on the head, and I don't remember anything before that. Not even my name—my real name, that is."

"But you saw him?" he persisted.

"Yes, I saw him. But it was dark and I didn't get a good look at him."

"Have you heard two more women were murdered last night?"

"Yes, I have."

"Did you hear about the message?"

I had no idea what he was referring to. "What message?"

"There was a message scrawled in chalk on a wall in Goulstone Street." He looked down at the little notebook in his hand. "'The Jews are the men that will not be blamed for nothing.'" He glanced up at me again. "They're pretty sure he wrote it because they found a piece of the second victim's apron there with blood on it."

I tried to push this last detail out of my mind. I didn't want to think about blood-soaked aprons.

"What does it mean?" I asked.

"That a Jew did it, I suppose."

"The Ripper is Jewish?"

Young Bill Tanner shrugged. "More likely he's trying to stir up trouble. There was a near riot after that last killing. He probably gets a kick out of seeing the police rush about trying to throw water on the fire."

Lucy came up behind me with a feather duster in her hand. "Bill Tanner, what's the meaning of this?"

"I've a right to be here," he said defensively. "It's a free world, isn't it?"

"You want to get me sacked?"

185

"Who said I was here to see you? I come to talk to Mrs. Smith. She doesn't mind."

"Well, *I* mind," Lucy said.

They glared at each other.

"Perhaps you should come in," I suggested. Despite his insistence that he had come to interview me, I suspected Lucy was the true reason for his visit. There was far too much tension in the air to think they had no feelings for each other.

He stepped inside, looking proud of himself for having gotten past the door.

For her part, Lucy was not about to leave us alone. She followed us into the drawing room and flung herself into a wing chair still holding the feather duster.

Bill Tanner sat down between us in Dr. Ellman's chair and glanced about the room with curiosity.

"Well, get on with it," Lucy snapped. "We don't have all day. You're wasting people's valuable time."

He ignored her. "What is your opinion about the killer, Mrs. Smith?" he asked, pencil hovering over notebook, face earnest.

"I have no opinion," I said.

"You must have. For instance, some people think he's an escaped lunatic, some a moral degenerate, some say he's a sailor, some a doctor—that's on account of how he cuts up his victims and removes their organs. They say it shows a knowledge of anatomy. For the same reason some say he's a butcher. Some say he has an accomplice or that he's a member of a secret society."

"I really have no idea," I said. "I just glimpsed the man."

"There, you see," Lucy said.

He ignored her again. "About the message—"

"What message?" Lucy demanded.

He explained all over again about the message scrawled in chalk on a wall in Goulstone Street and the bloodied piece of apron found beside it.

"You can't even be sure he wrote it," Lucy objected. "A bloodied piece of apron isn't much to go on."

"The police seem pretty sure."

"Well, it wouldn't make any sense for him to write it if he was a Jew, now would it?" Lucy pointed out.

"Who knows how someone like that thinks?" Bill retorted. "He's got a twisted mind."

"He must have wanted people to know he wrote it," I said. "Otherwise he wouldn't have dropped a piece of his victim's apron beside it."

"That's right," Bill said, happy that I was on his side.

"I want to see it," Lucy declared, springing up from the wing chair as if ready to be off at once. I assumed she meant the wall and not the piece of apron, which without doubt would now be in police custody.

"You can't," Bill said.

"And why not?"

"It's gone. They washed it off. I didn't even see it myself. I went along with my friend, Mr. LaRue, who was supposed to photograph it, and when we got there, it was gone."

Lucy sank back down in the wing chair, disappointed.

"Do you know who the women were?" I asked. "Do you know their names?"

He shook his head. "Not identified yet."

"I just don't see how he gets away with nobody seeing him," Lucy muttered.

"It's dark," Bill said. "He's just one more bloke out there on the streets who could be on his way to work or on his way home or just out for a walk because he doesn't feel like sleeping. If he's got some blood on his hands or his clothes, who's going to notice?"

There was a loud rap at the door and we all jumped. Lucy sprang up to answer it. She hardly had time to fling open the door before Abberline charged in. His eyes leaped from me to Bill Tanner as if he suspected us of plotting against the Crown.

Bill was up in a flash, hand extended. "Inspector. It's an honor."

Abberline stared at him. "Who the devil are you?"

"Bill Tanner. The *Star.*"

"A reporter. I might have known. What do you want?"

"A little information," Bill said. "And seeing as how you're here, sir, care to give me a statement regarding the two latest murders?"

"What?" Abberline said.

"A statement. Do you have any suspects?"

"I'm not at liberty to say. Now off with you. Mrs. Smith has nothing to say to you."

I thought that was rather high-handed of him, and I felt sorry for Bill Tanner, but before I could object, Lucy leaped to his defense.

"You can't talk to him like that."

"Oh, can't I?" Abberline glared at her.

"He's got as much right to be here as you do," Lucy said, lifting her chin defiantly.

"That's right," Bill Tanner said.

Abberline looked at me.

I shrugged. "He's just doing his job."

Bill and Lucy looked smugly triumphant.

"Fine," Abberline said. "I'll just sit down here and listen." And he dropped down on the sofa.

I turned back to Bill Tanner, ready for more questions, but

he suddenly seemed to have forgotten what he wanted to ask. He fidgeted with his pencil and then tapped it on his notebook nervously. Finally he blurted out: "You're American, aren't you?"

"Yes, I am."

There was an uncomfortable pause while he jotted down my answer in his notebook. Then he tried again. "Will you be staying long? I mean, here in England. That is, London."

"I don't know," I said.

"Right." He jotted this answer down in his notebook as well.

Lucy rolled her eyes and groaned. "Come on. I'll make you a cup of tea."

A look of relief swept over Bill's face, and he followed her out of the room like an over-sized puppy.

"What was that all about?" Abberline asked with a frown.

"He's a friend of Lucy's."

"But I thought he said he was a reporter."

"He is. He's also Lucy's friend."

Abberline stood up, strode to the doorway, and looked into the hall, probably to make sure that Lucy and Bill were out of earshot. Satisfied that they were, he turned back to me.

"I guess you know why I'm here."

"Yes. There were two more murders last night. I assume that's why you're here."

He watched me warily, nodded, then sat down again. "Why were you out there last night? And don't say you just went for a walk. Tell me the truth."

"I had nothing to do with the murders," I said. "Just ask Purkiss. Apparently I was never out of his sight."

"You were walking in Whitechapel alone. Do you have any idea how dangerous that is? That maniac was out there on the streets last night. Don't you realize it could have been you he found?"

"It wasn't me, and I wasn't alone. Purkiss was there."

He pulled a square of paper from his pocket, unfolded it, and spread it on the carpet between us. It was a map of some sort, hand-drawn.

"What is it?" I asked, leaning forward so I could see it better.

"A map of East London."

He pointed with his finger. "That's Berner Street, where the first victim was killed shortly before one this morning." He moved his finger. "That's Mitre Square, where the second victim was killed less than an hour later." He moved his finger to a spot midway between. "That's where you were at about half past, according to Purkiss."

A shiver ran down my spine.

"Do you realize what that means? The killer may have passed you on his way from his first victim to his second. If Purkiss hadn't been there—"

"It's not possible," I said, staring at the map.

"What in god's name were you doing there?"

I shook my head. I had a sinking feeling in the pit of my stomach. Could Jack the Ripper have been looking for me? Had he somehow known I would be abroad last night? Had two other women died because he hadn't found me? No, I didn't want to believe it. Surely it was just a coincidence.

"Purkiss can't tell me. He says you were lost. But you must have been there for a reason. I want to know that reason."

"I was going back," I said faintly.

"Back? What do you mean?" He frowned.

"To Buck's Row."

"For god's sake, why?"

"I thought I could—" I stopped. What was the point? The map before me blurred as tears filled my eyes. What was the use of trying to explain? He would just think I was crazy. The truth wasn't what he wanted and I didn't have anything else to give him.

He handed me his handkerchief. "You were trying to go home. That's it, isn't it?"

Now I really did start crying. It was like a dam bursting. All the feelings I had held in for so long. All the loneliness and despair.

"Is everything all right?" Lucy asked from the doorway.

"She'll be fine in a minute," Abberline said.

I heard Lucy's footsteps retreat. When I finally could look at Abberline again, he seemed embarrassed.

"Does she know?" he asked.

I shook my head. "So you believe me?"

"I don't know what to believe. I've never been one to believe in ghosts or boogeymen. Our Jack out there is boogeyman enough for me."

"I'm not a ghost," I said, dabbing at my eyes.

"No, you're flesh and blood all right."

"So you're not going to haul me off to Colney Hatch?"

"Not unless you go around telling people you're from. . . ." He left his sentence unfinished.

"I won't," I said and handed him back his handkerchief, damp now.

"So is there anything you can tell me about this Jack the Ripper?"

I shook my head.

"But you said he's famous—in the future." His eyes shot to the doorway warily, then back to me. "I'm not saying I believe you are from. . . ." He cleared his throat. "I'm just saying if you *were*, what's his name?"

"I don't know."

"You mean you don't remember?"

"I mean no one knows. It's a mystery that never gets solved."

He stood abruptly. "No, that can't be right." His brows knitted in a frown.

"I'm sorry," I said. "If there were anything I could tell you, I would."

He began to pace, and I sat waiting.

"There are different theories about who he was," I explained, "but no one ever knew for sure."

"How many?" he demanded, stopping.

I thought he meant theories, or suspects. I tried to think. There was one about the Queen's son, the Duke of Clarence, wasn't there? And about her physician, Sir William Gull. And another about a Polish immigrant. Or were these just ideas invented by the movies? What did I really know?

"Victims," he said. "How many women does he kill? Can you give me their names?"

"I don't know," I said, feeling hopelessly inadequate. Why should he believe I came from the future if I couldn't answer his questions?

"I'm going to catch him. I refuse to believe he can't be caught."

My eyes fell on the map again. "Do you think somehow it was my fault? That if I hadn't gone out last night, those women wouldn't have died?"

"Of course it's not your fault. It's a coincidence that you were there when they were murdered." He too stared at the map, as if to convince himself. "And your daughter, is she here too?"

"I don't know. I don't think so."

"She's in the future?"

"Yes."

"How far in the future?"

I hesitated. "A hundred and thirty years."

He shook his head. "This is insane. All right. Let's suppose it's possible. So you haven't been born yet. In fact, your parents haven't been born."

"That's true."

"And in your future, I've been dead for at least a century, and so has Jack the Ripper, whoever he is."

"Yes."

"And what is he, the worst killer who ever lived?"

"No. Just one of the first."

"First what?" he said, frowning. "He's certainly not the first man to commit murder."

"Serial killer," I said.

He studied me with narrowed eyes. "That's the second time you've used that word. What did you say it means?"

"He kills more than one person, and it's not for money or revenge, and sometimes it involves mutilating the body . . . and he takes pleasure in it."

Abberline stared. "Pleasure?"

"Well, in a perverse sort of way."

"Are there many of these serial killers in the future?"

"Yes, I suppose there are."

"And he's the first?"

"I guess so. I'm no expert."

He stood up and paced again. "Pleasure, you say? He takes *pleasure* in cutting up women? He's a lunatic then. No sane man would take pleasure in cutting someone up."

"You're right," I said. "But he still might be hard to spot.

He could seem perfectly normal when he's not killing."

"Like Dr. Jekyll," he said grimly.

"Yes, like Dr. Jekyll."

He looked at me thoughtfully. "What if you can't get back to your own time?"

"Then I suppose I'll have to get used to this one."

He nodded. "Meanwhile we do have a killer on the loose, and you seem to have some possible connection to him, even if I'm damned if I understand it, and so I'd like to ask you to please not chase about the streets of Whitechapel at night. I'd rather not find he's made you one of his victims."

"All right," I agreed.

He looked at his hat. "And if you want to go to Buck's Row, let me know and I'll send a man with you. Or I'll come myself. Day or night."

"All right," I said again.

He scooped up his map from the carpet, folded it, and tucked it back into his pocket. "How's the ankle?"

"Better, thank you."

He looked as if he might say something else and then changed his mind. Neither of us said anything as I walked him to the door.

He paused before stepping back out into the brisk air. "Mrs. Smith," he said with a nod and put his hat on. He was all business again.

"Inspector Abberline."

I watched him walk away without looking back. He might not have stood out in a crowd, but how many men of his time would have been broad-minded enough to make the leap that he had just made? Not many, I suspected.

Closing the door, I went in search of Lucy and Bill. I found them in the kitchen cozily sipping tea. Mrs. Haslip had gone home to Banstead for the day so they had the kitchen to themselves. They appeared to have settled their differences.

"Are you all right?" Lucy asked the moment I walked in.

"I'm fine now," I said.

"What did Inspector Abberline want?"

"He was hoping I could give him more information about the killer."

"And could you?"

"Not really."

Lucy rolled her eyes. "Listen, we've been talking. Bill knows this man who's taking photographs of the bodies for the police. He said he could introduce us to him."

Bill looked uncomfortable. "Maybe it's not such a good idea. He's kind of a strange chap."

"It's a great idea," Lucy said. "Maybe he would even let us look at his photographs."

"Why would you want to do that?" Bill asked, grimacing.

"To look for clues of course."

He looked doubtful. "I don't know."

"Maybe we could notice something the police missed," she insisted eagerly, "and we could figure out who the killer is." She looked at me. "You'd come too, wouldn't you, Virginia?"

I looked from one to the other. I wasn't sure I wanted to see photographs of the dead women and my ankle still ached, but Lucy was so eager that I hesitated to refuse. Besides, it would give me an excuse to get out of the house for a while. It wouldn't be like I was breaking my promise to Abberline. We would be out in broad daylight and I wouldn't be alone.

Once we had decided, Bill dashed off to make the arrangements. An hour later, after leaving a note for Mrs. Ellman in case she returned and found us gone, we set off, all three of us, to catch an omnibus to Soho.

* * *

Mr. LaRue lived in several cluttered upstairs rooms in a dingy boarding house on Dean Street. Yellowed curtains blocked out the light, dust powdered the surface of a small table by the door, and clothes had to be removed from the chairs before we could sit down. Mr. LaRue himself was a man approaching middle age with overlong greasy hair, circles under his eyes like dark bruises, and dirt embedded under his fingernails. He wore a rather shabby coat and down-at-the-heel boots. There was a kind of glaze to his eyes that made me suspect he was on drugs. He struck me as creepy, and I began to wonder almost as soon as we stepped into his rooms if maybe Bill was right about this not being a good idea.

The row of photographs tacked up on the front wall just reinforced this impression. Side by side with portraits of stern-looking Victorians who had posed for him were photographs of the Ripper's victims. Lucy gasped audibly when she stepped up for a closer look. I'm not sure what I had expected. In some photographs the women were discreetly draped and what we saw were their lifeless faces, eyes closed, looking more like waxworks from Madame Tussaud's than real women. In others they were nude, their wounds and the crude stitching of the surgeon's needle clearly visible, making them look like broken dolls that someone had tried to mend. They were all horrible to look at, but LaRue didn't seem to realize that. He took obvious pride in his work.

"This is the first victim, Mary Nichols," he said, pointing to the photograph nearest the door. "Her throat was cut and her abdomen split open." The sepia photograph showed a woman in a coffin, her eyes closed, her round face framed by wisps of hair. With her body hidden beneath a cloth pulled up to her chin, she looked like a child who had been tucked in for the night.

He pointed to the next photograph. This woman wore a dress, curly hair framed her face, and her lips were slightly parted. "That's the second victim, Annie Chapman. Throat cut of course, but this time our fellow really went to work, split her open down the middle like a melon, pulled out her entrails, and walked off with her womb."

I was repulsed by the relish with which he recounted their injuries. His interest in the details struck me as ghoulish.

The photograph of the third victim was similar to the first two, eyes closed, an unnatural sleep, but this woman had a more commanding presence even in death. There was a hint of sensuousness about her full lips. She looked as if she had liked to laugh and have a good time when she was alive.

There were three photographs of the last victim, who had been photographed nude to show the extent of her wounds. In the first she lay with her head thrown back, the gash in her throat clearly visible, the wound in her chest gaping. Her face was so badly mutilated that it was difficult to make out her features. The second photograph showed her face from another angle, with an ugly cut across her cheek. The third showed her after the surgeon had stitched her up. It looked like a zipper ran down the front of her torso. I shuddered and looked away.

"These last two beauties are from this morning," LaRue said. "The police are still trying to identify them. They think the second one had just been let out of jail for drunk and disorderly. If they're right, it's a pity for her the coppers didn't keep her locked up a few more hours."

"Poor thing," Bill said under his breath.

"Do you suppose they knew each other?" LaRue asked.

"Maybe shared a gin at the same public house? Was it fate that put them in the path of the Ripper? Makes you wonder, doesn't it?"

I clenched my hands, trying not to think about the man in the alley at Buck's Row, to push from my mind the sounds of an animal feeding.

"The first lady was lucky," he continued. "She only got her throat cut. Of course that was enough to kill her. They think the killer got interrupted. But he wasn't ready to call it a night. He hadn't gotten what he came for." LaRue gave a crooked grin. "Of course there weren't a lot of tarts out on the street to choose from. The ladies of Whitechapel are scared, and they don't go out alone now in the middle of the night unless they're desperate for a few pence to pay for a bed to sleep in or they've had a drop too much to care."

He pointed at the last three photographs and again I noticed his dirty fingernails.

"This lady wasn't so lucky. Not an hour out of jail, and she runs into the Whitechapel Fiend, or Jack the Ripper as he calls himself. How's that for bad luck?"

I shivered again, remembering that I had been midway between the two victims. Abberline said the killer may have passed me in the dark. I felt sick at the thought.

"You see how he cut pieces out of her face. He cut her lower eyelids. He near cut her nose off. One ear lobe's gone. And of course he cut her torso open. Some say he's a doctor or a medical student, some say he's a butcher. In any case he seems to take an interest in their internal organs. He carried off this last victim's womb, just like Annie Chapman, and one of her kidneys for good measure. Why do you suppose he took just one? Why does he take anything at all?"

"Christ!" Bill said, looking rather pale.

I stepped back. I had seen enough. A minute later Lucy did the same. She looked rather pale too.

"He could sell the organs," she said.

"He's insane," Bill muttered.

"He's taking souvenirs," I said softly.

LaRue cast a sideways glance at me. "Strange sort of souvenir."

"Oh, that's just sick," Bill said.

"A pity I couldn't get a photograph of the message he left on that wall in Goulstone Street," LaRue said. "The police could have compared it to the handwriting in the letters they're getting. And if they caught him, they could have taken a handwriting sample and compared it. The police are such asses sometimes."

"Better not let them hear you say that," said Bill. "You might have to find yourself another job."

LaRue shrugged. "They're lucky to have me. My photographs will be famous someday. These chaps like Foster who sketch for the police—they'll be obsolete. Mark my words. Who needs a sketch when they can have a photograph? That's the future."

"Doesn't it ever bother you?" I asked.

He blinked at me. "Beg your pardon?"

"Doesn't it bother you to photograph women who have been brutally murdered?"

"Not really," he said. "Why should it? They're dead. Does it bother the doctor who autopsies them? Or the undertaker who buries them? Like them, I'm just doing my job."

I looked back at the wall. What was it that bothered me so much about the man? Was it the way he had the photographs displayed on his wall? Was it the interest that he took in cataloguing their injuries? Was it his apparent lack of feeling?

Whatever it was, it disgusted me. He didn't care that these women, who had been alive a very short time ago, caught up in their own joys and sorrows, no doubt just as attached to life as any of us, were now dead. Jack the Ripper, who had cut short their lives and viciously mutilated their bodies, may have been worse, but this man was twisted too.

"Do you think the police have any leads?" Lucy asked.

"I think they have a great many leads," LaRue said. "That doesn't mean they'll catch him."

"Oh, I expect they'll catch him sooner or later," Bill said. "It's just a matter of time."

"Is it?" LaRue said, his mouth twitching into a lopsided smirk.

CHAPTER 18

We rode back on a crowded omnibus that pitched ominously whenever we turned a corner.

"Well, there'll be two more inquests now," Lucy said. "It will start all over again."

"Will you be there?" Bill asked her.

Lucy glanced uncertainly at me.

She couldn't go unless I went, but I was not eager to sit through any more inquests. I didn't want to end up like LaRue with his photographs of murdered women mounted on his walls like pornographic pinups.

Lucy's face fell.

"But couldn't you go?" Bill persisted. "Like before?"

I felt guilty for disappointing them, but I had had enough of death.

I had no way of knowing if or when I might ever get back to my own time. Maybe I was stuck here, and maybe it was time I faced that and started living in the present. However, I couldn't indefinitely take advantage of the Ellmans' hospitality.

I needed to find a way to make money so that I could live independently.

After we were back at the house, I followed Lucy up to her little garret room and asked for her advice.

"What can you do?" she asked, frowning, as she donned a freshly laundered apron.

"Perhaps I could get a job as a maid," I suggested, sitting on the edge of her narrow bed.

"Oh, no," she said, shocked.

"Why not?"

"Anyone can see you're not a maid. And besides, you're an American."

I had no idea why being an American meant I couldn't be a maid but didn't argue. I had a feeling I wouldn't like being a maid. "Well, there must be something I can do to earn money," I said.

"Can you sew?" Lucy asked doubtfully. "I know someone who works in a dress shop. She said they're in need of another seamstress."

I thought this was a wonderful suggestion. I may not have had the skill to do needlepoint of the sort Mrs. Ellman did, but I did know how to sew. There was nothing to it. Anyone could sew.

The next day Lucy took me to a small dress shop in Marylebone Road near Madame Tussaud's. The proprietress, Madame Girard, had a ramrod straight back and a painted on smile that hardened when she realized Lucy and I weren't paying customers. She eyed me skeptically as Lucy explained the purpose of our visit.

"Enough," she said, stopping Lucy in mid-sentence with an upraised hand.

Her hawk-like eyes appraised me. I smiled at her but she did not smile back. She took in my grey skirt, my grey jacket, my gloves, and my hat, and her lips tightened in disapproval.

"Have you ever worked as a seamstress?" she asked. I had assumed she was French, but she spoke without any trace of a French accent.

"No, but—"

Her hand shot up. "Can you sew?"

"Yes, of course," I assured her.

"Let me see your hands," she demanded.

I tugged off my gloves and held my hands out for her inspection.

She turned them palms up and her lips grew tighter. "They don't look like the hands of a seamstress," she declared.

I wondered what the hands of a seamstress were supposed to look like. My confidence was waning and I was ready to retreat when she abruptly changed her mind. "All right. We'll see what you can do. Follow me."

She led me to a back room crowded with stools, tables, and colorful bolts of material, where five seamstresses were busily at work. She snapped her fingers at an empty stool. Realizing she meant for me to sit on it, I did so. The other women did not look up. Madame Girard flung two scraps of fabric at me, a bit of black worsted and a piece of brown silk. I looked at them nervously. What was I supposed to do with them?

"Miss Harding, show her."

Without waiting to see if her employee complied, she turned on her heel and swept out of the room.

Miss Harding, a thin pale young woman wearing spectacles

and with her mousy brown hair pulled severely back in a bun, pointed along the edges of the fabric. "You're to sew it here." She pushed needles and thread toward me, then resumed her perch on her own stool and bent over her own piece of fabric.

I began to feel confident again. I could do this. It had not been so difficult after all to find gainful employment. I did not care for Madame Girard, but I could put up with her for the sake of a paycheck. I wondered how much the work would pay.

I had been stitching for about ten minutes when Madame Girard returned. She held her hand out for the sample, put her spectacles on, and squinted at it.

"Is this a joke?" she said, looking up.

I felt my stomach twist into knots.

"This is atrocious," she said. "You can't sew. Why are you wasting my time? Get out. You're obviously not a seamstress."

I felt miserable when I stepped back out on the pavement. Was there nothing I could do in their world? Was I hopelessly unskilled?

I found Lucy peering in the window of the hat shop next door. One glance at my face told her I had failed.

"Never mind," she said, linking arms with me. "We'll think of something else."

But it wasn't easy to think of something else. I couldn't be a governess, Lucy said. I would have to go away to do that and I would probably hate it. Most governesses did. I could work in a shop, but I would probably have to know someone in need of a shop assistant. The fact was that women of the upper and middle classes didn't work and the only jobs for women were too menial for me to undertake or not respectable. The situation seemed hopeless.

Later that afternoon Mrs. Haslip was making a stew for supper and I was sitting at the table shelling peas and feeling discouraged when Mrs. Ellman came into the kitchen looking for me. She had just gotten back from visiting a friend and was still wearing her dark blue dress and pearl brooch.

"I heard Lucy tried to help you find employment today," she said.

"I'm afraid we weren't successful," I said ruefully.

"You know it's really not necessary. You're welcome to stay here as long as you like. If it's money—"

"You've been very kind," I told her, "but I can't keep living here like this."

"I don't see why not."

"I'm a grown woman. I should be taking care of myself."

"Nonsense. Lots of grown women don't take care of themselves. In fact, I know very few who do."

"There must be something I can do," I said.

"How about a governess or a schoolteacher?" Mrs. Haslip suggested. She was standing at the stove, cutting up an onion. "Clearly you have an education. You made a great impression on my Jenny."

"I've got an even better idea," said Mrs. Ellman. "You could give piano lessons."

"But I have no studio," I objected.

"You could use our piano. You could give lessons here. Dr. Ellman wouldn't mind. He's hardly ever home during the day."

"I couldn't."

"Why not? You know how to play a piano. You have a talent, my dear. You should use it."

"It's very kind of you, but—"

She put her hand over mine and looked into my eyes. "I had a daughter, and if she were in a faraway land among strangers and could not remember who she was, I would like to think she might find some kind soul who would help her. Let me be that kind soul for you."

Tears sprang to my eyes at her generosity. "But where would I find students?"

"Leave that to me, my dear," she said, patting my hand.

With Lucy's help I tracked down a trove of sheet music in a bookshop in Fleet Street. By the end of the week I had given lessons to my first five students. I was never quite sure how Mrs. Ellman had found them all. She refused to take credit with a modest wave of her hand. "I just told their mothers you were a wonderful teacher," she said. My students ranged in age from six to thirteen except for a young woman of twenty-one who had recently married above her station and felt she needed to learn the piano in order not to be a disgrace to her husband. Giving piano lessons came to me as naturally as breathing. I felt as if I had been doing this all my life. For all I knew, maybe I had.

I soon began to look forward to these lessons. Because of them, I could forget about Jack the Ripper for long stretches of time, although not entirely. Two new inquests were underway, as Lucy had predicted, and the newspapers were full of them. Letters from Jack the Ripper to the police appeared almost daily in the newspapers. According to the press, the police were preparing to use bloodhounds to hunt for him. The number of police patrolling the streets of the East End had been doubled. Suspects were rounded up, then released again. Letters flooded in to the newspapers, some deploring the living conditions in the East End, where so many lived in poverty, and others criticizing Scotland Yard and the Whitechapel police for not having caught the killer.

The two women who had been killed in what the press called "the double event" had now been identified. The first, Elizabeth Stride, was forty-four years old and, like the previous Ripper victims, had been killed while trying to earn money to pay for a bed in a lodging house for the night. Several people had seen her with a man, but their descriptions of him varied and in any case he may not have been the killer. The second woman, Catherine Eddowes, age forty-six, had been picked up by the police earlier in the evening for drunk and disorderly, then released. She had been on her way home when she crossed paths with the Ripper. According to the surgeons who examined her body, he had spent at least five minutes slashing, gouging, and carving her up with his knife. Yet no one had seen or heard anything.

Every day Lucy read the newspapers, searching them for clues. Meanwhile I tried to push the murders out of my mind, refusing to live in a state of fear. Abberline had said it was coincidence that I had been midway between the two victims, and so I tried to believe that. The focus of my life became the piano lessons. I looked forward to the arrival of my students, who showed up with smiling faces and the eagerness of youth. Never mind that they were inexperienced and hit wrong notes and sometimes failed to practice. For the hour they were with me, I forgot everything else. I corrected them gently, praised them lavishly, and shared their joy when they mastered a new piece. Slowly I was adjusting to my new life.

It was in the second week of October when another memory came back. My youngest pupil, six-year-old Lydia

Tomkins, was there for her lesson when I had to leave the room for a minute to get another sheet of music. When I came back, she was playing a Brahms' lullaby with such concentration that I paused in the doorway and watched her. As I stood there, a sense of déjà vu swept over me. I had stood before like this and watched a little girl at the piano. Then like a wave crashing over me, I remembered Courtney when she was about the same age sitting at the piano in our living room, playing the same song. The memory was so vivid I seemed to hear her voice calling to me just as she did in my dreams. I reached out and touched the door frame to steady myself.

"Are you all right, Mrs. Smith?" Lydia asked. She had stopped playing and was looking at me with large black anxious eyes.

With Courtney's voice still echoing in my head, I forced myself to smile. I didn't want to frighten her. "Yes, I'm fine."

"Was it all right?"

"It was lovely. It was perfect."

The worried look vanished and she resumed playing, unaware that she had just given me back a small piece of myself, a shard of memory. I felt overwhelmed with hope. Maybe my memory was coming back.

With the first money I earned, I bought a new pair of shoes for myself that didn't pinch and books for Jenny. I couldn't wait to take them to her. I made the trip to Banstead on my own, proud that I could find my way about without help. Gradually I was mastering the terrain of my new world. Jenny was delighted to see me and thrilled about the books. She insisted we sit down at once and begin to read, or rather she read haltingly and I helped her when she needed help. Sometimes we had to stop to hunt for her grandfather's glasses or retrieve the newspaper that had fallen under his chair. Susan required tending too, and we took turns holding her, but when she was crawling we did not make much progress with the reading lessons. Then her younger brothers arrived home and it was impossible to continue. Jenny needed to start cooking the evening meal, so I said good-bye, promising to return again soon, and set off to catch the train back to London.

My visit to Jenny was the first time I had ventured out alone since the double murders. Only a week had passed and people were nervous, myself included. However, I told myself I was safe so long as I was home before dark. I felt like Little Red Riding Hood wandering in the dark wood where a dangerous wolf lurked. So long as I stayed in the light and steered clear of the shadows, I would be safe. Nevertheless, I looked around me with a certain amount of unease, taking note of the men reading their newspapers on the omnibus, especially those traveling alone, and those hurrying along the streets, their heads lowered against the drizzling rain. I glanced behind me from time to time as I walked under my umbrella, always on the watch for anyone suspicious, but no one gave me cause for alarm, and gradually I grew more confident.

With confidence also came restlessness. I decided that since I was trapped in this place and time, I might as well get to know it. I had seen Madame Tussaud's queer wax museum, thanks to Lucy, and I had been to the Lyceum Theatre with Inspector Abberline, but there was a great deal of London that I had not seen. So on a day when the sun had peeped out for a change, I took an omnibus to Great Russell Street to see the British Museum after Mrs. Ellman recommended it one evening at dinner.

The museum was an imposing Greek style edifice with

massive Ionic columns topped by a pediment showing a relief sculpture of figures from Greek mythology. I felt a sense of anticipation as I mounted the wide steps to the portico. Within was a hall leading to a maze of galleries through which I wandered happily for the next hour, looking at sculptures from ancient Egypt of gods with animal heads, mummies, and funerary jars, glass cases displaying pottery, vases, and countless objects of ivory, gold, silver, bronze, and glass. I saw the Rosetta Stone, feathered cloaks and helmets from the South Seas brought back by Captain Cook, and a pair of huge half-man, half winged lion stela from Ancient Assyria. Eventually I came to the Greek antiquities—statues of gods and goddesses, busts, vases, friezes, even a small temple façade—a wonderful assortment of ancient artifacts sprawling through several rooms. I was so absorbed that I failed to recognize the man standing at the far end of the gallery until I was only yards away.

"Inspector Abberline!" I said in surprise when I turned and saw him standing there.

If I had caught him unawares, he didn't show it.

"Mrs. Smith. This is unexpected." He glanced around the room. On the far side of the gallery a fashionably dressed couple were contemplating a headless statue of a winged goddess. They were the only other people besides us in the room. "You're here alone?" he asked.

"Yes," I said. "It so happens that I am. You also appear to be alone, or is Purkiss lurking about?"

"Purkiss? No, he had to go up to Cambridge." His eyes swept about the room again, as if assessing it for potential threats. So far as I could see there were none. The fashionably dressed couple looked harmless enough.

"I hardly think I'll be attacked in the British museum."

"No?" He smiled. "Are you so sure the Ripper isn't about, waiting for his opportunity?"

"I hardly think he would risk being seen in so public a place." The words were hardly out of my mouth when there flashed through my mind the image of the man who had followed Lucy and me through the Chamber of Horrors at Madame Tussaud's. I pushed it away.

"A pity. We might have a chance to catch him then."

"Do you come here often?" I asked.

"When I need to think. This room is my favorite."

I looked at the fragment of frieze before us, which had once graced the Parthenon in Ancient Greece, according to the placard. It depicted a long-ago battle—a tangle of human limbs, horses, spears, and shields.

"Is it your first time to see the marbles?" he asked.

"I don't remember being here before," I said.

He nodded. We stood there a moment in silence looking at the frieze.

"I heard you're giving piano lessons."

"Yes, I'm trying to earn my keep."

"I'd like to hear you play sometime."

I could think of nothing to reply to that. There was another silence.

"We've heard from him again, you know."

I nodded. "I've seen the letters in the papers."

"Not just a letter this time. He sent half of a kidney to George Lusk. Do you know who he is?"

"No."

"The head of the East End Vigilance Committee. I'm sure it'll be in all the newspapers by evening."

"Was it the kidney he took from Catherine Eddowes?" I asked, remembering what LaRue had said.

"Who knows? Whether it is or not, people will think it is." There was resignation in his voice.

I felt sorry for him. Without thinking, I touched his arm. We both looked down at my gloved hand on the arm of his jacket. Aware that I may have been too forward, I withdrew it.

"May I buy you a cup of tea?" he asked.

"Yes, that would be nice," I said.

He knew a shop about a block from the museum that served tea, so we went there. After our walk in the brisk October air, the mug of hot tea warmed me pleasantly.

"What a nice place," I said, looking about at the other tea drinkers and the fire crackling cozily in the fireplace.

"My wife liked it."

This caused an awkward pause in the conversation. I would have liked to ask him about his wife, but I didn't want to pry.

"Do you regret not having children?" I asked since children seemed a safer topic.

"I regret a lot of things," he said. "How about you? Just the one daughter?"

"Yes."

"You don't suppose there are more children that you've forgotten about?"

I couldn't tell if he was teasing me. "I don't think so."

"But if you've forgotten your husband, surely you might have forgotten a child or two as well. Who knows, maybe you have a dozen of them." He was looking at me with those shrewd blue eyes and I couldn't tell if he was serious or not.

"I think I'd remember."

"But you don't remember your husband," he pointed out.

"No."

He was right. Maybe I did have a husband. Maybe I

212

shouldn't be sitting there with him, drinking tea and feeling like a girl on her first date.

"Maybe you're a widow," he suggested.

"Maybe," I agreed.

"I don't really believe that of course."

"Why not?"

He shrugged. "Call it a hunch."

I smiled. "Then why can't I remember him?"

"For the same reason that you can't remember your name. You took a blow to your head. You should be grateful you've got a hard head."

"I suppose so."

"And maybe it will turn out in the end that you have a husband who's very much alive and looking for you. Maybe your conviction that you're from the future is only a delusion after all." His eyes met mine steadily.

I didn't say anything. Had he changed his mind about me since our last meeting? Had he gone back to thinking I was delusional?

He pulled his watch out of his waistcoat pocket and glanced at it. "It's almost four o'clock. Perhaps I should see you home."

"That's really not necessary," I said. "I don't need an escort. I'm perfectly capable of finding my way by myself."

He reached out and laid his hand over mine, startling me. "I thought I might like to go down to Wiltshire next Sunday and see my sister. Would you like to come along?"

I didn't know what to say. It was so unexpected. There were probably a good many reasons why I should say no—including the fact that I could be married—but instead I pushed my reservations aside and said, "Yes, I would like that."

CHAPTER 19

When I got home, I found Lucy and Mrs. Haslip in the kitchen. Mrs. Haslip was kneading a batch of dough. Lucy was talking excitedly but stopped when she saw me, whipped a piece of paper from the pocket of her apron, and waved it at me.

"He's coming!"

"Who's coming?" I said, taking the piece of paper.

"Mr. Keating. Go on. Read it."

She waited impatiently while I read the following short note, written in ornate handwriting:

Dear Miss Callaghan,

Please be advised that I will call at half past four on a matter of utmost gravity. I trust the time will not be inconvenient.

Respectfully yours,

Roderick Bartholomew Keating

"Utmost gravity!" Lucy said. "He's going to propose!"

It seemed to me that this cryptic message could mean

many other things, but I kept that to myself. I didn't want to dampen her enthusiasm. I knew this was what she had been hoping for.

"Mrs. Ellman won't like it if she finds him here when she comes home," observed Mrs. Haslip, vigorously kneading her mound of dough.

"Well, it can't be helped," Lucy said. "This is my future, you know. Am I to be a servant all my life?"

"Unless you want him to see you with that flour on your apron, you'd best change now," Mrs. Haslip said.

"There's flour on my apron?" Lucy said, dismayed. "How did that happen? Oh, but what if he comes while I'm upstairs changing? Who'll answer the door?"

"I will," I said.

She bit her lip. "Well, I suppose I should be wearing a clean apron when he asks me to be his wife."

"Of course you should," said Mrs. Haslip. "We wouldn't want Mr. Keating turning you down over a bit of flour."

"No, we wouldn't," Lucy said decisively and dashed off.

"Is there anything I can do to help?" I asked Mrs. Haslip after she was gone.

"Oh, just go wait in the drawing room for her Mr. Keating," she said, pounding the dough, then kneading it again with her strong hands.

"Have you met him?" I asked.

"Mr. Keating? Just once."

"What's he like?"

"Oh, a lawyerly sort of man. A little dry some would say, but aren't most lawyers?"

"Do you know how they met?"

"At court. Lucy was there as a witness to an accident. A carriage collided with a hay wagon. The carriage driver had been drinking. One of the horses pulling the hay wagon was injured. They both claimed it was the other's fault."

"Do you think he'll make her a good husband?"

Mrs. Haslip shrugged. "Who knows? He's got a respectable income, so I suppose they'll do all right."

"An income isn't everything."

She gave the dough another slap. "It puts food in the stomach and a roof over the head."

I felt a stab of guilt, knowing how hard she worked to support her brood in Banstead. Indeed, where would I be had it not been for the generosity of Dr. Ellman and his wife? There was a lot to be said for food and a roof over one's head. Still, I hated to see Lucy end up in a loveless marriage just for the sake of security.

Leaving Mrs. Haslip to her dough, I wandered to the drawing room, where I could not resist sitting down at the piano. At the opening chords of the Moonlight Sonata, I felt a wave of calm wash over me. I started thinking about Abberline's invitation to visit his sister in Wiltshire. Had I made a mistake when I accepted? Would I regret this later? Did he have some ulterior motive for inviting me? Ulterior motive or not, I was looking forward to it. I would see him again, and I would have a chance to get to know him better, which was something I very much wanted.

I was brought back with a jolt by a rap at the door. I had forgotten all about Mr. Keating.

When I opened the door, I found myself face-to-face with a tall man probably in his forties with a long face, a small mustache, and a monocle. He wore a tall black hat and a black suit and carried a walking stick. If I had not known he was a lawyer, I would have mistaken him for an undertaker.

"I've come to speak to Miss Callaghan," he announced stiffly. "I believe she is employed at this domicile?"

"Yes." He was so pompous I had to resist the urge to laugh.

"I believe she is expecting me."

"Won't you come in?" I said, trying to keep a straight face.

He stepped across the threshold and looked around with an air of boredom.

"If you would wait here," I said, waving my hand toward the drawing room.

He pulled out a gold pocket watch and consulted it. "Will she be long? I did specify half past four and I dislike being kept waiting. Time is money."

"I'm sure she'll be right down," I said. "I'll just go and see."

He did not strike me as a man who had come to propose to his future wife. I wondered if Lucy had misinterpreted his note. Besides, how could she want to marry a man as ridiculous as Mr. Keating? Surely she couldn't seriously be considering tying herself to him? He must have been twenty years her senior, far too old for her. I climbed the stairs, intending to beg her not to marry him, but when I saw how excited she was, patting her hair and biting her lips to make them red, I didn't have the heart to say it.

"Do I look all right?" she asked anxiously.

"You look very pretty," I assured her.

"Wish me luck."

She flew downstairs. I followed more slowly and retreated to the kitchen to give them privacy.

"Has he arrived then?" Mrs. Haslip asked, still kneading dough, her hands white with flour.

"Yes, they're in the drawing room."

"Well, they'd better be quick. Mrs. Ellman will be home any minute now."

"Do you really think he's here to propose to Lucy?" I asked.

"Why else would he be coming to the house? And you saw his letter."

"But are they in love?"

"You'll have to ask Lucy about that. I'm sure I don't know."

I told myself it was none of my business if Lucy got engaged to Mr. Keating. She had a right to marry whomever she chose. But the prospect of her marrying the man in the drawing room disturbed me. I thought she deserved better. What kind of life could she have married to a man like that?

"What about Bill Tanner?" I asked.

"What about him?"

"He loves her."

"Did he tell you that?"

"He didn't have to. Anyone with eyes can see."

"Look here," Mrs. Haslip said. "This is Lucy's life. You've got to let her choose for herself. Bill Tanner's a nice young fellow, but he doesn't make much. I doubt he could afford a wife. If they got married, they'd be pinching every penny to make ends meet. A lawyer, on the other hand. . . . Well, she wouldn't have to worry about how to put food on the table."

I was about to argue when Lucy burst into the kitchen, all smiles.

"I'm engaged!"

"Congratulations," I said, trying to sound as if I meant it.

"When's the wedding?" asked Mrs. Haslip.

"He wants to wait until mid-January. It'll take time to get things ready."

"I wonder what Mrs. Ellman will say. She'll be sorry to lose you."

"I'm not going to tell her just yet. He wants it to be a secret. But I had to tell both of you."

"Why is it a secret?" I asked, immediately suspicious.

"Because he's a very private sort of man, and he doesn't want people to make a fuss about it. It'll just be a small wedding, and then we'll announce that we're married, and I'll be Mrs. Keating, not Lucy Callaghan anymore."

The words were hardly out of her mouth when Mrs. Ellman appeared in the kitchen doorway. "Who was that man I saw leaving?" she asked as she pulled off her gloves.

"I think it was very careless of Lucy to let a total stranger in this afternoon," Mrs. Ellman said over dinner that evening. "I can't imagine what she was thinking. He could have been this Jack the Ripper everyone is talking about."

Lucy had told her that Mr. Keating had knocked on the wrong door, and not until she had invited him in did they realize his error.

"I hardly think he'd come to the door," said Dr. Ellman, reaching for the potatoes.

I pretended to be completely absorbed in the meat pie. It seemed dishonest of me not to blurt out what I knew, but that, of course, would mean revealing Lucy's secret, which I had sworn to keep.

"You'll never guess who I ran into today at the British museum," I said to change the subject. "Inspector Abberline."

Immediately I had their attention. Mr. Keating was forgotten.

"How is he doing?" asked Mrs. Ellman. "All this awful

business. People are being quite hard on the police and Scotland Yard. I'm sure they're doing their best."

"He seemed well," I said. "We met in the Greek antiquities."

"Odd," Dr. Ellman said, frowning. "He'd better not let any journalists see him there. Next thing they'll have a caricature of Scotland Yard in the papers. Show him staring at statues instead of catching the killer. That sort of thing."

"Did he offer to buy you tea?" Mrs. Ellman asked.

"As a matter of fact, he did."

"Perhaps we should invite him to dinner," she said. "Charles, what do you think?"

"About what?"

"Inviting Inspector Abberline to dinner."

"Whatever you think, dear."

"He's invited me to Wiltshire next Sunday to meet his sister and her family," I said.

"Wiltshire?" Mrs. Ellman said. "Oh, I really don't think that's a good idea."

"Why ever not?" Dr. Ellman said.

"Well, a single woman. . . ."

"My dear, she's from the States. Everybody knows Americans do as they please."

"I suppose you're right," she said, casting an uncertain glance at me. "Did you tell him you'd go?"

"I did, but if you think I shouldn't, I won't. I'm a stranger here. I'm not used to your customs. I didn't realize there would be anything wrong with accepting his invitation."

"Nice area, Wiltshire," Dr. Ellman said. "Very pretty."

"I suppose I *am* a bit old-fashioned," Mrs. Ellman said. "Times are changing. Women are much freer today than when I was young."

And so it was settled. I would go to Wiltshire on Sunday.

While I had the outing to Wiltshire to look forward to, I still felt concerned about Lucy's engagement to Mr. Keating, and so after dinner instead of joining the Ellmans in the drawing room, I climbed the narrow stairs to Lucy's little room, hoping she had not gone to bed yet. Her room was at the top of the house where the roof sloped and you could only stand up in a few square feet. But despite the lack of space, she had made it cozy with a patchwork quilt on her narrow bed, a small oval hooked rug on the floor, an old trunk, a squat bedstand, and a wardrobe that had somehow been wedged in despite the low ceiling. During the day light poured in through a little round window that gave a glimpse of house roofs and chimneys against the sky. Now it was dark in the room except for the lamp by her bed. Lucy laid down the book she was reading. I saw it was *Dr. Jekyll and Mr. Hyde*.

"Aren't you afraid it will give you bad dreams?" I asked.

She grinned. "Not likely. I sleep like a baby. But that's not what you came up here to talk about, was it?"

"No, it wasn't," I admitted.

I sat beside her on her bed—the only place to sit besides the floor.

"Are you sure you want to marry Mr. Keating?" I asked.

"Of course I'm sure," she said. "I'd be daft not to jump at a chance like this. Girls like me don't get offers from the likes of Mr. Keating every day. I'm lucky he wants to marry me."

"I'm sure there are many men who would want to marry you," I said. "But you shouldn't be in such a rush to get married. You're only eighteen."

"And I'm a housemaid. I have no money and no prospects."

"But what about love?" I argued. "You can't tell me you're in love with him. You couldn't be."

"You're like a babe in the woods," she said. "How could you know so little about the world? You may be old enough to be my mother, but you haven't a clue when it comes to life."

This made me smile, but I wasn't ready to give up. "You'll be miserable. He can't possibly make you happy."

"How would you know?" she said. "Maybe having a nice house to live in and nice clothes to wear and servants to wait on me would make me happy as a lark."

"Maybe at first," I conceded. "But later you'd see it's not enough. Marriage is hard. Even when you marry for love, it can be hard."

"And is this the voice of experience speaking? Have you been married then?"

"I'm just saying, can't you wait a bit? You're young. You've got your whole life ahead of you."

She closed her eyes, took a deep breath, then opened them again. "You saw where Jamie is. I've got to get him out of there. It breaks my heart when I see him. It's my fault he's there. Do you know what it's like to see your little one at the mercy of strangers who don't love him and not be able to do a thing about it?"

I didn't have an answer to that. "What about Bill Tanner?"

"What do you mean?"

"He's in love with you."

"Don't be silly," she said. "Bill's just a friend."

"I don't think that's how he sees it."

"I couldn't marry Bill. He knows that."

"Does he know about Mr. Keating?"

"Of course he does."

"Then you'll tell him you're engaged?"

"I can't do that. It's a secret. If I tell him, it won't be a secret, now will it?"

"And that's another thing," I said. "I don't see why it has to be a secret."

She sighed. "Virginia, one of these days you're going to wake up and remember who you are, and you'll step back into your comfortable life." I tried to protest. "And, yes, I'm sure it was comfortable. But me, I don't get to wake up. This is it. This is all I get. And I want more. I want a good home for my little boy. I want to hold him in my arms. I want to give him things—nice things—and send him to a good school and give him a future that won't include sweating for every farthing he makes. Is that so terrible?"

"Of course not."

"So be happy for me."

I nodded and tried to smile.

"Let's not quarrel," she said. "Let's talk about something else. Tell me about the museum. Did you like it? Did you see the mummies?"

"Yes."

"You had no trouble getting there or back?"

"No, no trouble."

"It put some color in your cheeks."

I felt more color rush to them. "I ran into Inspector Abberline."

Her eyes widened. "Did you now?"

"I'm going to Wiltshire to meet his sister on Sunday."

"Are you?" Now would that be on police business or a social call?"

CHAPTER 20

When Sunday came, Abberline and I traveled by train to Salisbury, where we were met by his brother-in-law, a jovial red-faced man with thinning hair, who was waiting to take us in an open carriage to the pleasant little home on a tree-lined street where his family of six lived. We were welcomed at the door by Abberline's sister, Sue. She had the same intense blue eyes as her brother, as well as the same quickness and intelligence but lacked his reserve and secretiveness. I felt at ease at once, and any qualms I had felt melted away in the first few minutes. There was a flurry of introductions to the children—Ben, age six; Joe, nine; Agatha, twelve; and Sarah, sixteen.

I saw right away that Abberline was doted on here. His sister scolded him good-naturedly for looking as if he were not eating properly, and young Joe wanted to know if he had caught any criminals. I could see him relax as they fussed over him. At the same time Sue was careful to include me. She managed to ask me a number of questions about myself without making me uncomfortable. Evidently Abberline had told her about my amnesia, because every time I couldn't answer a question about myself, she breezed on to something else.

Joe followed his uncle about like a puppy. As I listened to Sue's bright chatter about a neighbor's chickens which kept straying into their yard, I happened to look up and see Abberline tousle the boy's hair. Joe ducked his head but looked pleased. It gave me a glimpse of Abberline's love for his nephew. I knew at that moment that I loved him, and I feared that he might not love me back, that he might decide loving me was a mistake because I didn't really belong here in his world.

"So what about this Ripper chap?" his brother-in-law Henry asked, puffing on a pipe he had just lit.

Sue cast her husband a reproachful look, while nine-year-old Joe looked up at his uncle with wide eyes, waiting for his answer.

"We'll catch him," Abberline said confidently.

"Did they really use bloodhounds?" Joe asked. "My teacher said they used bloodhounds."

"Yes, they did."

"Did you see them?"

"Now that's enough of that," Sue said. "You don't need to be pestering your uncle with questions about work on his one day off."

"It's all right," Abberline said. "I don't mind. Yes, indeed I saw the hounds. Burgho and Barnaby—those were their names. They led us a fine chase, but in the end they had no better luck than we did at tracking him down. It wasn't really their fault. There probably wasn't much of a scent trail to follow once they were brought in."

"All right, that's quite enough talk about the Whitechapel

murders," Sue said. "Who wants to help me make pies?"

It turned out all the children were eager to help make pies. While they pulled out bowls, pie tins, a roller pin, and more with a great deal of clatter and clanging, Sue produced a picnic basket with a blue cloth cover and handed it to Abberline.

"If you wait much longer, it could decide to rain," she said, glancing out the window at the overcast sky.

I realized then that we were not going to eat lunch with his family. I wondered where we were going. Abberline had not mentioned any plans, and even after we were settled into the family's open carriage, he refused to tell me. He just smiled and said, "You'll see."

He drove us into the country, our two horses clopping along at a steady pace. I couldn't help thinking how much nicer it was to travel like this than in a car. We were in the open air, and we traveled slowly enough to enjoy the countryside, passing quaint old thatched roof cottages that looked as if they had sprung from a children's storybook. Then we came over a hill and saw a sight that took my breath away—stone megaliths in the distance jutting up against the grey sky.

"Stonehenge!" I said, hardly able to believe my eyes.

"You know it then?" he asked, looking pleased.

"Of course," I said. "Who doesn't? But I've only seen pictures of it in books."

"I grew up with it," he said. "My family used to come here for picnics when I was a boy. I carved my initials on one of the stones."

He tied the horses to a post, and we climbed a footpath up to the megaliths, which were even more impressive up close. Some of the lintels were in place and others had fallen. We spread a blanket on one of the fallen stones and unpacked our basket of cold chicken, bread, cheese, and wine. Except for some children playing nearby, we had the megaliths all to ourselves.

"I've always liked this place," Abberline said, looking around him after we had finished off the meal and sat sipping the wine. "It dates back to the Druids, you know."

"Why do you suppose they built it?" I asked.

"People say it was connected to their religion."

"It's amazing that after all this time it's still here."

"And after we're gone, it'll still be here."

I didn't say anything. I didn't want to think about the future. I wanted to be here in the present with him.

He reached for my hand. From the other side of the circle of stones, we could hear the voices of the children as they played.

"Why didn't you marry again?" I asked.

He thought a moment. "After my wife died, I didn't think I'd want to get married again. I just couldn't imagine coming home to anyone else. Then I guess I got used to living alone. My job takes up so much of my time. There isn't much left over. It didn't seem fair to ask a woman to put up with the kind of hours I work—and the uncertainty, not knowing if I'll come home again. Then you came along—" He glanced at me.

The blood was pounding in my head. I wanted him to love me, but I was afraid. How could he when he hardly knew me, when I hardly knew myself for that matter? He could have a younger woman. He could have a woman from his own time and place. Why should he want me?

He touched the side of my face and our lips met.

It was like a dam bursting inside of me. The memories came rushing back. My life had just flashed before my eyes. My mother, my father, our house on Monroe Street. Mark kissing me on our first date when I was seventeen. How crazy I had been about him. Our wedding. Courtney. Moving from Philadelphia to New York, where Mark had worked on Wall Street and I had taught at Julliard. The quarrels. How we had shouted at each other. Terrible things, unforgivable things. How we had separated, then gone back together. Then the really bad period and the divorce and the trip to London, which had been Courtney's idea. "It'll cheer you up, Mom," she had said.

"What is it?" Abberline asked.

"I was married. I remember everything."

He looked at me with troubled eyes.

"We divorced."

"Divorced?"

"I was a teacher. I taught piano. I lived in New York."

"And this is in the future?"

"Yes." Had he hoped that when my memory came back I would remember that I was from his time?

"But then why aren't you there? Why are you here?"

"I don't know."

"You have a husband," he said.

"No, we're divorced."

"He was unfaithful to you?"

"Yes, but it was more than that. We didn't get along anymore."

I was so overcome by the rush of painful memories that I scarcely knew what I was saying.

"What's your name?" he asked.

That simple question stopped me cold. It was like being doused with cold water. I remembered so much but not my name.

I shook my head. "I don't know."

There was a rumble of thunder and drops of rain began to

fall. We scrambled to pack our basket then and get back to the carriage.

Abberline was the only one who knew my memory—at least part of it—had returned. I couldn't tell Dr. Ellman, because revealing that I was from the future could still get me locked away in a hospital for the insane. Over the next few days more memories surfaced. At times my mind felt overwhelmed with them. But still my name was not among them. Nor could I remember the ending to that piano piece which haunted me so much. Every note of it was in my head until I reached that one place, and then I hit an invisible barrier. I could not get beyond it. At last, thoroughly frustrated one afternoon, I asked Lucy for paper and pencil and set about guessing what came next. I sat at the piano, drew a staff, treble and bass clefs, bar lines, and the notes that came before, then began to try notes. It was a slow laborious process, but I was determined to figure out what came next. Lucy wandered in to see what I was doing. She looked with amazement at the score I had scribbled.

"You make it up out of your head?" she asked, astonished. "You write the notes?"

I looked at the paper propped in front of me at the piano. It had not struck me as odd before. Writing down the notes had seemed the logical thing to do.

"I guess I do," I said. And in a flash it hit me. I didn't know the ending to this piece because I hadn't finished writing it yet.

Abberline came around every few days, although often he could stay only ten or fifteen minutes. He was busy following up leads. Everyone was tense, wondering when the Ripper would strike again. Almost three weeks had passed since the 'double event,' and there had been no sign of him, unless you counted the torrent of letters pouring into the newspapers, all claiming to be written by him. Abberline didn't like me going about alone, but I was not going to stay cooped up indoors, and now I had a little spending money from the lessons I was giving, so when I had an afternoon free, I went out. Sometimes I took the train to Banstead to see Jenny. Sometimes I went to the National Gallery or the British Museum. Sometimes I went to the shops in Regent's Street to look at the latest fashions. Occasionally I would come home with an object that had caught my fancy—a hat, a reticule, a pair of earrings. Other times I browsed in a bookshop or walked by the river and watched the boats. I missed my old life, but I thought if I had to live here, I could do it. I was beginning to think in fact that it might be a good thing. There was such a cloud of unhappiness hanging over my memories that I preferred to forget them as much as I could. I had been very unhappy when I came to London with Courtney. There had seemed little to go on living for, and I thought that the best years of my life were behind me. Now I was looking forward to the future. In this so improbable time and place I had met someone who made me feel alive again. He was intelligent, caring, hardworking. When he took me in his arms, I felt as if nothing else mattered. Since that day at Stonehenge when we had first kissed, I had begun to think I might want to stay.

One day in mid-October I was shopping for a pair of gloves in Piccadilly when I saw Mr. Keating emerge from a shop with a young woman on his arm. From the way she simpered and looked up at him, I doubted she was his sister. They didn't notice me. I decided not to tell Lucy what I had seen because I didn't want to upset her. However, the next day I took the omnibus to Fleet Street, climbed the narrow stairs to the offices of the *Star,* and sought out Bill Tanner among the maze of desks and workers. He was sitting as before at his corner desk.

"Mrs. Smith! This is a surprise!" He glanced past me expectantly, but when he didn't see Lucy his face fell. "You're here alone?"

"Yes, I've come on my own," I said. "I hope I'm not interrupting."

"You've got something you want to tell me? You've remembered something more?"

"I didn't come here about the Whitechapel killer," I said. "I came about Lucy."

"What about Lucy?"

"She's had a proposal."

He fiddled nervously with his pencil. "What do you mean? Someone's asked her to marry him?"

"Yes. Mr. Keating. A lawyer. Do you know him?"

"So she sent you here to break the news? She couldn't tell me herself?"

"Actually she doesn't know I'm here," I confessed. "Her engagement is supposed to be a secret, but I thought you should know."

He frowned at the paper in front of him on which he had been writing. "When will she marry him?"

"Mid-January."

"I see. Was there anything else?"

"You're not going to try to stop her?" I had expected him to be upset.

He looked at me blankly. "Why would I do that?"

"Because she's about to ruin her life," I said. "Because you're her friend. And because you love her. Or at least I think you do."

For a minute he didn't say anything. He just stared at the half written page in front of him. Then he looked at me. "What can I do? I can't stop her from marrying him. Yes, I love Lucy. I've loved her since I first met her in a bookshop down the street. But I wouldn't stand in her way. Why should she marry me when she can have a lawyer? I can't compete against a man like that. I can't give her the life he can give her."

"She doesn't love him," I said.

"I never really thought she did. And now, if you'll excuse me, I have work to do."

I was not going to be put off so easily. "I saw him yesterday. He was coming out of a shop in Piccadilly with a woman on his arm."

"So?"

"They looked like more than friends."

He thought about this. "Did you tell Lucy?"

"No."

"Why are you telling me?"

"Because I think she's making a big mistake. There's something not right about Mr. Keating. Why does he want to keep the engagement a secret? Why is he shopping in Piccadilly with another woman on his arm?"

He sighed. "What do you want me to do?"

"You're a reporter," I said. "Investigate him. Ask questions. Snoop. Find out what you can."

"Snoop?" he said, grinning. "Is that what you think we do?"

"What I'm saying is that if you really do care about her—if

you're her friend—you'll try to stop her from marrying this man."

He ran one hand through his hair. "You're sure the woman wasn't his sister?"

"Absolutely."

I didn't have long to wait to find out the result of Bill Tanner's sleuthing. The next afternoon he showed up at the Ellmans'. Except for Mrs. Haslip, I had the house to myself. We went into the drawing room and Bill told me what he had found out.

"You were right," he said. "Keating stands to inherit a considerable sum from an uncle if he marries. However, he will forfeit the inheritance if he marries his cousin, a certain Miss Graham."

"The woman I saw him with?"

"That's my guess. The old man swore her side of the family wouldn't get a penny of his money."

"Not a first cousin I hope?"

He nodded. "I presume so."

"Isn't that illegal?"

He shrugged.

"So why Lucy?"

"Well, she's pretty. It's not as if he's marrying some cow. And no doubt he'll expect her to be grateful and not complain."

It was just as bad as I had feared. "Do you think he'll be unfaithful?"

"He'll probably be discreet about it."

I stood up and began to pace. "We've got to tell Lucy."

He didn't look happy about this. "Why don't you tell her?"

"She may not believe me."

"Well, she probably won't like hearing it from me neither. Where is she anyway?"

"She went to the chemist on an errand for Dr. Ellman. Why don't you have a cup of tea? She'll be back soon."

"Maybe I should go," he said.

"At least have a cup of tea first," I urged.

He nodded and followed me to the kitchen, where Mrs. Haslip was cooking a stew and the air smelled of simmering onions.

"What's this all about?" she asked when we walked in.

"Bill found out something about Mr. Keating," I told her. "He's marrying Lucy so he'll get his inheritance, but he's really in love with his cousin."

"I don't suppose you could keep this to yourselves?" she said and sighed.

"She has a right to know," I insisted.

Bill looked embarrassed and said nothing.

We were still drinking our tea ten minutes later when Lucy burst into the kitchen, her blonde curls damply clinging to her cheeks. "It's raining," she announced. Then she saw Bill. "What are you doing here? Come to interview Virginia again?"

He hung his head guiltily and didn't answer.

"Tell her," I said.

"Tell me what?" Lucy looked from one to the other of us.

Mrs. Haslip stirred the stew with an unnecessary clattering of spoon on cast-iron pot to make it clear she was not a part of this.

"What's wrong?" Lucy said.

"When were you going to tell me?" Bill asked, looking up at her with hurt eyes.

Lucy shot me a look of reproach. "You weren't supposed to tell. It's supposed to be a secret."

"Mr. Keating is using you," I said. "He doesn't love you." I turned to Bill. "Tell her."

Bill told her everything he had found out about the inheritance, the deadline, and the cousin. I thought Lucy would be devastated, but she wasn't.

"So?" she said. "You think any of that matters to me? And what right do you have to pry into Mr. Keating's affairs?" She glared at Bill. "You ought to be ashamed. I thought we were friends."

Bill looked miserable.

"But doesn't it bother you at all?" I said.

Lucy tilted her chin up stubbornly. "He's asked me to marry him, and I said I would, and I will."

"You don't have to marry him," Bill said. "You could marry me."

Mrs. Haslip stopped stirring. There was complete silence as we all waited to hear what Lucy would say.

I felt like cheering Bill for having gotten up the nerve to say those words. But Lucy would not budge.

"I wouldn't marry you if you were the last man alive," she declared and marched out of the kitchen.

"She didn't mean that," I told Bill.

He nodded grimly. "Guess I'd better leave."

"Well, that didn't go so well," said Mrs. Haslip when she and I were alone again.

"At least he asked her," I said.

I felt bad about what had happened and began to wonder if I had misjudged Lucy's feelings for Bill. Was she really so set on the comfortable life she thought Mr. Keating could give her that nothing else mattered? I just hoped she would come to her senses before it was too late.

CHAPTER 21

I thought that after our outing to Stonehenge I would see more of Abberline, but he was busy with the Ripper investigation, and aside from an occasional meeting in a restaurant or the British Museum, we didn't see much of each other. He avoided coming by the house, but generally he would take me out on Sunday afternoon to show me something I had not yet seen—Westminster Abbey, the Tower, Kensington Gardens, St. Paul's Cathedral, Hampton Court.

After that first time at Stonehenge, I didn't have any more dredged up memories of Mark when we kissed. I thought only of Abberline. Even now that I knew his first name was Frederick, I thought of him as Abberline. Sometimes he asked me about the future, but I wasn't very good at explaining. I told him about fingerprinting and psychological profiling and DNA testing, but I had to confess I had no idea how these were done.

It was November now and a month had passed since the murders of Elizabeth Stride and Catherine Eddowes. People were beginning to relax a bit and think maybe there would be no more. They said maybe the Ripper was a sailor whose ship had left or a lunatic who had been apprehended and safely locked away in an asylum.

Then on the 7th of November I had the dream again. In my dream it was dark and I was being pursued through a maze of rooms. I tried to run faster, but the menace behind me kept drawing closer. I tried to scream, but no sound would come. I searched frantically for the door to the next room and the next, trying to find a way out. Finally just as my pursuer was about to overtake me, I awoke in a sweat, my heart pounding. I had not had the dream since the double murders. I was seized by the fear the Ripper was going to kill again. Even after I was up and dressed, I was so upset I could think of little else. As soon as possible I went in search of Lucy and found her in the drawing room lighting a fire on the hearth against the morning chill.

"I'm sure it doesn't mean anything," she said after I had told her about my dream. "It's probably because you were reading *Varney* again last night."

Which was true. I had found the book with the luridly illustrated cover the day before in the study when I was looking for something to read and decided to give it another go. But I doubted that was why I had had the dream again.

"I had the dream before," I told her, "and then those women were killed."

She looked skeptical. "You're letting your imagination run away with you."

"Please, we have to do something," I said.

"Well, if you're really worried, you could send a note to Inspector Abberline about it," she suggested.

Post or telegram seemed too slow. I wished I could just

pick up a phone and call him. I wanted him to know as soon as possible. What if the Ripper struck again that very night?

In the end I decided to go to the headquarters of Scotland Yard in Whitehall to find him if I could. Once my mind was made up, I set off to catch an omnibus to the West End. Although I hadn't been to Scotland Yard's headquarters in Whitehall before, Lucy had pointed out the tall grey brick building with its rows of windows, so I had no trouble locating it. I entered through its arched doorway and was directed by a guard to a desk where a young man in spectacles sat with papers in neat piles in front of him.

"He's not here," he told me in answer to my question.

"Well, can you tell me where I can find him?" I asked politely.

"Sorry, I'm not permitted to do that, but if you leave a message I'll see that he gets it."

Since this apparently was the best I could do, I followed his suggestion. I didn't want to stir up suspicions, so I merely wrote 'Urgent' on the piece of paper he offered me, signed it 'VS,' folded it, and wrote 'Inspector Abberline' on the outside. The young man looked at me curiously but didn't ask any questions.

Abberline turned up in the early afternoon. I felt a wave of relief when I opened the door and saw him standing there.

"What's this all about?" he asked when he stepped into the hall. He had my note in his hand.

"It's going to happen again," I said as calmly as I could. "I think he's going to kill someone."

He didn't ask me who. "What makes you think that?"

I took a deep breath. "I dreamed he was chasing me through a house of many rooms."

"This is about a dream?"

"Not just a dream," I said. "It's a sign. He's going to kill again."

"You can't be sure of that," he said. "Not just because you had a dream."

"But I dreamed it before, and then those women were killed."

He frowned. "Why didn't you tell me this before?"

"I thought you wouldn't believe me."

"It was probably just a coincidence," he said. "People dream things all the time and then they happen. It doesn't mean anything."

"It wasn't a coincidence," I insisted. "He was looking for me."

Abberline touched the side of my face. His fingers felt cool against my skin. "I'll put a man back on your door if it will make you feel better."

"You don't understand."

He pulled me into his arms. "I wouldn't let anything happen to you. You know that."

"You have to do something," I said. "If you don't, it'll happen again."

He looked at me, studying my face as if searching for the answer to a question. "What do you want me to do?"

"Stop him!"

From the window that night I could see a man standing on the opposite side of the street in the pouring rain under an umbrella. I didn't think it was Purvis. Seeing someone on watch made me feel a little better. I listened to the rain and the creaking of the house as it grew quiet for the night. Mrs. Haslip had retired to her small room at the top of the stairs and Lucy to her garret. The Ellmans had gone to bed. I had asked Mrs. Ellman if I could stay up and read in the drawing room for a while. It felt comforting to have a light on, to keep the darkness at bay. I hoped the rain would keep the women of Whitechapel indoors, but I knew there would always be some who braved the elements to pick up the four pence for a bed in a lodging house or another glass of gin at a public house. I had laid *Varney* aside in favor of *Ivanhoe*. No night terrors lurking there.

It seemed like a long night. I was still reading when the grandfather clock chimed four, but then I must have dozed off. Next thing I knew it was morning and Lucy was shaking me.

"Didn't you go to bed at all?" she asked.

"I guess I got caught up in the book I was reading."

She picked it up and wrinkled her nose as she read the title. "*Ivanhoe*? Don't tell me *that* kept you up!" She rolled her eyes in disbelief.

I glanced out the window and saw that my sentry was gone. The day was dawning greyly, but at least it had stopped raining.

"What time is it?" I asked.

"Past six. Didn't you hear the clock chime? The doctor will be down for his breakfast any minute."

"No one's come for him?"

"Of course not. Besides, you would have heard. Did you have a bad dream again?"

"No, I didn't." I realized with relief that this was true. I vowed to stick to *Ivanhoe* for my nightly reading, never mind how boring it was.

For the next hour I half expected a knock at the door to call Doctor Ellman away, but no knock came, and breakfast passed as usual. Then the doctor left for the hospital, Mrs. Haslip set off for the market, Lucy went upstairs to start her morning chores, and Mrs. Ellman went out to visit a sick friend. I tried to work on my piano composition, but I kept glancing at the grandfather clock until finally my eleven o'clock pupil showed up, Vera Walsh, a self-assured young lady of twelve who always chattered to postpone as long as possible the moment of reckoning when she would have to play for me.

She was still playing when Mrs. Ellman returned from her sick bed visit. She stood in the doorway listening to Vera finish her piece.

"That's lovely, dear," she said when Vera was done. "Your mother must be very proud of you."

Vera beamed at the compliment.

I thought Mrs. Ellman looked troubled, but waited until Vera was gone to follow her into the kitchen, where Mrs. Haslip was making tea for her.

"Is everything all right?" I asked.

"Something's happened," Mrs. Ellman said. "In Dorset Street."

A chill ran through me. I knew what was coming next.

"They're saying another woman's been murdered."

So I had been right after all.

"It's not safe to go out on the streets," said Mrs. Haslip. "What's the world coming to?"

I had to know more about it. "I'm going out," I told them.

"Be careful, dear," Mrs. Ellman said.

Grabbing my jacket and hat, I headed for the door. Lucy was just coming down the stairs.

"And where might you be off to in such a rush?" she asked.

"There's been another murder," I said, pulling on my jacket. "On Dorset Street."

She opened her eyes wide. "Wait. I'm coming too."

It took her a few minutes to run back for her coat, and then a few more to run to the kitchen to beg permission from Mrs. Ellman to accompany me. I wanted to be on my way and felt impatient at the delay.

"He killed someone in broad daylight?" Lucy asked as soon as we were out the door. "Surely someone saw something this time."

I had less confidence than she did. There seemed to be no stopping this monster. If only I knew how many women he had killed. And their names! If I knew their names, maybe Abberline could protect them.

Dorset Street was not far away. It took only about fifteen minutes to walk there. When we arrived, we found it cordoned off by the police, who were letting no one in. Word had spread rapidly, and already a crowd had gathered.

"There's Bill," Lucy said. I spotted young Bill Tanner standing beside the cordon. "Maybe he can tell us what happened." She grabbed my hand and started pulling me through the crowd in his direction.

I wasn't sure Bill would want to talk to her after she had told him she wouldn't want to marry him even if he was the last man alive. However, she seemed to have no qualms about that.

"Bill!" she cried out and waved her free arm to get his attention.

People complained as we pushed between them. Bill's face lit up in a smile when he saw Lucy. He also seemed to have forgotten her words from the last time they met.

"What have you found out?" Lucy asked when we finally succeeded in reaching him.

"Not much. It was like this when I got here."

"Where's the body? Have they taken it away?"

He shook his head. "I'm not sure they've even gone in yet."

"What do you mean?" I asked.

"He murdered her in her room."

That sent a shiver through me. I had just assumed the crime had occurred in a street like all the others.

"Where did it happen?" Lucy asked, frowning at the nearly deserted street beyond the cordon. Except for a few police standing about, the street looked empty.

"In Miller's Court." He pointed at an open archway halfway down the street between the brick buildings.

"If they haven't gone in, how do they know someone's been killed?" I asked.

"There's a broken windowpane on the side, and they've looked through it. I talked to one of the men who looked inside. He said it was the most awful sight he's ever seen. Blood everywhere. What's left of her body lying on a bed."

Just hearing him describe it made me feel sick.

"What are they waiting for?" Lucy asked. "Why don't they go in?"

"I think they're waiting for the bloodhounds. If they go in, they'll interfere with the scent."

"The bloodhounds will find him," Lucy said. "They'll catch him this time."

"Maybe," Bill said.

"Is Inspector Abberline here?" I asked.

"Yes, I saw him a while ago. He's in there." He nodded toward Miller's Court.

Just then there was a commotion not far from us as police pushed through the crowd, escorting a man through the cordon. He was carrying a black box about the size of a hatbox and something long like a walking stick. It was Mr. LaRue, the photographer from Soho, with his camera and tripod.

"Why is he here?" Lucy asked.

"To take photographs, of course," Bill said.

I shuddered, remembering the photographs of dead women mounted on the wall of his lodgings. Now he would have another Ripper victim for his ghoulish collection.

We watched as he walked up the street with his police escort and disappeared through the narrow entry into Miller's Court.

"He's never gone inside before," Lucy said. I knew she meant the killer, not LaRue.

"No," Bill agreed.

"She probably thought she was safe."

"Do you suppose she knew him?" I asked.

"The women around here aren't over particular who they invite into their rooms," Bill said. "Plus one fellow over there told me she'd had more than a drop to drink last night."

"Maybe he's here right now," Lucy said, and we all glanced around nervously. There were a lot of down-and-out, rough-looking men in the crowd. She was right. Who would notice him in a crowd like that?

"She was twenty-five," Bill said. "Pretty girl. Everybody liked her."

Not in her forties, I thought. Not like the others.

"What was her name?" Lucy asked.

"Mary. Mary Kelly."

"What?" The name hit me like a physical blow. I reached for Lucy's arm to steady myself.

"What's the matter?" she asked. "Are you all right? You look like you just saw a ghost."

I remembered my name. It was as if someone had opened a door and I had walked through it and found myself on the other side. I was Mary Connor, born Mary Maddox. I kept saying it over and over, frightened that I might lose it again. It had been the sole remaining piece of the puzzle. All the pieces had slipped into place now.

"I'm sorry," I said. "I just felt faint for a minute."

"Are you sure you're all right?" Lucy asked anxiously.

"Yes, I think I'll be fine now."

"Maybe you should take her home," Bill suggested.

"She said she feels fine now."

I knew Lucy didn't want to leave. She didn't want to miss anything.

Fifteen minutes passed, then an hour. Word spread through the crowd that the police were going from room to room in Miller's Court, questioning people, searching for the killer in case he was hiding close by. LaRue emerged with his camera and tripod and after making his way through the crowd rode away in a hansom cab. A rumor spread that the bloodhounds were not coming. At 3:30 the crowd parted for a horse-drawn wagon bearing a wood coffin, which passed the cordon and disappeared through the narrow brick archway into Miller's Court. Twenty minutes later it came back out. People jostled each other trying to touch the coffin. Women cried and men took off their caps as it passed. Mary Kelly may have had little to call her own in a life of hard knocks, but in death she was everybody's sister, daughter, and friend.

After the coffin was gone, the crowd began to disperse. Lucy and I walked home and Bill headed back to Fleet Street. I wondered when I would have a chance to talk to Abberline. I wanted to let him know I had remembered my name. And yet I was reluctant to tell Lucy or the Ellmans. If people knew my name, they would try to trace me and there was nothing to trace. Mary Connor was just as much a fabrication as Virginia Smith, more so in fact. She didn't exist. Virginia Smith did.

CHAPTER 22

Dr. Ellman did not come home for dinner that night. No doubt he was busy with the autopsy of Mary Kelly. Mrs. Ellman and I were sitting alone at the dinner table when a knock came at the front door. Lucy was just setting a plum pudding before us and nearly dropped it. We all looked at each other in alarm.

"Well, Lucy, better see who it is," Mrs. Ellman said.

"Yes, Ma'am."

"I'll go with her," I said, rising before Mrs. Ellman could protest.

Lucy shot me a grateful look.

"What if it's him?" she whispered as we headed for the door.

"Why then we scream and fight," I said. "There are two of us against one of him."

She smiled half-heartedly. I think we were both relieved when the door swung open to reveal Abberline. He looked tired, but just seeing him standing there made my heart beat faster. Lucy hurried back to the dining room to let Mrs. Ellman know who had arrived while we stepped into the drawing room and took advantage of our first minutes alone to exchange a long kiss.

"Sorry, I can't stay long," he said. "I suppose you've heard about this latest murder?"

"Yes."

"You were right. I don't know how you knew, but you were right."

"I told you, I dreamed it."

"It's a shame your dreams can't tell us who he is."

"I'm sorry I'm not more help," I said.

"You're a help just by being here."

"I was there at Dorset Street this afternoon," I told him. "I went with Lucy."

"Did you? I wish to god I hadn't been there. I've never seen anything so terrible before. It's a sight I'll not soon forget."

I could smell the damp wool of his coat. He kissed me again and then traced the side of my face with his finger.

"I couldn't bear it if anything happened to you," he said.

"Or I to you," I said.

"We've got to catch him. This has to stop. There'll be a riot if it keeps up."

"Why didn't they bring in the bloodhounds?" I asked.

"They weren't here. It turned out the police never reached an agreement with the owner about how much he'd get paid. He took them back to North Yorkshire. But even if we'd had them, it's doubtful they could have caught a scent after so many people had moved about the area."

"No one saw anything? No one heard anything?"

"Several people claim they saw Mary Kelly with a man last night, but no one knows if he was the killer, and the descriptions don't agree. One woman says she saw her with a rough-looking man who had whiskers and a carroty mustache while another says she saw her with a well-dressed man who had a trimmed black mustache and carried a black bag. As for hearing anything, a woman in the room above thought she heard someone scream 'murder' a little before four in the morning, but she didn't think anything about it. It's a rough neighborhood. People quarrel. They get drunk. There are a lot of prostitutes in the area."

"Why do you think he went inside this time?" I asked. "He's never done that before."

"Maybe no one invited him in before. Maybe there are too many police out on the streets now. Whatever the reason, it gave him ample time to do his business. She was such a bloody mess that her boyfriend had trouble identifying her, and then it was only by her eyes and her ears."

I shuddered. "You would have thought she'd be more careful about inviting a stranger in after all that's happened."

"Maybe she was too drunk. Maybe he seemed harmless enough. Maybe she knew him."

I found it difficult to believe that someone she knew would mutilate her like that. It was too horrible to imagine. The killer had to be some sort of monster.

"Somewhere, somebody knows him," Abberline said. "He lives somewhere. He has neighbors. He has parents, aunts, uncles, cousins, a brother or a sister, maybe even a wife and children. He can't just live in a vacuum. Somebody knows him."

"No one saw anyone leave her room?"

Abberline shook his head. "He's either incredibly careful or damned lucky." He put his hat on. "I'd better get back. Don't go out. You won't, will you? Not while this maniac is out there."

"Of course not," I said. We kissed again. I wished I could stay in his arms forever, warm and safe, tasting his lips, feeling the tickle of his mustache. Yes, this was where I wanted to be.

When he opened the door, I saw Purvis standing across the street, his collar turned up against the cold, his hands jammed in his pockets to keep them warm, patiently waiting for him.

"You'll be careful, won't you?" I said.

It was ten that night before Dr. Ellman came home. I had a lamp on in the drawing room, where I was curled up on the curve-legged sofa, wrapped in a shawl, reading *Ivanhoe*.

"Still up?" He looked tired as he stood there in the doorway, his spectacles reflecting the light from the lamp.

"I couldn't sleep," I said.

"My wife's gone to bed?"

"Yes, I think they all have."

"You heard another woman's been killed?"

"Yes."

He lifted one hand to his temple as if he had a headache.

"Are you all right?" I asked.

He nodded. "It's a bad business."

"We heard this one was worse than the others."

"I've never seen anything like it," he said. "In all my years I've never. . . ." He shook his head. "What he did to that poor young woman was horrible, just horrible. He's no surgeon. No surgeon would ever have carved her up like that. No butcher either. Only a madman could have done such a thing."

"Would you like me to make you a cup of tea?" I asked.

He shook his head. "No, I think I'll go to bed now. God knows if I'll be able to get a wink of sleep. I think if I close my eyes I'll see that poor unfortunate young woman."

He turned to go, then stopped. "We couldn't find her heart."

For a few seconds I didn't understand. Then, with a quick intake of breath, I did. The killer's souvenir, his trophy. He had taken her heart. I stared unseeing at the book in my lap as Dr. Ellman's footsteps trudged up the stairs. How could I read after that? My mind would not let go of the awful image of the killer carving up his victim and carrying away her heart. What fluke of nature or terrible childhood trauma had created such a monster? How could such evil exist?

Dr. Ellman left the next morning immediately after breakfast. It was Saturday, but nothing seemed quite as it should be. Mrs. Ellman was upset about the murder and did not want us to talk about it in front of her. Lucy dashed out to buy a newspaper, and when she returned, we spread it out on my bed and pored over it together. The headline blared 'Another Whitechapel Murder.' There was an illustration of a woman standing in a doorway, one hand on hip. The caption said she was Mary Kelly. Her body had been found by a young man sent to collect overdue rent. Her door was locked but he had looked through her broken windowpane and seen the gory scene inside, where she had been murdered and mutilated on her own bed. He ran back to tell the landlord, who after looking for himself, ran to the Commercial Street police station to summon the police. As we already knew, they had waited hours to go inside. When they finally did, they found a scene of horror. Mary Jane Kelly had been eviscerated and mutilated to the point of being barely recognizable. It had been the most gruesome of all the Ripper's murders so far.

"I don't see how he could commit such a murder and get away unseen," I said.

Lucy sighed. "It was probably still dark when he left. He would have looked like just another man stepping out of a prostitute's room. No one would have looked twice."

"I suppose so," I agreed. "But still you'd think someone would have seen something."

Mrs. Ellman put her head in the door and pretended not to notice the newspaper. "I'm going out in a bit to a meeting of my women's society. Would you like to come along? You might find it interesting."

"I have two lessons today," I told her. "Perhaps another time."

She didn't seem too disappointed, and now I had the rest of the morning free to work on my piano composition until my first student arrived. Composing was a struggle, but gradually I was making progress on the piece. I didn't like to disturb Mrs. Ellman so I tried to work on it only when she went out.

I was at the piano later when Lucy walked in frowning with an envelope in her hand which had just arrived in the post.

"Why do you suppose she's written to me?" Lucy said, looking worried.

"Who's it from?" I asked.

"Mrs. Lynch in Epping. I'm afraid it's something bad. She doesn't ever write to me."

"Would you like me to open it?" I offered.

She nodded and handed it to me.

It was so unlike Lucy to be afraid of anything. I gave her an encouraging smile and tore the envelope open. The message within was brief, barely legible, and riddled with misspellings.

"Well, what is it?" she asked anxiously.

"Jamie is sick," I said after reading it through twice. "Mrs. Lynch says he has . . . ague."

Her hand flew to her mouth.

"She says if you want to see him, you should come right away."

Lucy sank weakly down on the sofa. "No! Not my Jamie!"

"Maybe it's not as bad as it sounds," I said, trying to comfort her.

She shook her head. "I should never have left him there. I knew they didn't take good care of him, but I turned a blind eye. I didn't know where else I could take him."

"It's not your fault," I said.

"Yes, it is! I left him there. It serves me right. I don't deserve him. The sweetest little boy in the world! Oh, god, what am I going to do?" She jumped up and started wringing her hands.

"Go to him," I said. "See for yourself if it's as bad as she says."

She nodded distractedly. "Yes."

"I'll go with you," I offered.

"But your pupils?"

"They can wait."

She nodded, fighting back her tears.

We caught the afternoon train and arrived half an hour later in Epping. Soon we were knocking on the door of Mrs. Lynch's cottage. The girl with a sore on her lip and her hair hanging in her eyes admitted us. In the next room a child was crying.

We could hear Mrs. Lynch scolding the child. She gave us a wary look when she saw us standing in the doorway.

"Where's Jamie?" Lucy asked, looking around anxiously.

"He's upstairs," Mrs. Lynch said in a sullen voice. "I don't want him giving the ague to everyone else. I'd have a right mess on my hands if that happened."

Lucy's eyes flew to the narrow stairs.

"Wait, I'll take you up," Mrs. Lynch said sharply. "Annie, watch these brats for a moment. If any of them give you trouble, smack them."

We followed her up a narrow stairs to a bare little room on the second floor where Jamie lay curled up on a small pallet on the floor. There was little else in the room, and it looked as if no one had bothered to sweep or mop for a long time. Lucy dropped to her knees beside him, heedless of her skirts.

"Jamie," she said, all her pent-up worry packed into those two syllables.

He opened his eyes and looked at her dazedly. She put a hand on his forehead.

"He's burning up," she said in alarm. "How long has he been like this?"

He's been sick for about a week now," Mrs. Lynch said. "We brought him up here two days ago so the others wouldn't be catching it. I had the doctor in. He says it's ague and there's nothing he can do about it."

"Has he been eating?" Lucy demanded.

"He wasn't hungry."

"When did he last eat?"

Mrs. Lynch squinted one eye and thought. "Yesterday maybe. No, maybe the day before. I don't remember. There's so many mouths to feed around here. I can't be spending all my time looking after one brat."

"I want a glass of water for him," Lucy said, her voice steely.

"There's water downstairs," Mrs. Lynch said. "You'll have to fetch it yourself."

I laid a warning hand on Lucy's arm. "I'll get it."

Hoping she wouldn't say anything rash to Mrs. Lynch

while I was gone, I hurried downstairs. In the kitchen I found a smudged-looking glass in the cupboard, wiped it hastily on my skirt, which seemed to be the cleanest thing around, then filled it with water from a faucet. When I got back to Lucy, she was cradling Jamie in her arms. Without a word she took the glass of water from me and held it to his lips. "Ssh. Drink, baby." He looked very sick. If we had been in my own century and he had been my child, I would have rushed him to the nearest emergency room. There would have been medicines—antibiotics—fever reducers—doctors who knew what to do.

"He can't die!" Lucy said, struggling to hold back her tears.

I wracked my brain, trying to remember. What should you do for a child with a fever?

"Do you have aspirin?" I asked.

She looked at me blankly. So no aspirin. I would have to think of something else. Then I remembered that you could reduce a fever by lowering body temperature, such as placing a person in a bathtub of icy water. I knew there was no ice but it was worth a try.

"We could put him in cool water," I said. "Try to bring his temperature down."

Her eyes filled with desperate hope.

After I explained what we wanted, Mrs. Lynch reluctantly gave us a round washtub which she used for the children's weekly baths. Lucy insisted on carrying the water herself from downstairs in the bucket Mrs. Lynch grudgingly provided us, while I sat with Jamie. Once the tub was half full of cold water, we undressed him and lifted him into it. He cried and protested at the coldness of the water but was too weak to fight us off.

"It'll be all right, sweetie," Lucy said, blinking back her tears.

I hoped we were doing the right thing. Jamie didn't like being submerged in cold water one bit. But soon his fever began dropping, and then he started to shiver.

Lucy lifted him dripping from the tub, dried him off with a towel, and wrapped him in a blanket. She sent me downstairs to get clean clothes from Mrs. Lynch, who at first was reluctant to give them to me.

"What good is it going to do when he's just going to die anyway?" she said.

She finally relented when she saw I wouldn't go away without them.

"I'm going to take him home with me," Lucy said when I returned with the clean clothes. "If I leave him here, he'll die."

I thought she was probably right. "Then let's get him dressed."

So we dressed Jamie, wrapped him in a blanket, and set off for the train station. I offered to help carry him, but Lucy insisted on carrying him herself, big bundle that he was. We had to wait about thirty minutes for the train to come, and she held him all the time and on the train too, as if she feared letting him out of her arms would mean losing him.

CHAPTER 23

It was dusk when we got back to Whitechapel. The doctor and his wife were not home, so we had no trouble smuggling Jamie up to Lucy's garret room. She thought she could keep him hidden there and swore Mrs. Haslip and me to secrecy. But I doubted she would be able to hide his presence for long, and I worried about what would happen when Mrs. Ellman found out. She was a gentle and charitable woman, but would she be broad-minded enough to keep a servant girl with an illegitimate child?

"You can't hide him forever," I told Lucy as she sat on her narrow bed beside Jamie, who was snugly wrapped in her quilt. "She's bound to find out."

"It's only till he's better. Then I'll find another place for him, and when I'm married to Mr. Keating, he'll come live with us."

"Poor little tyke," said Mrs. Haslip, who had come up to check on them, and she hurried off to heat some broth.

When it was ready, Lucy couldn't get him to take more than a few sips. Watching him lie there pale and listless, I wondered if Mrs. Lynch was right when she said he would die. My heart went out to Lucy. I wished there were more I could do.

Around nine o'clock the Ellmans returned. I was reading in the drawing room when they came in.

"Thank god, that's over," Dr. Ellman said as he hung his hat on the hat rack by the door. "Why did they have to sit me next to that awful Mrs. Fitch? She thinks she has every malady known to man and some besides."

"I'm sorry you couldn't go with us," Mrs. Ellman said to me as she pulled off her coat. "I'm sure you would have enjoyed it. It was a lovely dinner."

"I thought Lucy could use the company," I explained. "She was quite upset when the letter came."

"Yes, of course," said Mrs. Ellman. "How is the little boy?"

"He's better now, I think." I didn't tell her he was upstairs in Lucy's bed at that very moment, but at least it wasn't a lie.

"Good. I'm glad to hear it."

I pretended to stifle a yawn then. "I guess I'll turn in now." I would have liked to stay up reading, but then she might ask me more questions about Jamie, and I was afraid I would end up giving away the truth.

I fell asleep quickly and was not disturbed by bad dreams, but in the middle of the night Lucy woke me to tell me Jamie was worse.

"I don't know what to do," she said, her voice full of worry. "Do you think we should bathe him again?"

"We should wake the doctor," I said, throwing off my blanket and swinging my feet to the floor.

"No!"

"He'll know what to do. You've got to tell him."

She shook her head, then nodded, biting her lip.

"I'll wake him," I said, taking charge of the situation. A child's life was at stake. It was no time to be concerned about what people might think. "Go back up to Jamie."

Without a word she turned and I followed her in the dark through the silent house and up the stairs to the door of the Ellmans' bedroom while she hurried up the little stairway that led to her garret room.

I took a deep breath and rapped on the door. "Dr. Ellman," I called softly. In a few minutes it opened and he stood before me in his nightshirt and slippers.

Suddenly I realized how I must look, standing there in my cotton nightdress, my hair disheveled, my feet bare.

"What is it?" he said. "What's happened? Has there been another murder?"

In the background I could hear Mrs. Ellman asking what was happening.

"It's Lucy's little nephew, Jamie," I said. "He's upstairs in her room and he's sick."

The doctor didn't ask me why Jamie was there. He just set off for the stairs with me close on his heels.

Lucy's door stood open and her lamp was lit. She sat on her bed with Jamie cradled in her arms. Dr. Ellman felt the child's forehead, took his pulse, and laid his head on Jamie's chest to listen to his breathing. "How long has he been like this?"

"Mrs. Lynch said he's been sick for a week," Lucy said. "She's the woman who looks after him."

"While we were in Epping, we got his fever down with a cold bath," I added.

The doctor shot me a look of disapproval. "And then you brought him all the way back here from Epping on the train?"

"We couldn't leave him there," Lucy said. "If you'd seen the place—"

"Of course you couldn't," said Mrs. Ellman from the doorway. She had thrown a robe over her nightdress and her grey hair hung down in a braid.

The doctor sighed. "I have some quinine downstairs you can give him in tea. Maybe that'll break the fever. Meanwhile he's got to be kept warm. We'll need more blankets. And lay him down on the bed. Holding him like that just exposes you to the illness as well. What good are you going to be to him if you catch it too?"

For the next twenty minutes we ran about fetching blankets, a hot water bottle, and warm tea. When we had done everything we could, the Ellmans went back to bed, leaving Lucy and me to watch over Jamie, with instructions to wake the doctor if Jamie got worse.

I must have fallen asleep because light was creeping in through the little garret window when I woke. I had fallen asleep leaning against the trunk with my head pillowed on my arms and a blanket thrown over me. Lucy was awake, but Jamie was sleeping peacefully, his lips slightly parted.

"His fever broke," Lucy whispered. "His skin feels almost normal now."

"You should try to get some sleep," I told her.

"I can't," Lucy said. "When I think how close I came to losing him. . . ."

"Dr. Ellman is right. You're no good to him if you get sick too."

She nodded and closed her eyes and I tiptoed out of the room.

After getting dressed, I went to the kitchen and found Mrs. Haslip fixing breakfast.

"How's the little fellow doing?" she asked.

"Better."

"It would about kill Lucy if anything happened to him."

"I wonder what she'll do with him now," I said.

"Well, I hope she has the sense not to take him back to Epping."

"I doubt she would trust him to Mrs. Lynch's care again." I looked at the platters of food on the kitchen table. Usually Lucy carried them to the dining room. Without a word I reached for the nearest platter.

As I carried them in one by one, I tried to think of how to explain to Mrs. Ellman why I hadn't let her know Lucy had brought Jamie back with her, but in the end I didn't have to explain. When she came down for breakfast, she merely asked how Jamie was doing, and when I told her his fever had broken, she nodded and said, "Good."

That afternoon Abberline came by and took me to Regent's Park for a stroll in Queen Mary's Gardens. He said they had finished questioning everyone who lived in Miller's Court but had come up with nothing. The killer had left no clues behind. Nobody had seen anyone suspicious. The public was demanding results from the police, but what were they to do?

"We can't put a policeman on every corner," he said, "and we can't protect the women of Whitechapel if they persist in going into dark alleys with strange men and taking them home to their beds."

"Well, I promise not to do that," I said as we passed a fountain. The sky was pearly grey and the air chilly. I turned up the collar of my new coat and returned my hand to the crook of his arm. It felt so right.

He smiled ruefully. "Sorry. I am a bit single-minded, aren't I, darling?"

"I'm just happy to be with you," I said. "And I know it's hard for you to think about anything else."

"It'll be different after we catch him. I promise."

I glanced at him.

"I do intend to catch him," he said.

Two days after Jamie's arrival, Mrs. Ellman insisted on moving him to Henrietta's old bedroom down the hall from her and the doctor so Lucy could get a proper night's sleep in her own bed. She said she did not want Lucy falling ill, for then who would see to the housekeeping? Although Lucy would have preferred to keep Jamie with her, she agreed to this arrangement. Meanwhile, Jamie was steadily recuperating and by the fourth day he was out of bed. At first he followed Lucy from room to room, as if he didn't want to let her out of his sight. But soon he grew bolder and ventured into the drawing room when I was playing the piano or giving lessons. I would look up and see him standing there solemnly watching me. Then he would smile shyly, duck his head, and run away. He soon made friends with Mrs. Haslip too and found she had good things in her kitchen to eat and a wood spoon and a pan lid he could play with. Mrs. Ellman also made a fuss over him and even the doctor wasn't immune to his charm but let the boy climb on his lap and look at his pocket watch.

On the fifteenth of November a letter arrived from Mr. Keating announcing that he would pay a visit to Lucy again *on a matter of utmost importance*. Lucy was in a state of nerves as the appointed hour approached, darting into the drawing room every five minutes to check the time on the grandfather clock. I was sitting in a wing chair reading and Jamie was playing under the table in the corner with some toy soldiers Mrs. Haslip had given him.

"What do you suppose he wants?" she fretted. "You don't suppose he's changed his mind about marrying me, do you?"

"I doubt it," I said. "Where else would he find anyone as pretty and intelligent?"

She sighed. "You forgot penniless."

"When are you going to tell Mrs. Ellman that you're getting married?" I asked. "Sooner or later you'll have to tell her."

"She'll probably be glad to get rid of Jamie and me. He's always underfoot."

"I don't think that bothers her. In fact, I think she's grown rather fond of him. We all have."

"Well, you'll all just have to make do without us," Lucy said. She glanced at the grandfather clock again. "He'll be here in thirty minutes and Mrs. Ellman is still upstairs. What am I going to do?"

"You're going to answer the door and invite him into the drawing room. Leave Mrs. Ellman to me."

I envisioned keeping Mrs. Ellman occupied in her room with conversation, but as luck would have it, at 4:15 Mrs. Ellman came downstairs pulling on her gloves and announced that she had just remembered she had to go to her dressmaker's for an alteration. As soon as she was gone, Lucy rushed upstairs to check her hair in the mirror and take off her apron. Mr. Keating arrived punctually at half past four. I admitted him and left him in the drawing room while I went to find Lucy. Halfway up the stairs I remembered Jamie and hurried back down. When I got to the drawing room, Jamie was standing in front of Mr. Keating, who was seated in one of the wing chairs eyeing him warily. I knew I should get Jamie out of there before Mr. Keating figured out who he was.

"Oh, there you are, Jamie!" I said, rushing forward and taking him by the hand.

"Is he yours?" Mr. Keating asked stiffly.

"No, he's . . . visiting."

"I must say he gave me a bit of a start. I was not aware there was a child on the premises."

"He just arrived on Saturday," I explained.

"Well, he oughtn't to be left about to hide in corners and startle people," Mr. Keating said. "Doesn't he have a nursemaid or governess to watch him?"

"No, he doesn't."

"How peculiar."

Just then Lucy appeared in the doorway, smiling and looking very pretty. Her eyes flew from me to Jamie to Mr. Keating. "Is anything wrong?"

"I was just telling—" Mr. Keating gestured vaguely at me. "I beg your pardon, but I've forgotten your name."

"Mrs. Smith," I murmured.

"Quite. I was just telling Mrs. Smith that this little boy ought to have a nursemaid or governess to watch him."

"I'm sure you're right," Lucy said sweetly.

Jamie looked up at her, then flung himself at her skirts. She ran her hand fondly over his blonde curls. If Mr. Keating could not see a doting mother's love in that simple gesture, he was blind.

I knew I should leave, but I thought Lucy might want me to take Jamie so I lingered.

"You had something to tell me," Lucy said, making no effort to detach herself from Jamie.

"Yes, I did." He glanced at me with annoyance, but I stood my ground. "It's about the date of our . . . er . . . nuptials."

"Yes?" Lucy said with a quick intake of breath.

Now I would not have left for the world. If Mr. Keating

was going to break off the engagement, I wanted to be there for Lucy.

He hesitated and gave me a last look of irritation. "I fear we must move the date up. I hope that won't be inconvenient."

Lucy smiled, visibly relieved. "It's not inconvenient at all."

I wondered why he was moving the date up. Did it have anything to do with his uncle's will? Had the old man given him a deadline? I was certain there was some ulterior motive at work.

"Will the fifteenth of December, one month from today, be acceptable?" he asked.

"Perfectly." She flashed him a brilliant smile.

He stood, holding his hat. "Then that's settled." He nodded to me. "Mrs. . . . Smith." He nodded to Lucy. "Miss Callaghan." He put on his top hat and headed for the front door.

"Wait," Lucy said.

He stopped. "Was there something else?"

She looked down at Jamie, still clinging to her skirt. "Yes, it's about . . . my nephew."

He looked down at the boy and frowned. "What about him?"

She took a deep breath. "His mother—my sister, that is—died recently of a fever."

"That is unfortunate. I'm sorry for your loss." His voice was cold. He turned and reached for the doorknob.

Maybe he guessed what Lucy would say next and hoped to stop her, but now that she had worked up her courage, she forged ahead. "He doesn't have anyone else to take care of him. You see, there's only me. So I was wondering . . . that is, if you don't mind . . . I'd like him to live with us. He wouldn't be any trouble. He's a very well-behaved child. I'm sure you'd grow fond of him with time."

After this rush of words, Mr. Keating was looking at her with such consternation that there was no doubt as to what he thought of her suggestion.

"Impossible. What would people say? How would it look? They would think he was yours. I have my reputation to think of—yours too since you'll soon be my wife. No, I'm afraid you'll have to make some other arrangement for him. Perhaps find someone in the country who will take him in. There are many women who do that for a fee."

Just then the front door swung open and Mrs. Ellman stood there blinking at us in surprise. "I beg your pardon. What's this all about?"

I had a sneaking feeling she had suspected something was going to happen in her absence and returned on purpose to see what it was. She could not possibly have had time to go to her dressmaker and come back.

"I am here on a little matter of business," Mr. Keating said, drawing himself up with dignity. "Now that it's taken care of, I'll be on my way."

"What matter of business?" Mrs. Ellman asked politely, not budging. He couldn't very well leave when she was standing in the way.

"Private business."

"This is my house," Mrs. Ellman said. "I think I have a right to know why you are here, sir."

"Really," he said. "This is a private matter between Miss Callaghan and myself. It doesn't concern you."

"She works for me, and therefore it concerns me," Mrs. Ellman said, shoulders squared as if for battle. I had never seen this side of her before. Was this the mild-mannered woman who could not bear talk of murder at her table?

"Very well," he said. "If you must know, Miss Callaghan and I are engaged. It was in regard to our nuptial arrangements that I came here to speak to her today. We have spoken, and now, if you don't mind, I will take my leave."

"Is this true, Lucy?" Mrs. Ellman demanded, still blocking the doorway. "You're planning to marry this man?"

Lucy scooped Jamie up in her arms. "I was, but I've changed my mind."

"What?" Mr. Keating stared at her.

I could have cheered, but I followed Mrs. Ellman's lead and kept my face expressionless.

"I said I've changed my mind," Lucy repeated and kissed Jamie's cheek.

Mr. Keating looked appalled. "You can't seriously say you'd turn me down because I declined to take in your nephew? You should be grateful for an opportunity to marry someone of my station. Good god, do you want to be a maid all your life?"

Mrs. Ellman stepped aside, leaving the doorway unobstructed. "I think you should leave now. Lucy's given you her answer."

CHAPTER 24

When Mary Jane Kelly was interred the following Monday at the Roman Catholic Cemetery in Leyton, the place was mobbed with people, especially the poor of Whitechapel, who had turned out in droves to mourn her. It was a grey and overcast November day and the wind was chill. Even in my new coat I was shivering. I was there with Abberline, who had not wanted me to come, arguing that it could be dangerous. The police were afraid that with emotions running so high there might be an outbreak of violence. But I was determined to go. I wanted to pay homage to Mary Kelly in whatever small way I could, not turn my back on her as if her death had not mattered. It did matter. She had not deserved such a terrible death. No one did.

Around me the crowd stretched in all directions. There was some pushing, especially near the open grave. Everyone wanted to get close enough to see the wooden coffin lowered into the ground. Men doffed their hats and women wept. Then while the priest intoned a prayer in Latin, the first drops of rain began to fall, as if even the heavens would weep for the death of Mary Jane Kelly.

When it was over, Purkiss joined us.

"Any sign of him?" Abberline asked. "Do you think he's here?"

"Could be," Purkiss said. "Half the men here look like they'd just as soon slit your throat as look at you. I'm sure there are plenty of pickpockets about, probably murderers too."

Abberline nodded. "Unless he has more pressing business elsewhere, I'll bet he's here, standing right under our noses laughing at us."

"Well, how we're supposed to pick him out in a crowd like this beats me," Purkiss said.

Bill Tanner was suddenly beside us, notepad in hand. "Mrs. Smith," he said, tipping his hat. "Is Lucy here?"

I shook my head. "No, she stayed at the house to take care of. . . ." I hesitated, uncertain if he knew about Jamie. "Her nephew."

"I didn't know she had a nephew. I thought her family was all dead. She still planning to marry that lawyer?"

"No, as a matter of fact she isn't."

"Come to her senses, did she?" He squinted at the sky. "Looks like we're in for some rain."

"Yes, it does," I agreed.

"Do you think I have a chance then?"

"I think you might have a very good chance," I said.

"She was very definite when she said no before. I'd feel like a right idiot if she turned me down again."

"You won't know unless you try."

He narrowed his eyes, scanning the crowd. "Quite a turnout, isn't it? Poor kid. She probably had no idea there would be such a turnout for her funeral. Not that that's much consolation." He tipped his hat again. "Well, I'd better get back and write my story. I might just take your advice."

Abberline was still talking to Purkiss. They had moved a little farther away. From time to time he glanced at me, as if to assure himself I was still there. Then a young woman who had been standing nearby turned to me. "Can you spare a few shillings?" she asked. She looked familiar although I didn't think I knew her. She was dressed in several layers of clothing with a black shawl pulled tightly around her. The hem of her skirt had mud on it and her auburn hair under her hat was coming loose. I tried to think where I might have seen her before as I fished a few shillings from my reticule and offered them to her.

"Thanks, Lucy," she said, pocketing them. "You've a good heart."

I was about to tell her she had mistaken me for someone else when I remembered her. "You were in the Whitechapel jail that day."

"So I was," she said. "It looks like you and the governor are friendly now."

We both glanced at Abberline.

"He's a good man," she said. "Some of them look down on us and think we're dirt, but the governor, he's a real gent."

"Yes, he is," I said.

"Did you know Mary Jane?"

"No. Did you?"

"I did," she said. "Mary Jane would give you the dress off her back if you asked. Not a mean bone in her body. I hope to hell they catch the blackguard who did this."

Just then a dark-skinned boy careened into her, knocking her against me.

"Watch where you're going, you young ruffian," she cried.

The boy was already gone, lost in the crowd.

"You best check your money, love. That's how they pick pockets." She was checking her own.

"I know him," I said, trying to spot the boy in the crowd. "I've seen him before."

"Are you all right?" Abberline said, rushing up.

"I've seen that boy before. He's the boy who took me to Buck's Row to search for my pocketbook."

"What happened?" asked Purkiss.

"Some boy just ran into her," Abberline said. "Did you check to see if he took anything?"

"No, I don't think so," I said. "It wasn't me he ran into. It was—" I remembered her name then. Kate. But she was gone. When Abberline and Purkiss had rushed to my side, she had melted into the crowd. I didn't blame her. She lived in a netherworld where the police were distrusted. I looked around, trying to find her or the boy in the crowd.

"Are you quite sure he didn't take anything?" Abberline asked.

"Quite sure," I said.

"There must be at least a thousand people here," he said. "You would think the Queen had died."

"I meant to tell you," I said. "I remember my name. It's Mary."

He stared at me. "Mary? Are you sure?"

"Yes."

"Like the dead woman?"

"Well, yes."

"When did you remember this?"

"That day in Dorset Street."

He frowned. "Why didn't you tell me before? Why did you wait until now?"

"I don't know," I said. "It didn't seem important."

"Not important? He's killed two women named Mary and your name is Mary too. That doesn't strike you as odd?"

"It's a common name."

"Christ," he muttered.

"Anyway our last names are different." I hadn't expected him to get angry.

"So what's your last name?"

"Connor. Mary Connor."

"I don't like it. I don't like it one bit."

"I don't see why you're making such a big deal of it," I said.

"You told me in your dreams it's *you* he's stalking. And what about that night of the double murder when you were midway between the two women who were killed? Suppose it's you he's been looking for all along."

I shook my head. "No, it was a coincidence. You said so yourself."

"Come on," Abberline said, taking my elbow. "Let's get you out of here."

He was grim on the ride home in a cab. Nothing I could say would shake his mood. I wished now that I had not told him my name. What did it matter if I was Mary Connor or Virginia Smith?

"I'm sure it's just a coincidence," I insisted. "London must be full of Mary's."

He glared out the window at the passing city. "Just like it's full of Jack's," he muttered.

That night I dreamed again that I was back in the house of many rooms. It was dark and there were shadows everywhere. I thought I heard Courtney calling to me from a great distance. The Ripper was coming and I was desperate to escape him. I thought if I could find my way out of the house, I would be safe, but every room led to another room. It was a maze with no way out.

In the early hours of morning I woke up in a sweat, my heart pounding, and made my way in the dark to the drawing room, where moonlight slanted in through a gap in the lace curtains. Through the gap I saw a man standing across the street in the shadows. Purvis. No doubt posted there by Abberline to watch over me. Knowing he was close at hand made me feel safer. I was tempted to rush out and talk to him, but I was in my nightdress and he would have thought I had lost my mind.

So instead I curled up in a wing chair and fell asleep. That was where Lucy found me a few hours later when she came down to help Mrs. Haslip prepare breakfast.

"Whatever are you doing sleeping here?" she asked. "Don't tell me you've been here all night?"

"I couldn't sleep," I said. "I got up to look for a book."

"Well, you'd better go get dressed before Mrs. Ellman sees you. She'll think something's wrong."

I looked out the window again. It was just starting to grow light. Purvis was gone. I watched a hansom cab roll past in the street. Did the dream mean the Ripper would strike again? Maybe it was all coincidence. Maybe the dreams had no connection to him at all. What was the point of telling Abberline about them? It only upset him. No, I would not tell Abberline about last night's dream, I resolved. I was not going to let some boogeyman steal my life from me.

In the afternoon Bill Tanner stopped by the house to see Lucy, but she was out on an errand, so I left him to wait in the drawing room while I went to the kitchen to ask Mrs. Haslip to make some tea. When I returned with the tea tray, Jamie was showing him a toy soldier.

"It's a fine soldier," Bill said. "See how he stands so straight? Must be one of the Queen's Guard. You know, the ones that guard the palace. You've seen them, haven't you?"

Jamie shook his head.

"You haven't? Well, you ought to. Maybe I can take you one day. Would you like that?"

Jamie nodded.

"Is this Lucy's nephew?" Bill said. "He's a handsome little chap. Funny, she never mentioned a nephew before."

"It probably just didn't come up," I said.

"It's just him?"

"Yes, his mother—" I stopped, unable to say she had died in front of Jamie, especially when it wasn't true. But Bill took my meaning.

"Poor little tyke. So Lucy took him in?"

"Yes."

"The Ellmans don't mind?"

"No, actually they're quite fond of him. We all are."

"They're good people. Not everyone would treat their servants like family."

The front door opened and closed. Then Lucy appeared in the doorway, her cheeks rosy from the chill air. "What's he doing here?" she demanded, pulling off her coat.

"I came to pay a visit," Bill said, "but if I'm not wanted, I can leave." He stood up, as if intending to do just that. Jamie tilted his head back to look up at him as if he were a giant.

"A visit to Mrs. Smith or a visit to me?" Lucy asked.

"To you, as a matter of fact. I have a question to ask you."

"I can't imagine what you have to say."

We all paused at the sound of the front door opening and

closing again. Mrs. Ellman looked into the drawing room. "My goodness. What's going on here? And who might this young man be?"

There was an awkward moment of silence. Then Bill snapped to life. "Bill Tanner, of the London *Star*."

"A reporter?" Mrs. Ellman said. "Did you come to see my husband?"

"No, ma'am, I came to see—" He glanced at Lucy. "Miss Callaghan."

"You seem to be very popular lately," Mrs. Ellman remarked to Lucy. "First that lawyer and now a reporter."

"I'm sorry," Lucy said, reddening. "It won't happen again."

"I invited him," I said. "It's not Lucy's fault he's here."

"Anyway he was just leaving," Lucy said.

"No, I wasn't," Bill said. "Not until I've had a chance to say what I came to say."

We all looked at him. I held my breath.

"Very well," Mrs. Ellman said. "What do you wish to say? I assume you don't mind saying it in front of all of us. It's nothing that would offend a lady's ears, is it?"

He looked uncomfortable. "No, ma'am." Then he turned to Lucy. "Mrs. Smith told me you're not planning to marry that lawyer anymore."

Lucy shot me a look. "So what if I'm not?"

"Well, if you're not planning to marry him, I was wondering if you'd reconsider my offer the other day." He dropped down on one knee. "What I'm asking, Lucy Callaghan, is will you marry me?"

Just then the grandfather clock began to chime. It was four o'clock.

"I know I don't make much," Bill said when the chiming

275

had died away. "I'm not a lawyer or a doctor or such, but we could get by."

"It's not that," Lucy said. "I have Jamie to think about."

Bill glanced at the boy. "He could come live with us. You'd like that, kid, wouldn't you?"

"Could I see the soldiers?" Jamie asked.

"Why of course."

Lucy bit her lip. We were all looking at her. "Are you sure about this?" she asked him.

"Of course I'm sure," Bill said. "I wouldn't be asking if I wasn't sure."

She looked down at Jamie, who was watching her, and then at Bill. "Well, then, yes, I suppose I could marry you."

Bill was on his feet in a flash and had her wrapped in his arms. "You won't be sorry."

Lucy was laughing now. Jamie plowed into her skirts, wanting to be hugged too.

"And to think if I'd come home any later I would have missed this!" Mrs. Ellman murmured to me.

Bill Tanner's proposal was not the only event that day. In the evening I went out with the Ellmans to what Mrs. Ellman called a musical evening. She told me she was sure I would enjoy it and besides Abberline would be there. As the hour of departure approached, I felt increasingly excited. Lucy fussed over my hair. I wore a rose-colored gown of Henrietta's that showed more neck and bare arms than any of her other dresses and a jeweled comb in my hair, tear drop earrings, and a ribbon choker with a garnet. I was determined to forget about Jack the Ripper for one night and enjoy myself.

This social event took place in a home in West London

much larger and more fashionable than the Ellmans' small house on Whitechapel Road. I knew almost no one besides the Ellmans and Abberline, who arrived soon after we did and at once was surrounded by men eager to talk about the murders. There was punch to drink and then we were invited by our hostess to seat ourselves on chairs facing the piano. I had had my eye on the piano from the minute I walked in the door. It was a grand, far more expensive than the small piano in the Ellmans' drawing room. I was hoping to take a closer look when I got the chance.

As we seated ourselves on the chairs, Abberline claimed the one next to me. "Thank god they're ready to start," he said in a low voice. "I don't think I could have endured another question about why we haven't caught the Ripper. You'd think it was like picking up a stray dog. I'd like to see them try it. Why didn't you come rescue me?"

"You looked like you were managing quite well," I told him.

"Whatever gave you that idea? By the way, you're looking stunning this evening. Have you spread the word that we're engaged? I don't want any of these toffs getting any ideas."

Our hostess, a tall regal-looking woman, gradually silenced us with her Medusa stare. Then she introduced a Miss Clements, the daughter of a banker, who proceeded to play a Schumann etude correctly but without much feeling. When the etude concluded, we all applauded politely. Next a Miss Wilcox played a Chopin ballade accompanied by a young man on violin. I liked sitting there with Abberline beside me and wondered how many future evenings like this we would share. My past, although I remembered it now, seemed far away, as if it had happened to someone else. Had I realized how unhappy I had been in my marriage? In fact, it seemed to me that I had been looking for something all my life, and now I had found it.

After the piano and violin duet had finished, our hostess announced: "And now we have a very special treat. Mrs. Smith, who is visiting us from the States, has kindly agreed to play something for us."

I couldn't believe my ears. I hadn't agreed to play for them. Where on earth had she gotten that idea?

Mrs. Ellman leaned closer. "I hope you don't mind," she said behind her gloved hand. "I really couldn't refuse her after she's been so generous to our little branch of the Society for Women's Suffrage."

There was no time to argue about it. Everyone was clapping politely. I saw I would have to play for them, although if I had known beforehand, I would have refused. It wasn't that I hadn't played for an audience before. I had. In fact, many times, on stages and in competitions, but that was when I was younger, before I had become a teacher and a composer. However, with everyone looking at me, I had to be gracious and pretend that I didn't mind.

I tried to think quickly what to play. It would have to be something I knew by heart. I thought about my own composition but knew it might sound strange to an audience that had never heard Bartok or Schoenberg, and I wasn't quite satisfied with the ending. By the time I seated myself on the piano stool, I had made my decision. My fingers touched the smooth ivory keys and I began to play one of Beethoven's sonatas. It was a wonderful piano, with a clear rich sound that rose up to the chandelier and filled the room. For a few moments my eyes closed and I forgot my audience. There was just me and the music and I knew in those moments that I could be happy anywhere if I had my music. They applauded when I finished, and I slipped back to my chair, while two more women were introduced. One sang an old troubadour song in French in a sweet soprano while the other accompanied her on the piano. Sitting beside Abberline, I wished that I could hold onto this moment forever.

When the music ended, conversation resumed and Abberline and I wandered out on the terrace that overlooked a garden in back of the house. A few other people also wandered out and stood in pairs and clusters talking. The air was cool and damp, but it wasn't raining. There was a smell of wet earth and vegetation. Overhead a pale moon shone through the clouds.

"Why didn't you tell me you could play like that?" Abberline asked. "I had no idea."

"Does it matter?"

"We'll have to get a piano."

I smiled. "I'd like that. Then I could go on giving lessons and composing."

"Maybe you'll become famous in the future," he said.

"I rather doubt that."

"Whatever do you see in a dull fellow like me?" he said. "Are you sure you won't be bored?"

"Of course I won't be bored. I can't imagine ever being bored by you."

"I don't always chase about after murderers. In fact, I've been thinking of retiring soon."

"I don't care what you do," I told him. "Just so long as I can be with you."

His hand squeezed mine. Around us I could hear the low murmur of the voices of the other couples who had come out onto the terrace. I wondered how many of them were in love. Some things didn't change no matter what century you lived in.

"By the way, thank you for having Purkiss watch the

house," I said. "It does make me feel safer, but poor Purkiss—it can't be much fun for him. He'll catch cold standing about like that in the damp at night."

He looked at me oddly. "Purkiss was watching your house?"

"I assumed you asked him to."

"When was this?"

"Last night."

"That's impossible," he said. "I know for a fact Purkiss was trailing one of our suspects the last two nights. He can't have been at your house."

"Well, if it wasn't Purkiss, who was it?"

He squeezed my hand more tightly. "What did he look like?"

I tried to remember. "I don't know. He was in shadow. And he wore a hat. I couldn't see his face. I thought it was Purkiss."

"No, darling, it wasn't Purkiss."

CHAPTER 25

Abberline stopped by the house the next day as Vera Walsh was leaving after her lesson. He set a small wood box on the side table in the drawing room. I wondered what was in it, but the kiss he gave me made me forget about the box for the moment.

"Why don't we marry before the end of the year?" he said.

"Tomorrow would be fine with me," I replied.

"Well, that might not be possible," he said, "but if you wouldn't mind moving it up a bit. . . . I'm so afraid you'll come to your senses, darling."

I had the feeling he had been about to say something else. "Is anything wrong?"

He sighed. "Sometimes I think you can see right through me."

"What's happened?"

"He's sent me a telegram."

I felt my blood run cold. "You? Why?" Of course the Ripper would know about him. All he had to do was read the papers to know Abberline was in charge of the case. But until

281

now he had sent his letters to the Metropolitan Police Commissioner or the press or the Vigilance Committee. In fact, Abberline had told me the police considered many of these letters to be hoaxes.

"He says he wants to give himself up. He wants to meet me on the bridge tonight at midnight."

"No. You can't."

"I have to. We've got to stop him before he kills again. This might be our only chance."

"Can't you send someone else? I don't want you to go."

"I know, darling, but I have to."

"You won't go alone, will you? Promise me you won't go alone."

"Of course I'll take Purkiss along. I'd be a fool not to."

He pulled the telegram from his pocket and handed it to me to read. It was addressed to Inspector Abberline, Scotland Yard.

Jack the Ripper wishes to give himself up. Will Abberline meet him on the Bridge at midnight Friday next with this end in view?

The message was written in red and signed Jack the Ripper. Scrawled at the bottom were these words: "*This is written with the 'Blood of Kelly.' All Long Liz's blood is used up.*"

"It's not really written in blood, is it?" I said, a shiver running through me.

"No, I'm pretty sure it's red ink."

"Have you showed it to anyone?"

"No, not yet."

"But you're going to, aren't you?"

"Yes, of course."

I knew by the tone of his voice that he probably would

not, or at least not until he had had a chance to meet the Ripper on the bridge. He had already made up his mind.

"Don't do this," I pleaded. "Please don't go. I couldn't bear it if anything happened to you."

"It'll be all right," he said, folding the telegram and tucking it back in his breast pocket. "He's not going to kill me."

"You don't know that," I said. "Look what he did to Mary Jane Kelly. And those other women. He's a psychopath."

"They were women. All of them were women."

"You think he wouldn't kill you just because you're a man?" It struck me as a dangerous assumption. I felt inexplicably angry at him.

"You tell me," he said. "Did he kill any men?"

"I don't think so," I admitted reluctantly. "Not that I know."

"Then he won't kill me. I'll be safe."

I shook my head. "No."

"I have to do this. It may be my only chance to stop him."

"Please don't."

"Look, I've brought something for you." He lifted the lid of the wood box. Inside was a revolver.

"A wedding present?" I asked wryly.

"You might say that."

"I wouldn't know what to do with it."

"I'll show you," he said. "I want you to keep this where you can get to it fast."

"Why? Do you think I'm in danger?"

"You might be," he said. "I don't like the idea that someone is watching this house. I had one of my men posted outside last night, but he didn't see anyone."

He lifted the revolver out and placed it in my hands. I was surprised how heavy it was.

283

"It's not terribly complicated," he said. "It's already loaded. You just have to aim and shoot. Aim at the chest. You're less likely to miss that way."

"How many shots will it fire?" I asked.

"Five." He looked at me thoughtfully. "Have you shot a gun before?"

"No," I said.

"Then I'd better show you how it works."

After he left, I hid the box with the revolver under my bed, then realizing Jamie might find it, moved it to the top drawer of the bureau. It didn't make me feel any better knowing it was there. I was no longer concerned about my own safety. It was Abberline I was worried about. So far as I knew, Jack the Ripper had not killed any men, but suppose I was wrong? How much did I really know about the Ripper and his victims? I wasn't going to let him kill the man I loved. I had waited a lifetime and traveled across time for him. A crazed killer wasn't going to take him away from me.

So a plan began to form in my mind. I did not believe for a minute that the Ripper was going to give himself up to Abberline. He was playing a game of cat and mouse with him. Would he even be at the bridge? If he was, it would most likely be some kind of trap. And if Abberline was alone and his body was found floating in the Thames tomorrow, I might be the only person he had told about that telegram from the Ripper, and if the telegram itself disappeared—destroyed past recognition by the muddy waters of the Thames—there would be no evidence left at all. He had said he would take Purkiss with him, but suppose two men were no match for the deadly Ripper? Wouldn't a third person—armed with a revolver—help to even the odds?

I was nervous the rest of the day and frequently went to the bureau drawer to check that the wood box was still there. Every time I opened the drawer my eyes fell on my old clothes, the blouse, jeans, and jacket I had arrived in, all neatly folded and pushed to the back. I asked myself if I shouldn't wear them when I went out. If the house was being watched by the police, I would have a better chance of eluding them if I was disguised as a man. And in jeans and athletic shoes I could move faster than in a long skirt and high-top shoes. But looking at my old clothes made me uneasy. Wearing them might be tempting fate to take me back to my own time. I doubted clothes had anything to do with why I had transported, but I was taking no chances. No, I wanted to stay where I was. I had made my choice.

And so that night I lay down in Henrietta's brown dress, and when the church clocks chimed eleven, I got up and pulled on my high-top shoes. Then I tiptoed up to Lucy's garret and woke her.

"I need you to do something for me," I said. "I need you to distract the policeman who's guarding the house so I can slip out. Abberline is meeting the Ripper on the bridge."

"Tonight? Why doesn't he take his men along?"

"The Ripper will only show if he thinks Abberline is alone."

"But what can you do?"

Her eyes grew wide when I showed her the revolver.

She got out of bed and began to dress. "Are you sure about this?" she asked as she struggled into a dress. "Don't you think Inspector Abberline can take care of himself?"

"If you were in my place, wouldn't you do the same?"

"I suppose I would," she said with a sigh.

We tiptoed down the stairs. At the door we hugged each other.

"Be careful," she whispered. "Don't make me regret this."

Then she opened the door and sauntered out as if it weren't the middle of the night. She went down the walk and into the street, then turned right. Almost at once a police officer came trotting out of the shadows and fog to follow her.

I took advantage of the fact that his attention had been diverted to set off in the opposite direction, knowing the fog would soon obscure me. Lucy would engage the police officer in conversation for a few minutes, then return to the house. She would claim to have had an urge to take a walk or pretend to have been sleepwalking. Meanwhile I would be on my way to the bridge.

I would have preferred to take a cab, but there were few about and to hail one might draw attention to myself so I would have to walk to the bridge. At least I knew my way around the city now. I would go down Whitechapel Road to Whitechapel High Street and from there to Aldgate High Street and then down Fenchurch Street to Gracechurch Street. Knowing there was no time to lose, I walked at a brisk pace.

Before I had covered half the distance, I became convinced that I was being followed. I tried to tell myself that my pursuer was not the Ripper, who might be at the bridge even now, lying in wait for Abberline. The person shadowing me was more likely to be a thief bent on robbery, but I could not afford to be waylaid. I clutched the revolver hidden under my coat more tightly.

Perhaps if confronted by a gun, any thief would change his mind. Stopping, I turned to face him, the heavy revolver clutched in both hands. But there was no one there. Just the fog and the eerily empty street wetly gleaming. Had I only imagined I was being followed? I waited, but the street remained empty. I started walking again, and almost at once the feeling of being followed returned. My heart was hammering in my chest. I told myself not to run. There were footsteps back there. Surely I was not imagining that! I didn't look back until I reached the next gaslight, and then I whirled about, my gun ready. There was someone there, a shadowy figure wearing a hat, barely visible through the fog, but I recognized him. He was the terror that stalked me in my dreams at night. I was not in a house of many rooms, but I had the same feeling of something monstrous and evil drawing near. Had he known all along that I would go to Abberline's aid? Was it possible that the trap he had laid was not for Abberline but for me?

The bridge was still blocks away. If I could make it there, Abberline might be able to help me, but I would never make it. It was too far. I held the revolver as steady as I could with both hands and aimed at the man, who was closer now. Aim for the chest, Abberline had said. He was still at least eight yards away when I pulled the trigger. The explosion was deafening and the kick caused me to drop the revolver. I knew even as I scrambled to retrieve it that I had not hit my mark. His footfalls on the cobblestones were running toward me. But before I could fire again, the gun was knocked from my hand and he was upon me. I curled into a ball and screamed.

CHAPTER 26

Gradually I became aware of the murmur of voices, but they were indistinct so I lay there, uncertain whether I was awake or dreaming. When at last I ventured to open my eyes, I found myself in a brightly lit room. As my eyes adjusted, I realized it was a hospital room. The murmur grew more distinct and became the voices of two people nearby. I tried to turn my head to look in their direction. To my surprise Courtney sat beside my bed reading a paperback. She had circles under her eyes and looked tired. My heart leaped to see her, but the next instant I realized that I had lost Abberline and could hardly bear it. I closed my eyes, wanting to go back, but the voices, which were coming from behind a curtain beyond Courtney, droned on, a backdrop now to the impersonal voice paging doctors over the intercom.

I must have slept then. When I opened my eyes again, a nurse had entered the room. Courtney still sat reading her paperback, a slight scowl creasing her forehead. As I watched, she yawned.

"Your mother's awake," the nurse said.

Courtney whipped about. "Mom? Thank god!" She grabbed my hand.

"What happened?" I asked.

"You got hit on the head. Somebody dropped a bottle of wine out a window. We were on a walking tour. Don't you remember?"

"No."

"You've been in a coma. They didn't know—" She trailed off, leaving her sentence unfinished. Didn't know what? Whether I would live? Whether I would wake up? Just how badly had I been hurt?

"How long have I been here?" I asked.

"About forty-eight hours."

"That's not possible." It had been months surely.

"I thought—" Courtney had tears in her eyes. "The doctors said you could be like this for weeks, or even months. You can't imagine how frantic I've been. I called Dad."

"What did he say?"

She looked away. With one hand she swept back her long brown hair. "He couldn't come right away. He couldn't get away. He said if you were still in a coma a week from now. . . ."

"Don't tire her," the nurse said. "I'll fetch a doctor."

I felt a great weariness remembering all the problems I had returned to. But the hurt of my divorce was not so acute now. More like an ache. Worse was the emptiness I felt knowing I had lost Abberline. Where was he right now? Waiting on London Bridge for the Ripper to show up? No, dead. He had died years ago. I would never see him again.

"I was there," I told Courtney, my throat feeling dry and unused.

"What do you mean? There—where?" She was stroking my hand.

"In Whitechapel."

"Yes, we were there together."

"No," I said. "You weren't there. I was alone. And at first I felt so lost. And I heard you calling to me in my dreams."

"Yes, I tried to wake you up," Courtney said.

"You don't understand," I said. "I was there. In 1888. When those women were killed."

"It was a dream," Courtney said. "You were in a coma. You haven't been anywhere except in this hospital bed."

"No, I was there. I can't explain how or why, but I was there. I couldn't have dreamed it, not in that kind of detail. Not Lucy, or the Ellmans, or—" I had been going to say, *or Abberline.*

"How are we doing then?" said a doctor, entering the room. He was a short balding energetic man who looked like he might start jogging in place at any moment.

"She's a little confused," Courtney said. "She dreamed she was back in the days of Jack the Ripper."

"Dreams? That's not unusual. I've heard some pretty amazing dreams coma patients have had." He shone a small light in my eyes, first the right, then the left, no doubt checking my pupils. "You'll be right as rain in no time."

"You mean she'll be released?" Courtney said hopefully. "We can go home?"

"Well, not today," he said. "We want to be sure she's all right. But if all goes well, she could be out of here tomorrow, although you might want to give her a bit of time to recover before you put her on a plane to the States."

He was looking at my head now, lifting a bandage wrapped around my temple. I suddenly realized it hurt.

"You got a nasty cut and we had to take some stitches. There's a bump and a bruise. You have a mild concussion. You're lucky it wasn't worse."

I remembered how Jack the Ripper had lunged at me as I groped for the revolver I had dropped. I remembered seeing the glint of a knife in his hand. Yes, it could have been worse. Had I escaped him or was I lying dead with my throat slit in a dark London street in the autumn of 1888, another victim of the Ripper?

"How's she doing?" called a man's voice from the doorway.

I looked, startled, because it sounded like Abberline, and in fact he did bear an uncanny resemblance to Abberline, but without the mustache.

"She's awake now," the doctor said. "Do you want to ask her any questions?"

"Not really necessary," he said. "I was just here to talk to the woman in 315 about her attacker. Thought I'd stop by to see how this one's doing."

"She'll be out of here tomorrow."

"Very good," he said, and then he was gone. Just like that.

"Who was that?" I asked.

"Scotland Yard."

"I know. But what's his name?"

"Inspector Merriweather."

The resemblance had been uncanny. He was not Abberline, but he could have been his twin brother. I knew right then that I was not going to jump on a plane and fly home without first speaking to him. I had to find out if he was like Abberline in more than appearance.

"Well, rest," the doctor said. "If you feel up to it in a bit, you can try walking around, but better use a walker and have someone at hand to catch you if you fall. We don't want you taking any spills."

After that the nurse came back and took my temperature

and blood pressure and offered me some clear broth. When I had managed to get down about half of it, she found a walker and told Courtney if she wanted to walk me about I could try it.

I was surprised how weak I felt when I stood up. I supposed that was because I had had no solid food for two days, only the nutrition supplied by the IV in my arm. I was glad for the walker and glad to have Courtney help push the IV apparatus for me.

"So where shall we go?" I asked her.

"There's a lounge just down the hall," she said. "We could go there. Unless you think it's too far."

"The lounge it is," I said.

We set off at a snail's pace. The hall was longer than I had anticipated, but I was determined to reach the lounge that Courtney had set as our goal. I felt rather proud of myself when we finally reached it. I was glad there would be no one we knew waiting there, dressed as I was in a loose hospital gown, my hair uncombed, and no makeup.

"My pocketbook," I said, suddenly remembering that I had lost it in Buck's Row, along with my passport, credit cards, driver's license, currency, and cell phone.

"Relax, Mom," Courtney said. "I took it back to the hotel."

"So it *is* here," I said.

"No, it's not here," Courtney said, misunderstanding. "I just said I took it back to the hotel."

"But it's not lost."

"Of course not. Why would it be lost?"

"I thought I dropped it. I thought it was gone."

"Well, you did drop it, but I picked it up."

We had reached the lounge now. We stood in the doorway

looking in. There were about a dozen people in the room. Some glanced at us curiously. There was an Indian family—mother, father, teenage daughter, and two sons. One of the sons looked familiar. I thought I had seen him before. Suddenly he grabbed a small handheld game from his younger brother and dodged out of reach. The younger brother let out a wail of protest. The father spoke sharply to the older boy and the mother chimed in, speaking in a language I didn't understand. Reluctantly the boy handed the game back to his brother.

I knew where I had seen him before. He was the boy who had led me to Buck's Row to find my pocketbook and who had bumped into me at the cemetery.

"I know that boy," I said. "I've seen him before."

"That's impossible," Courtney said. "You couldn't have seen him before. You're feeling confused from the bump on your head. Remember, you've got a mild concussion. Come on, let's go back."

She helped me turn around. The walker made me feel old. Perhaps she was right about the confusion. It couldn't possibly be the same boy. That boy had existed in 1888. More than a century had passed. He wouldn't be alive anymore. My brain was playing tricks on me.

And then I heard something that sent a chill down my spine. Someone was whistling a tune. I knew where I had heard that before. I had heard it that night in Buck's Row as the killer had walked away and vanished into the fog.

"What's the matter?" Courtney said as I tried to turn the walker back.

"Did you hear that?"

"Hear what?"

"Someone whistling."

"Yes, but—you're going to knock the IV over."

"I've got to see who's whistling," I insisted.

"What does it matter?"

I had succeeded in turning around so that I could see the room again. The whistling had stopped. People stared back at me. The Indian woman put her arm protectively around her youngest son as if she thought I might somehow be a threat. They all watched me with their big dark eyes. Besides the Indian family, there was a rather corpulent man who had looked up from his newspaper. Near him a teenage boy was listening to his iPod. Also in the lounge was a middle-aged woman with an old man, who might have been her father. Not far from them, looking out a window, was an innocuous-looking man in wire-rimmed glasses who might have been an accountant. What had I expected—Jack the Ripper?

But the tune, a voice in my mind nagged. It had been the same tune. I was absolutely certain of it. And then the innocuous-looking man in wire-rimmed glasses who looked like an accountant turned from the window and looked directly at me with flat curious eyes. I had the vague feeling I had seen him somewhere before, but where?

"Mom, honestly, what is it?" Courtney said. "Everyone's staring."

"I think I've seen that man before."

"You haven't seen him before. Let's go back."

"I remember," I said as the scene flashed before my eyes. "I saw him at Madame Tussaud's."

"You did?" She sounded doubtful.

"Yes. In the Chamber of Horrors."

"I don't remember seeing him," Courtney said.

Of course she didn't. She hadn't been with me. Lucy had been with me that time.

Behind us in the lounge he had resumed whistling. There was no doubt about it. It was the same tune I had heard as I lay in the gutter in Buck's Row.

ABOUT THE AUTHOR

Deanna Madden has taught literature and creative writing at various colleges on the mainland and in Hawaii. Her previous publications include short stories, essays on literature, the novella *The Haunted Garden*, and the novel *Helena Landless*. She lives in Honolulu with her husband and daughter and is at work on her next novel.